# SEARCHING FOR MY LOVE

## SPINSTERS OF THE NORTH
### BOOK THREE

ISABELLA THORNE

MIKITA ASSOCIATES

Peggy's Story

Book 3 Spinsters of the North

Searching for My Love

Copyright © 2023 by Isabella Thorne

# PART I

# CHAPTER 1

THE JOURNEY HAD BEEN LONG AND MUCH MORE cumbersome than Miss Margaret Williams had anticipated. Mrs. Williams, she repeated to herself. She was Mrs. Peggy Williams now. She must accustom herself to the ruse that she was a widow for her son's sake. She hated the lying, but it must be done, else, her son would be branded a bastard. She sighed, exhausted in body, mind, and spirit.

Having been granted her freedom after four long years of unwilling servitude, Peggy had expected the vigor of her release to bolster her journey to the far north. Rather, having lived within the confines of Blackwell house and seeing nothing but its dreary walls for so many years, she had found her reintroduction to the outside world nothing short of overwhelming. The streets were busier than she remembered; even the long country roads were filled with carriages and passersby waving and shouting at one another. Their cheerful greetings unnerved her. The villages bustled with activity, and there was always some festival or another that brought out the crowds in droves.

Sounds and smells that she had thought were long forgotten came rushing back to her. She had chosen to rent a horse and travel amongst the wagons filled with troubadours that went from town to town singing and plying their goods rather than stuff herself into the mail coach, although the journey would have been much faster by coach. The thought of being confined in such close quarters, even for a short while, left her shaking and nervous.

She had wanted to feel the open air on her skin and smell the scent of the wide-open meadows that bordered the roadway, even though the weather was quite cool. She might have already reached Northwickshire within a fortnight—and the small village where her son was supposed to be—had she chosen another means of travel, but the stop and go of her merry little band had given her the time to prepare herself, she hoped, for what lay ahead. He had waited four long years. A few more days could not matter.

Her son. *Adam.*

At first, when her friend and solicitor, the dear Mr. Crowley, had given her the information that she needed to locate the child from whom she had been separated, she had raced off to plan her travels without hesitation. Now... well, she was not quite delaying, but she was glad that she had taken the long route. She had needed to think. Needed to ponder all of the possibilities.

What if Mr. Crowley's informant had been wrong and Adam had been removed to another location? The money that she had been given by the Duke of Manchester in restitution for her suffering seemed substantial, but she was a woman who, for ages, hadn't had a guinea to her name. What if it was not enough to buy her son from the family to which he had been sold and also provide the two of them with a suitable living afterwards? She couldn't very well take her child to beg on the streets. Worse yet, and her greatest fear of all, what if he did not want her? What if he did not even remember the mother from whom he had been parted at the tender young age of less than five years? What if he did not wish to see her? Or leave with her? What if the one thing that had given her strength these past years, the thought of starting a new life with Adam, was nothing more than a dream? She could not quite keep the abhorrent thought from her mind. What if he was happy where he was? What if he had made a home without her? What would she do?

What a wicked mother she was to wish years of unhappiness upon her own son. Of course, she tried to keep her thoughts focused upon a more positive outcome. Adam would recognize her in an instant and come running into her arms. They would embrace, and she would explain that she had never meant to leave him, and he would understand. He would accept her back into his life with all the gusto of the small boy who had once greeted her each morning with a smile and a kiss. They would be together again, a family, albeit a small one.

These long months on the road had given her time to think, to ponder the plan that had previously been filled with ridiculous fantasies of retrieving her son and then buying passage on a ship to a far-off land where she would never have to look at the cursed English soil again. Despite her fantasies, she had come to see that option as unreasonable. Where would they go? Certainly not to the colonies. That was no place for a lone woman and child, and she had no intention of marrying, even for the comfort of provisions or protection. Peggy was world weary enough to take care of herself these days, and she was certain she could care for Adam too, once he was back in her arms. That was all she dreamed.

So it was that she had decided to find a remote English town in which to settle, someplace far away from anyone who knew her or her troubles. There had been a small village between Nottingham and Lincoln that she had enjoyed. It had quaint little shops and kind people. Most of the neighboring land was filled with hard-working farmers and sheepherders, but her traveling companions had continued moving northward. She had thought it would be a good place for a boy to grow, but there were many such places. She would find a good town, a place for Peggy to start anew with her young son. She would find somewhere large enough to have protection and community, but small enough to go unnoticed by the world at large. Somewhere far removed from all of the horrors of her past in London. She was determined to purge all thought of her ordeal from her memory. She had been given a fresh start, and she was even more determined to make the most of it. There was only one thing missing. Adam. Soon enough, she prayed, that matter too would be a thing of the past.

The countryside was beautiful with the promise of summer on the horizon, although the spectacle of whispering willows blowing in the wind and the fields of wildflowers were lost on her in her introspection. She picked at her horse's mane, setting plaits into the coarse hair to keep her hands busy as they walked a slow pace.

They had long passed the boundaries of most cities and made their way further north each day, which she thought was not the best of routes since the weather was getting cooler, but she could not complain. She had not wanted to wait another full year until the weather was more conge-nial. No. She needed to do this now. Adam had waited long enough, and so had she.

This far north, many of the deciduous trees had shed their leaves and stood stark against the sky, but the pines sheltered them along the road and broke the cold wind that swept across the land as they traveled ever further north.

The trees told a story of the coming winter. At first, in the wetter southern soil, there were golden willows, and although many of the English oaks' green leaves had changed to brown, the tall trees stood resolutely against the wind. Soon, the wet land that the willows preferred became drier, and hawthorns with their bright red pomes dotted the landscape. At last, the colorful leaves were replaced by stark birch trees with their pale silver bark with only a few yellow leaves clinging to the branches. Rowans with their reddish leaves and orange-red berries gave a bit of color, but mostly, the deciduous trees were denuded.

They had taken the North Road and bypassed Halthaven entirely. With any luck, they would reach Northwickshire tonight, and shortly thereafter, they would reach a small village called Riversbend which was, according to Mr. Crowley, the place where Peggy might find her son.

Peggy was nothing but nerves all morning.

"Riversbend ahead!" the leader of their troupe called over his shoulder. He was a portly bard whose wife provided tinctures, tonics, and potions of affection to giddy young misses. The horses were spurred into a livelier step. All were eager to reach the village before dusk so that they might settle to their trades and rest the night. The children raced ahead to explore and find entertainments of their own.

Peggy hung back, her mount falling in beside the wagons that brought up the rear.

This was it. This was the moment for which she had been preparing for so long. She searched the horizon. Her son might be anywhere in the village, might even be right in the square playing as boys are wont to do, if only she could recognize him.

Her heart gave a thump. What if she did not recognize him? She had not thought of that. It was possible. At nine —nearly ten—years of age, he would be an altogether different child than when she had last seen him. In her mind, he was still barely more than a toddler, but now, she sighed, he was a boy, closer to manhood than infancy.

"It's all right dearie," Mrs. Banning, the bard's wife, clucked from where she sat with her legs dangling off the back of the wagon that had pulled past Peggy's creeping mount. "Chin up. It'll all go as planned, and you'll see, you'll be goin' south again with us at week's end when the trade is over. There's plenty of room in the children's wagon with me boys."

"Thank you, Mrs. B." Peggy attempted a trembling smile. The woman's words bolstered her, and she kicked the mare forward to keep up with her friend. Mrs. Banning was the only person to whom she had divulged the entirety of her sordid tale. The others knew that she had intended to join them on their northbound journey, but she had kept the details to herself. What a fool she would look if this were all for naught.

"Just remember that you've done nothing wrong," Mrs. Banning had continued. "You didn't abandon him. You were taken. There's no fault in that. You're here now, and that's what matters. A boy needs his mum."

Peggy nodded. She had been trying to convince herself of Mrs. Banning's constant refrain for weeks but was struggling with the thought that Adam must have been led to believe that she had abandoned him. How could he think anything else?

"Perhaps he's very angry..." she murmured for the thousandth time, once again letting the horse dawdle. With her inattention, the gelding snatched a lone bite of greenery. Peggy pulled up on the reins just as the horse came away with a significant stalk of thistle which she postulated could not be very tasty, but he munched contentedly through the bit as she kicked him into forward motion.

"Then you'll tell him your truth, and he will see reason," her companion replied as she drove the wagon beside Peggy. "He's a smart child with you as his mum."

Peggy's eyes shot to the older woman in shock. "I cannot tell him *all* of it."

"Why not? He'll do better to know."

Peggy shook her head. "Some of it can be shared, to be sure, but not all." There were things that would have to wait until her son was older to reveal. She could gloss over her capture and involuntary servitude in London's Blackwell house. She could even well tell him of the adventure of her escape and her journey to find him. But of his father... well, that was not a conversation that she had prepared herself to have with the boy. Soon enough he would know he was born outside of wedlock. She did not want to rush the matter.

"He'll want to know why he was left on his own at a convent with no family." The herbalist looked away from the road momentarily and pierced Peggy with a very motherly look of reprimand.

"I am his family," Peggy replied. "That is all he need know."

"Perhaps you are right." Mrs. B. sighed. "But if my boys are anything to judge by, he's of the age where he will have an endless stream of questions and the stubbornness to demand answers."

Together, they laughed. The bard and his wife had three sons, and all of them were as precocious and devilish as young boys ought to be. They provided endless laughs and entertainment for the travelers and always found some way or other to wheedle out of their punishments.

"I won't put the cart before the horse," Peggy said at long last when they drew up to the first of the fences that surrounded the village. "My first objective is to find him. I will let his behavior be my guide." She allowed herself a bolstering breath before lifting the reins and urging the horse onward with a touch of her heel.

# CHAPTER 2

Riversbend was a quaint town, like so many of the others before, with small sturdy houses clustered around a central crossroad from which sprung all the necessary shops and entertainments of country life. In the square, Peggy was surprised to see a charming little garden bordered by bushes that seemed to have been pruned and cared for with great attention even though any flowers were gone by this time of year. The homes and businesses were tidy and well kept. The overall initial impression was that it was a happy place to live and that its residents took pride in its appearance.

The inn was centrally located and easy enough to find. Peggy secured herself a room and a stall at the stables for her horse while the troop of peddlers, a small village in itself, made camp in a nearby field that was designated for such things—festivals, market days, community gatherings, and the like.

Tomorrow, there would be bonfires and storytelling in the cooling evening. Truthfully, Peggy would be glad of a fire. The weather had turned quite brisk. She knew Mr. Banning would sing his tales while his wife sold her wares from the cart along with the other tradesmen and women. The small town was already abustle with interest. Faces peered out of the windows, and children had to be coaxed inside with promises of exploration on the morrow. Peggy could not help but wonder if one of the young awe-filled faces was her sweet Adam.

She slept deeply that evening beneath a downy quilt. Exhaustion from her travels and a determination to have full use of her faculties the next day meant that her body gave in to the need. She might have dreamt of her worries, or even of an idealized outcome, but when she woke with the rising of the sun, she remembered none of it.

The day was cold but fresh and full of promise. She pulled a clean gown from her small trunk, one of a handful that her dear friend Marilee had gifted her upon release from their dreadful prison. It was actually a beautiful dress, of forest green, and Peggy wanted to look her best. Marilee had once been the lady's maid of Lady Charlotte, now the Duchess of Manchester, who had gowns aplenty that she often passed down to her tragic companions. The three of them shared a bond that could never be broken and that none, save those who had been likewise captured and forced to live the horrors of indentured servitude, could quite comprehend. So it was that Peggy had been given a small but fine wardrobe and purse enough to start her life anew. She brushed her hair until it shone and put it up in a rather elegant design just to prove to herself that she could do so.

Unlike the duchess, Peggy was no lady of noble birth. Her mother was the youngest daughter of a baronet who ran off from her own family to marry Peggy's father, a handsome merchant with delusions of aristocracy. Unfortunately, Peggy's mother, along with her father's patiently awaited infant son, had died of influenza some years ago. None of her mother's family even came to the funeral, her father had told her. Peggy had been too young to remember much about the event, only that her mother was not with her for much of her formative years. When her mother died, she was nearly the same age Adam had been when she had left him at the abbey, Peggy thought with a sigh. She didn't remember her mother. What would Adam remember of her?

Father had been a wealthy merchant who had educated his daughter in many things, including his trade, with hopes that she might marry them into a respectable position. A true upstart. His dream had very nearly been made reality, and possibly would have had she caught the attention of the lesser son rather than the heir to a great estate. Instead, she had found herself with child and rejected by her lover—and then by her father when she refused to abandon her son, Adam, a bastard.

That son was now all that mattered to her in this world. She had no care to ever see her father again, though she was sure that he was still making waves in Hampshire social circles. Without a child to marry off, and marry up, his progress would end with him. For just this reason, Peggy refused to let him know that she was alive and well. At least as well as someone who just escaped from years of servitude could be. Since the exact details of the last five years of her life were known to only a few, she intended to keep it that way. Now, due to the duke's generosity, she was presently a woman of somewhat decent means. If she could make it last, that is.

The gentleman she had once thought was the love of her life could rot for all she cared. She had been so foolish and naïve. No longer. But she could not hate him entirely since one good thing had come of their union—her son— but nothing else.

This far north, she thought, she could live well outside of his notice. He had been a London gent, and she had assumed a new surname to keep herself hidden. Williams. A common enough name that no one would think twice when she started a new life with Adam and gave him the future of a well-off working widow's son rather than the shame of a bastard title. She had concocted a story that her husband had died in the war. She would be a widow. That would be preferable. She would allow it to be her new past, after she had collected her child and when they settled anew. No one would know her shame, or her son's.

Mrs. Banning had helped her to form the new identity so thoroughly that all those they traveled with, save the woman herself, were none the wiser. It was a surprisingly respectable group of peddlers and tinkers, but all the same, gypsies were not well known for keeping secrets when the knowledge might be worth a hefty bag of coin. On the other hand, gypsies tended to keep to themselves and were often ostracized, so she did not think anyone would pay her any mind.

Although she had traveled unbothered, she still kept her secrets close at hand. With the papers provided by the solicitor, Mr. Crowley, who had been instrumental in the release of the imprisoned women, Peggy had everything that she needed to start her life anew. And today... Today was the first real beginning.

Although she had awoken early, Riversbend was already ablaze with activity at first light. She went down to the common room to see what news could be gleaned.

"My, you're up with the crows, Miss," the barkeep greeted her as he lined wooden tankards from the previous evening's entertainments back along the shelf above his head.

Peggy hummed her acknowledgement and accepted a bowl of leftover stew to break her fast.

"I've ne'er seen a lady down before half past midday." He continued laughing and inspecting her as if looking for the sheen of a fever.

She smiled. Apparently, her clean clothing and brushed hair had improved her appearance from last night if he was addressing her as a lady. Good. She wanted to seem respectable. Her son depended upon her good name.

The man plunked a steaming cup of tea with a chipped saucer down in front of her. "Somef'in wrong with the room?"

"Oh no. Not at all," she assured him. "I've always been an early riser."

Again, he narrowed his eyes at her, and so she felt compelled to provide further explanation, although the truth—that during her years as laundress in Blackwell house she had been forced to rise well before the sun— would not do. "My father always said a waste of daylight is a waste of progress," she replied, taking a sip of tea. The words were not entirely false. Her father had said such things; only then, she had often chosen to ignore him.

"Ah, a tradesman then." He pursed his lips and nodded with understanding. Again, Peggy hummed her assent but provided no further details to the curious barkeep. She busied herself sipping the hot tea, which was a blessing after so many days on the cold road.

"So, what brings you to Riversbend?" he continued, wiping the already spotless counter.

Peggy felt her heart leap to her throat, not that he could have any idea of the apprehension that surrounded her arrival. It was, after all, a perfectly acceptable question.

"I arrived with the others last night," she said, avoiding the question with her attention to her tea.

"Good gad, child," he gaped.

"I am not a child," she said somewhat tartly.

"But yer not travelin' with the gypsies? They are a rowdy lot."

"I have since London." She laughed, accustomed to the shock that always accompanied the revelation. A lady might not travel so, but a daughter of a tradesman would not find it so loathsome a pastime.

"But they're gypsies," he stuttered.

"I assure you that it's been much less eventful than some of my other journeys. Safety in numbers, and all that." That was certainly the truth. Thinking about the coach journey that had ended in her abduction so many years ago, she suppressed a shudder.

His brow furrowed in a frown, misunderstanding her shudder. "I can call you a coach," he murmured, as if the tinkers sitting in the far corner of the room with their ale might be offended if she were to abandon their party.

Peggy knew well enough that they would watch and protect her as long as she remained one of their number. The Bannings had made sure of that, but they also would not think twice about her once she said her farewells. "The mail coach will arrive tomorrow," he added.

"I appreciate the offer." She smiled. "But I've ridden in the mail coach and cannot say that I think highly of the experience." It was, after all, just such a vehicle from which she had been abducted all those years before. The very captivity that had broken her away from her son, from the life that she had known, had occurred on what had meant to be a simple and respectable jaunt between two abbeys. In retrospect, traveling with a horde of armed nomads willing to fight to the death to protect their families had been some of the most benign months of this decade for Peggy.

The barkeep huffed and shook his head as if he thought her mad, but he would leave her to her own devices if she were so determined. Peggy had enough time to ask him for directions to the local cobbler so that she might have the heel repaired on a particularly worn riding boot.

CHAPTER 3

Peggy hefted her bag with her broken shoe in it and pulled her cloak tightly about her shoulders as she thought about having the shoe repaired. *All the better to be prepared for a swift departure.* She made her way out into the frost-soaked morning, thinking perhaps it might even be possible to glean some relevant information about the local residents while she commissioned the cobbler's work. A young, supposedly orphaned lad from out of town who had been sent from a convent to aid in fieldwork or whatever sort of additional hands a small country farm might need would be few and far between in these parts. Someone must remember his arrival only four years before. She was counting on it.

The cobbler was a pockmarked young man with a stall that could hardly be classified as more than a drafty lean-to that was braced against the side of his small home. The door shut out the wind, but it was rather cold in the building with the want of a fire.

She learned that he was new to the area himself and far

more interested in finding out what sort of goods the tinkers had brought to the market square than answering her questions. She soon learned that he was new to the trade as well, and as such was not yet in the way of crafting shoes. He was only barely skilled enough to repair the damage that had been done during her travels. Still, her heel was mended, and that was all she had needed. If only he might be convinced to answer one or two more questions so that she might ascertain who best to approach next, she would be happy.

She had nearly given up hope of collecting any useful information from their encounter when the door opened and they were approached by an exquisite young lady with golden hair and startling green eyes. The combination was enough to declare her a diamond of the first water in even the most competitive of London seasons, but her wide, genuine smile led Peggy to believe that she would not place much stock in such titles based on features alone. A true lady would not smile at her so. Perhaps she too was a daughter of a tradesman.

In the few moments it took for the lady to greet the bumbling cobbler, Peggy, who considered herself a fair judge of character, had decided that this female was a pure, unsullied soul. A rarity in Peggy's experience. The poor cobbler, who had dipped into a bow so low that his cap tumbled off into the dusty clutter at his feet, blushed as red as a tomato while he attempted to brush the cap off upon his knee. He only succeeded in spreading the damage to his trousers, which flustered him further. The lady averted her eyes and pretended not to notice. Furthermore, she did not find humor in his discomfort. She did not even move to feign a stifled laugh. She simply focused her attention upon his collection of tools and began to talk, giving the young man time to collect himself without an audience.

"I wondered if you had found the time to mend the seam on my slipper?" the young lady asked by way of distraction. Her golden-yellow gown, just a shade darker than her hair, was a shock of color against the dull backdrop of the shop. The pastel would normally mark her as unwed, and Peggy thought it strange she was not accompanied by a groom or chaperone. Perhaps she was simply a young bride. Of course, this small village was not London, but still, a young lady should be chaperoned if she were unmarried.

"Of course, there is no hurry if you haven't," the lady continued. "I am aware that I had instructed that I wouldn't require it for at least a fortnight, but I thought that I might as ask since I found myself in the village."

The cobbler ducked his head in shame. "I meant to hop a wagon to the big house and tell you," he began sheepishly. "I might've broken the buckle a bit, but I was able to order a match through the catalogs. It arrived two days past, but I haven't put it on yet." He was speaking at an increasing pace as if afraid of her censure, and all the while his cheeks continued to darken. "I truly am sorry, M'lady. I know it was a foolish error, but I promise I am getting better. If you'll still accept my work, I can have it done within the hour. At no cost, of course."

Without warning, the young lady turned her piercing eyes upon Peggy, who had not meant to listen in on the conversation but could not have excused herself before she had paid for her own services.

"And you," the lady asked. "Have you been well served by this cobbler?"

Peggy was at first shocked by the question, so she fumbled to hold up her boot so that the lady might look upon the repaired heel for herself. "I have no complaints. He was efficient and well-mannered," she replied, noting the sigh of relief from the cobbler, who had perhaps been unsure if he had done a fair job of conversing with a female customer.

"I am pleased to hear it," the lady said with a nod. She smiled and pulled a coin from her wristlet, pressing it into the cobbler's callused hand before her. "I am perfectly satisfied with a new buckle. I appreciate your initiative in ordering a replacement. That is just the sort of workmanship for which Lord Belton was hoping to expand the shops in Riversbend. We appreciate you joining our small town and encourage you to continue to master the trade."

"Thank you." The cobbler beamed and bent once more at the waist. "Thank you a hundred times over. And please, tell his lordship that I find myself most at home here."

The lady turned to make her exit but stopped to wait for Peggy to complete her payment. "You're not from around here," she said with a tilt of her head, the gesture indicating that Peggy might walk with her if she pleased. She did.

"I'm not really from anywhere." Peggy laughed. "But yes, I have only just arrived."

The lady looked askance, just seeming to realize that Peggy was quite alone.

"Just arrived? With the peddlers?" The lady's brow shot up in surprise when Peggy nodded. She sighed, a secretive smile drifting across her lips. "My own father would never allow such a thing," she said, shaking her head. "It must be so romantic to travel from town to town, to see all the sights—the excitement—and meet new people every few days."

"I would not call it romantic." Peggy laughed. For herself, romance was the very last thing on her mind as she made the lengthy journey from London to Riversbend. Not once had she looked upon a strange man's face and felt even the smallest inclination to flirt. She'd felt eyes upon her, looks of male appreciation cast her way, and had pulled her cloak around her to hide her womanly curves. She had resolutely turned and walked in the opposite direction each and every time a man paid her notice. She was an attractive enough female, with thick dark brown hair, and was thin enough but soft, with the womanly curves that had presented themselves after her body had gone through the transition of carrying and birthing a child. But Peggy was old—eight and twenty to be exact. Too old to be bothered with thoughts of a husband. Perhaps five years ago, before her captivity and while Adam had still been young, but now she saw little point in the effort. No one would want her with a child, and she was not giving up her son. She had plans of her own and would not allow them to be disrupted by a stranger who thought he knew what was best for her.

The young lady at her side, at the very least a handful of years her junior, was still in the prime years of romantic musings. Of course, she would think that traveling cross country with a group of troubadours and traders would be a life filled with excitement. While there certainly had been men and women enough who found their comforts in each new village, most of those in the party were families, exhausted from the constant pulling down and setting up of their wares and sleeping under little more than a waxed canopy.

"Are you married to a gypsy?" she asked with a bit of trepidation. Clearly, the thought—combined with Peggy's fine clothing—had confused the lady.

"No," Peggy said.

"Then, how does one find themselves in such company? Your husband must be very accommodating." The lady giggled. "I swear, I'd have horses after me within the hour!"

It was then that Peggy realized that the young lady thought that she too was a member of the gentry, a married lady. That would be expected, given her age. Peggy glanced down at her gown, the cast-off of a very wealthy duchess, and laughed herself.

"I'm no lady of noble birth," she revealed, "and I have no family left to send horses after me, husband or otherwise."

The lady hummed to herself before looking upon Peggy with a sadness beyond her years. "I suppose that the care of my family, and sharing moments with them, can make up for my lack of adventure."

Peggy smiled, though she did not entirely agree with the sentiment. "If you have a loving family, then yes," she replied. She might have given the indication that she had no living relatives, but the reality was that she had none with which she ever cared to associate again. She had chosen to take to the road rather than seeing her father again. She had chosen Adam over her father once, and given the opportunity, she would choose the same if she had to do so again.

The lady's features transitioned from pensive to mischievous. "Did you enjoy traveling with this group?"

Peggy nodded.

"Have they exciting wares?"

Again, she gestured the affirmative.

The lady giggled. "Then I suppose I have some shopping to attend to. If you have not noticed, several of our shops are still without merchants, and many are without merchandise. I haven't been able to buy ribbon in half a year at least."

"There are ribbons aplenty in the tinker wagons." Peggy grinned. "Mabel has a secret collection she only brings out for special customers. I am sure that I can persuade her to part with some."

"I feel my purse becoming lighter already." The lady laughed as they left the cobbler's poor shop. "Do lead me to the purveyor of ribbons," she said as she waved Peggy ahead of her.

Peggy smiled and led the way towards the wagons as the woman spoke. "Allow me to introduce myself," she said politely. "I am Honora Belton of Whitefall Manor," her new acquaintance said.

"Lady Honora," Peggy whispered, surprised.

"I know I must look affright, but we don't stand on ceremony." She lifted her skirts slightly to show sturdy boots. "After all, we don't even have respectable sidewalks." It was true parts of the streets that weren't cobbled were given over to mud. In fact, with the recent rains, the dirt of the side street was becoming rather soft.

Lady Honora held out a gloved hand. "Please," she said. "Call me Nora." She gave Peggy an appraising look.

"Margaret Williams," Peggy replied with a dip of her head and slight curtsy.

"I'm pleased to meet you, Margaret," the lady replied.

"Peggy to my friends," Peggy added.

"Peggy then, and I do hope we will become friends," she said while hooking her hand through Peggy's bent arm.

# CHAPTER 3

THE TWO WOMEN, WARMED BY HOT DRINKS FROM THE gypsy wagons and carrying bags filled with ribbons and wares, entered the edge of the square. Lady Nora looked out upon the vibrant crowd with glee. "Isn't it marvelous to see the birth of a new town?" she asked.

"I suppose, but why haven't you shops in Riversbend?" Peggy asked as she looked past the carts and wagons to see empty storefronts that lined the square. "It doesn't seem to be a new town. On the contrary, it seems as if many of the shopkeepers have left the town."

Lady Nora nodded.

Peggy worried that if the town were struggling, or if vendors had chosen to leave, that it might not have been a pleasant or comfortable place for Adam to have lived. Had he been left to walk with his feet bare or in hole-filled shoes without a proper tradesman to care for the locals' needs? The cobbler was barely competent, and while ribbons would not matter to a boy his age, Peggy wondered what else he might have gone without.

"The Viscount is building a new estate twenty miles from here, and he offered to help anyone from the village who wanted to move with him to start a new town nearer his residence—a bonus of two years income to begin. Several took the opportunity, and so we have a half town in each location and are working to expand the pair. Perhaps they shall meet in the middle," Lady Nora said clapping her gloved hands together gleefully.

Peggy noted that the lady spoke as if she had taken an active role in the dealings herself. Therefore, she deduced, the lady must be affiliated with the baron or his family.

"Is the new tenant pleased with this situation here at Riversbend?"

"Tenant?" Her brow furrowed. "Oh, you mean Lord Belton? He isn't a tenant. He's the heir, and this will become his great house at least until he takes up the entail," the lady explained. "It's a significant investment and promises a substantial increase in the holdings, so I believe everyone involved, including the townsfolk and tenants, are quite pleased with the prospects, although the transition phase has required the patience of all the surrounding estates."

"I can imagine," Peggy mused. She well knew what it was like to try to work in a household that was under-staffed. She could hardly fathom the struggles of a village without certain trades and supplies.

"At least Nash has me!" her companion grinned. "Heavens knows if we ladies left it to the men, we would have poulters and tobacconists, but he'd forget all about the milliner and modiste. Men," she said, shaking her head.

Together, they laughed. "So, you are hoping for a milliner and a modiste," Peggy said.

"One can hope," she replied, "But if they are one and the same, I will not complain. I do not want to have to travel to London every time I need a petticoat, but I suppose there is Leeds or York or even Northwick."

"You could go to Scotland," Peggy teased, commenting on how far north the village was.

"Heaven forbid. No. I am hoping to shop right here in town, so if there are any of these fine, skilled travelers whom you think might be swayed into planting roots, I would beg you now for an introduction. We have barely enough tradesmen to make a town now that half the citizens have followed the baron."

Peggy felt fortunate that she had made such an acquaintance on her first day. Who better to be able to locate a local resident than a prominent member of a nearby estate? She could not say why exactly because Peggy was not one who easily trusted or opened up to strangers, but she felt at once that she liked this young lady and her frank manner of speaking. There was no artifice in her manner, no subtlety hidden beneath a veil of words. She was forthright and direct and unashamed to reveal her intentions. It was no wonder that this Lord Belton had chosen in his wife one who could stand by his side while he rebuilt the village and secured his future. Perhaps Adam had not ended up in so horrible a place after all. Only time would tell.

The square was abuzz with activity. It seemed that the entire town and neighboring estates had come out to pick through the offerings. Mr. Banning stood atop a wooden crate at the center of the square singing melodic renditions of knightly adventures and romances of generations past. Some had perhaps been based in fact; others had clearly been embellished to include meddlesome smallfolk and dangerous sirens of the deep. Tonight, he would regale the onlookers by the light of a large bonfire with stories of sea monsters, witches who could raise the dead, dragons, and wraiths who stole misbehaving children from their beds and forced them to sell their souls or labor for a hundred years in the darkness. The nightfall and shadows would make the tales all the more believable than they had been by day, and the coin would flow freely for the talented bard.

Peggy accompanied her new friend from stall to tinker's stall while the lady made thoughtful purchases and asked insightful questions of the merchants. She was shocked to find how quickly the young lady was able to earn their good graces and even overheard a few things about her companions that she had not known even though she had traveled with them for months. The lady was able to draw out confidences in a matter of a quarter hour's conversing. It was a talent that Peggy respected and felt that she, too often close lipped herself, did not possess.

Lady Nora convinced a young woman, plump with child and a handful of other hungry mouths at her hip, to remain behind and make an attempt as the new stockinger in Riversbend. The promise of a winter without iced roadways and a solid roof overhead left the woman sagging with relief.

Peggy had seen the woman's skill with the needles and had even purchased several pairs of knitted stockings herself in recent months. She would have no delay in making a success of the career and was impressed that the noble lady had had an eye for the talent straight away. Lady Nora sweetened the deal by promising a half year rent free so that the family might get settled. And so, it was done.

Nelly, the young mother, waved over her husband to share her good fortune. With a cheerful bounce to her step, she planted a kiss upon his bearded cheek.

"What say you to roots?" she asked.

"You know, we've spoken of it," he replied.

"Yes. We have considered leaving the road, and Providence has shown itself this day."

Her husband chuckled and looked around, scanning the vacant shops with eyes both wary of the emptiness and a keen understanding of the promise of a future to be built in this place.

"Got you a need of an iron monger?" he asked of the lady, taking her estimation as her slight form was dwarfed by his bulk. "I'm no blacksmith, mind you, but I've a collection enough to get started—with sturdy buckets, knobs, latches, and the like—and I know how to build 'em in for folk."

"We have a blacksmith. Mr. Hallows," Lady Nora replied, and the man's face fell.

But the lady continued. "I am sure he would be pleased to have commission of the pieces you might sell. In fact, the baron's new estate is not terribly far away and is still in need of all new furnishings, so I might suggest that your collection start its expansion this day." She gestured down an intersecting lane and instructed that the blacksmith might be found at the edge of the village. "Tell Mr. Hallows that Honora Belton sends you, and I look forward to a delicate lock and key for my letter box."

They left the couple, who embraced at their good fortune and walked on with their children clamoring for attention until they were out of earshot.

"Two for one," Peggy mused. "That was fine dealings."

The lady laughed. "Yes, I cannot wait to gloat to Nash and tell him that I intend to commission all new stockings and garters. He might laugh and call them impractical, but I assure you my feet shall say otherwise, especially with the weather turning cooler. I nearly forced him to take me to Town before the season to procure a warmer set, but we've been so terribly occupied here that there hasn't been the opportunity. Papa promises me a Season next year. The last was a positive disaster, and I refused to budge this year."

Peggy had thought the young woman married to the local lord, but now, it was clear she was not.

Just as Peggy was about to reply, they were accosted by a rush of no fewer than a dozen boys racing after a runaway hoop. The laughter and shouts were filled with merriment, and the rough and tumble gang did their best to catch the hoop as it plundered through the crowd and down a gentle hill. When it splashed into a small looking-glass pond, the boys stood upon the bank daring one another to jump in after it. It was, after all, past the time for swimming and wading. Although the pond was not yet ice covered, it was undoubtedly cold.

Peggy found herself watching them with her full attention, unaware that anyone was watching her. She studied each boy in turn. Might one of the youths be Adam? She searched face after face, her chest full of longing for recognition, but the quest went unanswered.

Adam had been light of feature when she had last held him, a plump little bundle who was full of giggles and mischief. Would his hair darken as he aged, she wondered? There was one who almost looked familiar, but his hair was too dark, surely, with a shine of russet as a glint of late afternoon sun reflected off of his locks.

The russet-headed boy was the one who took the leap and was received with shouts and cheers of encouragement from his companions. He emerged from the pond with the hoop in hand and stomped his feet to shed the water from them. He had a wide, toothy grin. He brushed back his mop of hair, and for a second Peggy felt her heart stop beating. His eyes were crisp and clear with excitement— mischief, she corrected—almost like the boy she had once known.

Adam? She opened her mouth to call out but was stopped short when a rosy-cheeked, plump woman with a mop of carrot red hair lumbered over with her hands on her hips and laughter in her eyes.

"Every time," the mother laughed, not even pretending to be stern. "You ought to have been born a fish, love," she said while tousling his hair. "Come on. Help Jemmy and your father load the wagon. We'll go back to the house, and you can remove those wet boots before you catch your death. You can put your feet under the blanket."

"Aww… But Mum…" the boy groaned.

"No buts. It's late and we've an early morn," the woman clucked. "Hopefully, your boots will dry by morning. Hurry up so you can take those wet boots from your feet." She kissed him on the forehead, and the boy ducked away, embarrassed. Then he raced off, apparently to help his father.

Not Adam, then. Peggy released the breath that she had been holding. He was tall, she thought, and probably a year or so older than Adam would be. How could she think of her baby as a young boy? Would it always be like this, she wondered? Would every child cause her heart to stop as she realized she did not know her own son.

Nora spoke softly at Peggy's shoulder. "I've always regretted that as one grows older, we must lose such joy and uninhibited play."

Peggy jumped. She had forgotten, in her musings, that the lady was present. That lady's watchful eyes scanned Peggy's face looking for an answer that she schooled her features not to reveal.

"Do you have any children?" Honora asked outright.

# CHAPTER 4

Peggy stared at her. She needed to deflect the question of children. She was not ready for this topic. Certainly, the lady played no games, Peggy thought. She came straight to the point.

"I apologize for being blunt," the lady said. "I never asked if you had been married, but you carry yourself in such a private manner, like one who has suffered but grown stronger for it. And… the way you looked at those children… as if you were struck by a memory. So, forgive me for being presumptuous, but I thought that since you were traveling alone perhaps you might be a widow."

"Oh, no. I am not…" Peggy could have kicked herself.

Didn't she plan to pass herself off as a young widow? Now she had ruined the ploy. The playing children had completely undone her. Peggy was well known for having complete control of her features, for not revealing what she was thinking or feeling, for maintaining the artifice of being without any care or concern. It was the only thing that had protected her during her long enslavement. It was the only thing that had kept her captors from finding out about her son and using threats to his person against her. Her friend Marilee had been the lone soul she had fully allowed to pass beneath her protective walls at that time. How was it then that this relative stranger had read her so well, and with only a glance? She did not know this woman. She could not trust her.

"That is, I'm not married. I…" she began to explain but halted as she considered her answer. She was not one for falsehoods and dared not risk any that might make it more difficult for her to claim her son. As the lady had asked the question direct, anything but the truth would, in fact, be a lie. Still, she was not yet prepared to release her secrets upon the town. The last thing that she wanted was word of her arrival to reach her son and his keepers before she had a chance to make the explanation herself. "I…" she began again but was saved in the moment by the arrival of a handsome young gentleman who swooped up behind Lady Nora and placed a beautifully embellished jeweled headpiece upon her curls. Nora squeaked her protest.

Peggy thought that he was quite the most handsome gentleman that she had ever laid eyes upon. Her heart did a little leap in her chest. In the next moment, she was berating herself for her foolishness. She had no time for such dalliances, and no doubt the man was the husband of her new friend. She demanded that the rush of emotion immediately cease. Her foolish heart ignored her.

"There now, my dear," the man declared with triumph, "you may no longer claim the woe of having not had a new coronet in *a-ges*." He droned the last word as the lady must have time and again in his presence.

36

"Goodness Nash." Lady Nora giggled as she removed the headpiece and inspected it more closely. "This is not a coronet at all, it is a bandeau, but thank you all the same. I do not suppose these gems are real." She touched them gingerly.

"Of course, they are," he laughed. "They are real glass, or perhaps real paste."

Peggy smiled at his wit.

Lady Nora chuckled. "I love it dearly, nonetheless." She raised to her toes and pulled his cravat so that he would bend down that she might press a kiss to his cheek.

The man was uncommonly good-looking, Peggy thought, as she attempted not to stare. His twinkling eyes were filled with merriment, and a swatch of dark hair begged a hand to push it from his sparkling eyes. She wanted that hand to be her own. The thought filled her with an uncommon heat which she resolutely denied. Hadn't she once let her passions run away with her? She could not allow such things now. She had a son to find.

She shook her head to rid it of the romantic notions. She was quite past such things at her age. She had a child to think of. In any case, the man was quite probably the lady's husband. She repeated the thought most sternly. Yes. That would explain why she was out and about without a chaperone. Her gentleman was here escorting her about the village. An unwelcome stab of jealousy rose within her.

Then, the lady groaned. "Good heavens, Peggy, you must think that I have unutterably poor manners. I must appear to be obsessed with buying new things, as it is all I've done today. As much as I love shopping, I promise it is not so. I only want Nash here to understand that a successful town must possess accommodations for the fairer sex. I'll admit that I have been needling him on purpose just to make the point."

"Well then!" The gentleman laughed and snatched the headpiece from atop her head. "If you have only tricked me, then I suppose I ought to take it back!" He bowed with much posturing to Peggy herself.

"You will not!" Lady Nora slapped at his arm and grabbed the jeweled contrivance back with far too much ease, indicating that he had intended her to keep it all along, or perhaps this was a game that they had played in the past. Lady Nora placed the hat on her head, shoved the man's other purchases into her own laden bag, and then pushed the entire bundle into his waiting hands. "Be a dear and carry that for me," she said with authority.

Peggy found herself smiling at the fashionable pair. Only a short while before, her new friend had been lamenting that adults were inclined to lose their playfulness, but she saw no evidence of that in the twosome. They smiled at each other and made the most attractive couple. Lady Nora with her golden locks and petite form stood in stark contrast to the towering gentleman with sable brown hair and close-cropped sideburns.

"My manners! Nash you always make me forget myself." Lady Nora shook her head and tucked her arm into her husband's elbow while offering him a feigned glare.

"You never had manners," he replied, only to find himself bent over with a sharp jab to the ribs. "Mother has said so, time and time again."

"I'd like you meet my new acquaintance, Miss Margaret Williams." Lady Nora gestured toward Peggy, who had done her best to hide her amusement at the pair.

"She has helped me to secure tenants for the Barbury house with trades each for husband and wife." Lady Nora had been more than happy to discover that almost all of the couples traveling with the group could boast no fewer than two skills among the pair, but Peggy knew that such was necessary to make any sustainable living on the road. "And Miss Williams," Nora turned, gesturing to the gentleman, "may I introduce, Lord Nashall Belton, Baron Whitefall."

Peggy dipped her head in acknowledgement, "It has been a pleasure to meet you both, Lord and Lady Belton."

At that, Lady Nora snorted and immediately covered her laughter with her gloved hand.

"No. No. No," she giggled. "I'm *only* Miss Honora, not Lady Belton." The Baron was shaking his head as if the situation were something of a reoccurring joke. Did others mistake the pair as husband and wife? "Nash is the heir to the Viscountcy with the cursory title of Baron Whitefall," Honora continued. "While I am merely the daughter of the Viscount and styled Miss Honora."

"Merely," Peggy blurted. She, in her years of isolation, had fallen out of practice of understanding the complexities of noble lines that had once been drilled into her for hours upon end by her father, who wanted a seat in that esteemed company by way of his daughter's marriage. She had shoved all thought of that tutelage away, but she knew that a viscount was a lofty title, although Nora was right. A viscount's daughters were not styled Lady, but ladies they were, nonetheless, as members of the aristocracy in Peggy's mind. She tried not to let the fact that they were aristocrats lower them in her esteem. They both seemed like surprisingly nice people.

"Merely," Nora repeated. "It would be presumptuous

39

of me to use the title 'Lady,' although the title Lord rightly belongs to Nash. He is my brother."

Peggy's mouth fell open in understanding of her mistake. "My apologies," she murmured and dipped into a truer curtsy. A baron was still far above her social status as a laundress, and perhaps more so as a fallen woman, and Miss Honora Belton was still a lady. She was still a member of the gentry, although she was surprised that they did not have a footman with them to carry packages and said so.

"Oh, my brother likes to drive the curricle himself, and I thought we had not need of a footman," Nora said with a gay laugh.

The lady was so friendly that Peggy had not credited it. Perhaps her experience with Lady Lydia had changed her more than she wished to admit. It might have hardened her to the fact that not all of the gentry, or even the aristocracy, were abominable. Perhaps she too was prejudiced. After all, Marilee's friend, Arabella, who was now the Duchess of Manchester, was also a member of the aristocracy and an amicable soul, for all that Peggy did not know her well except through Marilee.

"I did not recognize that you were siblings," Peggy admitted. "My mistake."

"Nonsense," Miss Nora giggled. "We look nothing alike. He's a big arrogant brute, and I'm…" She paused in thought. "Well, I'm not a brute."

Peggy frowned. The handsome cultured gentleman in front of her looked in no way a brute, and the boyish grin on his face was at odds with her characterizing him as either a brute or arrogant. She felt an uncommon rush of heat run through her as she looked at the man. He was certainly fine, not a brute at all in her estimation.

"Don't let my sister fool you. She's a pest. Meddlesome and mischievous as a wood sprite. And not much bigger than one." This earned him another jab to the ribs which Peggy realized he was completely unharmed by and only pretended for his sister's sake.

"Take that back!" Miss Nora demanded, pounding tiny hands on his chest.

Instead, he captured his sister under his arm and turned to address Peggy. "Has she convinced you to join her in one of her schemes perchance? Caught you up for a task? Lured you into her plotting with sweet intentions and the guise of doing good until you are promising something far beyond what you would have ever intended otherwise?"

Peggy had to grin. She wanted to deny the claim but was entirely flummoxed. Never had she been teased so by a gentleman. Like his sister, the brother seemed far too skilled at reading features with only an instant's glance. She did not want to entangle herself in any untruths, but she did have secrets, or at least *a single secret*. His name was Adam. Still, as far as she was aware, Miss Nora had not enacted any plans, but Peggy *had* helped introduce her to the travelers and find new residents for the village. Perhaps it was mischievousness, or perhaps their meeting had been a strike of serendipity. The thought must have shown on her face.

"Ah-ha! So she has!" The Baron laughed.

"There is no meddling when that family needed a place to settle!" Miss Nora defended herself. "The woman was with child and had no right to be on the road in her condition."

"Shocking," Lord Belton said, which of course it was, but his countenance showed no sign of being shocked. Instead, he raised one eyebrow and looked to Peggy for confirmation as if they shared some secret too.

She felt her face once again growing warm and looked toward her new friend. "It is truth," Peggy agreed. "A good deed all around. And Miss Nora has not put me out in the least. In fact, I've enjoyed her company."

"And a gentleman should be aware of the hardships of his people," Miss Nora added.

"Until a moment ago, she was a part of the travelers and not 'my people' at all," he protested with all the aplomb of a boy trying to explain away a stolen cookie in his hand.

"Nonetheless," Miss Nora chirped, "the family is your responsibility now. Furthermore, I offered the terms *you* suggested, my good sir, and they accepted without any so-called needling on my part. Besides, haven't you come to do the same? Surely, some people in the tinker's wagons will want to stay."

"Gypsies," Lord Belton said with a sniff. "Father will not be pleased."

"Father need not know," Miss Nora said flippantly.

Peggy felt a spike of annoyance at the prejudice. Surely, they would not be speaking to her so candidly if they knew of her family and her situation. Her fine clothing had obviously fooled them into thinking that she was of a higher status than she was. Should she tell them of her humble beginnings, she wondered?

"So, am I the only one who found a couple to stay?" Miss Nora asked, with her head tilted up to see her brother.

He pursed his lips. "I've come out of it with a fine

chandler and a young man who wishes to make a try at fish mongering, although I'm not sure how many fish are in the river or how skilled the man is at catching them. Still, it is all for father's new settlement," he confirmed.

"*Your* settlement in all good time." The lady grinned. "We have a draw, two persons each."

"Not so." Lord Belton released a deep, rich chuckle, and Peggy noticed the man had dimples, two round indentations in his cheeks which bore evidence that he smiled often. "Yours is only one household," he protested. "Mine is two."

Peggy could see that Miss Nora was prepared to dig her heels in and start a row, so she decided to settle the score, in her new friend's favor, of course.

"Two workers in one household makes room for even more to make their homes," she declared. "They are a family and of two different trades. Quite efficient of Miss Nora, don't you think? Two workers, and yet only one roof to be maintained over their heads."

Lord Belton turned sharp blue eyes in her direction, and Peggy was taken aback that she had not noted how vivid the color was earlier. They were quite arresting. She caught her breath. Then, those eyes softened and grew full of merriment. He nodded and declared his sister the victor, to which she cried out with joy and clapped her hands.

"This will suit for my spoils." Miss Nora grinned and waved her new headpiece at her brother.

Peggy did not bother to point out that he had already presented it as a gift to keep and that Miss Nora might have chosen another prize, but Peggy surmised that the victory was more in the words and decided that as she had never been graced with a sibling of her own, she was unused to the intricacies of what was very clearly a solid bond. They were clearly a gentleman and a lady, and yet they had the playful spirits that she had only seen among the common folk or the very young.

Confused, Peggy excused herself from her new friends and found her way back to the inn where warm tea and soup awaited her. Lord Belton's countenance followed in her mind's eye, and his handsome face would not cease to haunt her imaginings.

What was wrong with her? She could not possibly allow any feelings for Lord Belton to cloud her judgement. Hadn't she learned her lesson that noblemen could not be trusted, no matter how sweetly they smiled? She put Lord Belton firmly from her mind, but perhaps she could be friends with his sister.

# CHAPTER 5

THAT NIGHT, PEGGY FOUND HERSELF LYING IN BED WITH her mind racing like a bird on a strong gale. The trio had made their rounds through the market with Peggy introducing them to the vendors, while Lady Honora and her brother, Lord Belton, spoke about the promise of the regrowth of their village. Never had she seen those of such lofty position care so deeply for those under their charge. Certainly, there were other nobility of the like, she must admit, but she had rarely encountered them. Never had they accepted her so readily. She convinced herself that what she had seen was romanticized by the dream. Nobles did not act so, well, noble. At least, not in her estimation. There must be some trick. She found herself looking for the falsehood.

Blackwell House, her previous abode, was governed by the petulant Lady Lydia and her band of miscreants. The house had been nothing short of terror, a dungeon to those trapped inside at the whim of its greedy masters. Servants and lesser folk had been seen as little more than chattel, tools to be literally bought and sold as the need might arise. She shuddered and pushed the memories aside. That part of her life was over, and she need never go back.

How different this town seemed to be, and that was due to the gentry of the area, but she must not lower her guard. To be sure, the Baron and his sister knew all of their residents by name. Moreover, they knew intimate details of their lives and held conversations that gave credence to the fact that they had invested in the wellbeing of all who fell within their range. But they were not to be trusted. Somewhere was a hidden mendacity. She just had not found it yet.

Miss Nora, willful and full of spirit, laughed and encouraged, while the young lord offered poignant and practical advice, taking his tenant's concerns to heart and offering solutions or consideration where needed. It was so unlike anything that she had ever known, even before her London traumas, she was not sure how to react. Certainly, it looked as if they loved their people, and their people loved them in return, but appearances could be deceiving.

Hadn't she thought a lord loved her once upon a time? Look how that transpired. She was turned out without a farthing, with a babe in her belly, and even her own father condemned her as a fool and a whore. Only the kindly sisters had taken her in with true charity. They gave her a home for a time, but even the sisters' good will ran out eventually, and their immortal souls depended upon their sheltering the homeless and feeding the hungry.

Unlike the good sisters, who were stern with good hearts, the nobility smiled, but their smiles covered evil. Didn't she note many a time when Lady Lydia gave the illusion of kindness when she wanted something, but at heart she was cruel. No, it would not do to trust these people. She would be on her guard. She would find Adam and move on. That was her plan, and that was best.

When Peggy had been a child, even her own father used her. She learned from him that everyone wanted something. Her father, a newly moneyed merchant, had schooled her in the art of attracting just the right man so that his daughter, with all his riches at her disposal, might wed their family into a higher class. She had been thrown about like a jewel, voiceless and soulless—like nothing more than the goods he traded. Just another offering to increase his range and wealth. Her own father did not value her. How could she expect more from strangers? Women were, for the most part, little more than chattel. She knew this. It was best she kept her head down.

Blackwell house had been the same. She had been a thing, a nothing, a cost that was only as valuable as its output, and she had labored to earn her right to do nothing more than keep her life and a roof over her head. It was only luck that allowed her to retain what little virtue she had left.

This town seemed to be a different world, a happier world, almost like a fairy tale. But like a fairy story, it was likely to dissolve into nothing. She could not trust it. She could not trust the gentry; she certainly could not trust nobility. A deep, secret part of her was torn between the desire to be a part of it and the fear—no, the certainty—that it was all a façade. She was not sure her heart could take the pain if it all came crashing down once again. No. She would guard her self-respect and her heart. No matter that Lord Belton was uncommonly good looking. His good looks undoubtedly covered a heart of stone, just like every other member of the aristocracy she had known.

The face of the handsome Baron came into her imagination, but she shoved it away. She needed to find her son and leave, but she could not fit a question into the conversation, although she wanted to ask her new friends about *Mr. and Mrs. Finch.* That was all that she had to go on in the search for her son, just the surname, Finch. Mr. Crowley's resources had gleaned that her son had been sent off to live with a couple by that name in the town of Riversbend to the north. This was Riversbend, an uncommonly small town. It was more than she could have hoped for, and yet still so little.

It was only the first day, after all. That was what she kept telling herself. But it had been more than that. She had been afraid to pierce the veil of the day, the happiness that she enjoyed that she had not been truly a part of for so very long. She had been terrified to ruin it with the knowledge that her son was no longer here, or worse, that he had suffered in her absence. That, beyond all of her other sins, was one that she did not know if she could stomach. She had kept her ear to the ground lest one of the names she might recognize would be mentioned, but nothing was said so far. Still, it was a small village. Someone would certainly know the Finches. She had but to ask, but once she asked, the fantasy she had built in her mind might be shattered by cruel reality.

She was hesitant to involve her new acquaintances with her burden, though she recognized that they might be the most efficient resources on the subject. Still, they seemed to like her, despite knowing so little about her past, and she hated the thought that when they discovered how

48

marred her history, they would banish her outright or refuse to help. She was sure of it.

Hadn't her father told her that, *"No place in England will welcome a whore. You'll be an outcast. A wretch that even the lowest of the low won't deign to meet the eye."* That was before she had been sold as little more than a slave. That was when she had only been ruined and not also wretched. How much worse off she was now! Now, if the people of this town knew her true history, she was sure, they would not accept her. It would be best if she took her son and left the area before anyone really knew her. She had to keep her secret. Elsewhere, she could be a widow and her son, just as she had planned—not a whore with a bastard.

The words stuck in her head, and she labored to rid herself of them. She wasn't a whore. At least, she refused to think of herself that way. She had been in love, truly in love, or so she had thought. She had given herself to one man and one man alone. And… was ruined. As she increased with her child, a child she thought, foolishly, would be born of that love, that same man—she would not call him a gentleman, although the world would see him so —that man had abandoned her. He found instead a more reputable, more fiscally promising prospect to marry. Still, whatever lofty thoughts she managed to think of herself, they meant little in a society where the mother of a bastard child was considered tainted beyond repair. The truth of the situation be damned, she had been ruined. And *he…* he had gone on without a scratch. It was not fair, but life was not fair. She had seen that played over again and again in the past years. She was no longer a foolish, naïve girl.

A dalliance was a mark of pride for a man, the title of

rogue an intriguing challenge to other women. Such activities were a damnation for a female even when based in love, and even worse for a child born a bastard. She would not allow that taint to touch her child.

For years, she had dwelled upon how unfair it all was. She had cursed the roles and rules of society. She had cursed her father for rejecting her when she could no longer secure the profitable marriage that he desired.

She cursed her fate and then she cursed the blackguards who kidnapped her. Finally, she cursed Lady Lydia and all the wealthy, placing them all in the same ignoble vessel.

Now, she thought differently. She was alive. She was well and free. The past could not be dwelt upon. The future was... unknowable, and the present would be whatever it must be. Perhaps, it would be whatever she would make of it. She had a strength of character that gave her life. She would not waste it. She would find her son, and she would live. She could plan no more than that.

Such a mundane outlook, and yet it was the only thing that had given her courage. Put one foot in front of the other, and keep going. She could not relive the past. She could not amend it. She could not atone for mistakes that were considered, by rule of society, unforgivable. She could only move forward. She would move forward.

What she could do was find her son and protect him. She could give him her love and, she hoped, a life and a family in which he could take pride. She could use the money of reparation paid, albeit unnecessarily, by the Duke of Manchester to give her son a life of promise greater than she had ever dreamed. If she invested well and worked hard, she could send him to the best of schools.

She could make a name for him in deeds, if not in pedigree. It was too late for her, but not for her son. He could have the world. She would do all in her power to see it happened. Nothing else mattered.

On the morrow, she would have tea with Miss Nora Belton at her brother's estate. On the morrow, Peggy promised herself, she would crush the cowardice in her heart and ask them about the Finches. She would attempt to reunite with her son for the first time in years. On the morrow, she repeated as she drifted off into sleep. It would be a new day.

The carriage that had been sent for her arrived at the inn promptly at one in the afternoon. Peggy found that the ride in the private carriage was not nearly as taxing to her mental state as the mail coach might have been. First of all, the interior was spacious and lavishly upholstered with fine buff-colored leather and blue velvet. The interior had a pleasant wood smell, which meant it was fairly new, with its frescoed ceiling and fluted columns presenting a pleasing ride.

She pulled the curtains back so that she might look out upon the countryside as she made the short jaunt to the manor. After a few turns upon country roads that offered spectacular views of the season's changes, and a long winding drive that led through the estate grounds, she found the carriage pulling to a stop in less than half an hour's drive from town.

## CHAPTER 6

LADY BLACKWELL MAY HAVE BOASTED ABOUT HER esteemed London townhouse, but it was crowded by the surrounding structures and filled with stagnant city air. At least, Peggy thought, it felt that way since she was sequestered in the basement and laundry for most of the years she was imprisoned there. This place was a palace in comparison. She could not help but stare.

The country house was a vision of grandeur with its stone-front façade and wide windows that opened out onto the grounds. A terrace was lined with statuesque sculptures and enormous clay pots so large she could crawl into them, if they were not filled with flowers.

As the carriage rolled up to the entranceway, Peggy heard laughter coming from further down the grounds. A group of servants gathered, their hands and aprons filled with freshly picked apples. Shocked to see servants laughing and playing while going about their duties, Peggy stared in dumbfounded silence until the driver gave a subtle cough to call her back to her senses. Laughing servants? She could hardly believe it.

She placed her gloved hand in the footman's hand to alight from the carriage and made her way to the main entryway, expecting to be greeted by a stoic butler and made to wait for hours of discomfort before she was joined by her host. Such had been Lady Blackwell's technique for establishing dominance. Instead, Miss Nora picked up her skirts, scandalously showing ankle, and came rushing towards her with her wide grin and greeted her upon the step.

"You've arrived!" the lady cried. "How glad I am that you are here!" She grasped Peggy's gloved hands and gleefully bounced as she surveyed Peggy in her borrowed finery.

"I could not very well have become lost in your own coach," Peggy said with a chuckle.

"Just so," Miss Nora nodded as she led the way inside, "although you might have declined. I would not blame you if you had enough of us two yesterday. Father is always telling us we lack decorum."

At the mention of Miss Nora's brother, Peggy felt her heart leap in her chest. "Oh, is Lord Belton joining us?" she asked, a spate of uncomfortable heat rushing through her at the thought. She certainly did not mind if the young lord joined them. He was pleasant to look upon, and he had been amiable enough. It was only that she had hoped to get Miss Nora alone so that she might press her questions about Adam in private. That conversation, she thought, would be awkward with the lord present.

Miss Nora turned and looked at her with narrowed eyes, her hands on her hips, and then shrugged. "He's here.

Perhaps in the library dealing with all those stuffy financial matters." She grasped Peggy by the hand again, quite informally, and pulled her inside of the bright and airy foyer. "I would be neither surprised if he made an appearance or if we saw none of him. You never know with that one. I think he is quite happy to be out from under father's thumb, even with all the work needed in the town."

Peggy felt a shiver go through her. She certainly understood what it was like to be under a father's thumb. No doubt that was why both Miss Nora and Lord Belton were here instead of in their ancestral home. She wondered if the Viscount was very demanding.

Peggy found herself being led down a wide, well-lit hall, so different from the darkness that pervaded Blackwell house or the stuffy formality of her father's home which had tried far too hard to display its newfound wealth.

Once inside, Peggy admired the lovely sconces that lined the corridor and lighted their way. From the carved stone base to the intricate metal filigree, each fixture held a candle or two, and they all came together in perfect harmony. Each sconce was an individual work of art with its own unique metalworking, in brass or silver, reflecting the light and adding a touch of opulence to the already elegant interior. The light they gave off brightened the area with a gentle glow that was both warm and inviting, while a faint hint of smoke from the burning candles inside the sconces mixed with the sweet scent of polish and beeswax that wafted through the air. Peggy was amazed at the sheer number of sconces on the walls which shed such a glorious amount of light in the windowless corridor. She had been used to the shadowy corridors of Blackwood where the lord of the manor was likely to accost the female staff members. This home was filled with light and goodwill.

"Yes," Miss Nora laughed. "We shall have need of new candles soon, I am sure."

Peggy opened her mouth to speak but halted the comment as the ladies came to the tea room. The room looked as if it had been decorated to suit Miss Nora's personality to the minutest detail. It was decorated with light pastels and plush chaise lounges. Bric-a-brac littered every available surface, and a fat cat lay sleeping on one of the oversized stools. But Miss Nora did not stop there. She tugged Peggy straight out of doors and onto the terrace that was at the side of the house. The smell of freshly baked pastries wafted through the air.

Miss Nora caught one of the maids with a gesture. "Molly," she said, "do bring our tea now," she directed, and the woman nodded with a smile before hurrying on her way towards what was presumably the kitchen. Other maids and footmen were preparing an area by the rear lawns for a luncheon to be served alfresco.

Peggy realized that this was where the apple bearing servants had brought the fruit. There was a table laden with various fruits, tarts, and sweetmeats. An elaborate luncheon had been prepared beneath the shade of the large tree. As Peggy looked around, she noticed servants standing just off to one side making sure all was in order.

Other servants scurried about arranging silver platters and filling them with various delicacies—crusty loaves of bread, golden-brown roasted chicken legs, succulent seasonal fruits. No detail had been overlooked!

Surely this is not all for us?" Peggy asked.

"Why not?" Miss Nora laughed. "I need no excuse at all for a party."

"But if there is just the two of us..." Peggy began, thinking of the gratuitous waste of food.

"I have been just dying for feminine company," Miss Nora explained, "And soon we cannot be out of doors nearly as much so I thought we ought to soak in the sunshine while it lasts." Peggy nodded and joined her on the lawn with pleasure. "Soon enough the whole area will be soggy with rain." A footman brought a platter laden with biscuits and bite-sized sandwiches. Another brought a platter with a mountain of fruit for the taking. Presently, Molly brought the tea setting.

"It's just so much food for the two of us," Peggy said trying not to let any hint of censure show in her voice. Perhaps, she had just known want for too long to be comfortable with such excess.

"Oh well, when we are finished, the servants shall have their own party, shan't they?" Nora said, reminding Peggy of nothing so much as a young girl having a tea party with her dolls. Peggy surely did not fit that description, but she did not want to offend her new friend.

The ladies settled down opposite one another and dug in with a vigor. Peggy was pleased that Miss Nora was not one to pick at her food, slight though she might be. She ate as she did everything else, with full pleasure and focus. At least, Peggy thought, the food was not going to waste.

They chatted as they filled their stomachs. Not about anything much, just the village and the weather. Peggy looked for an opportunity to ask about that Finch family but found no opening that would allow her to be so direct without feeling uncomfortable. The problem was that she knew nothing about them. She did not know if they were farmers to be questioned about the yield of the crop, or if they raised cattle or sheep. Might the herds have been well fed? She did not know if they plied a trade or served in one of shops or houses in the area. She knew nothing and therefore found no entrance through which to lead her question. She let her mind wander, trying to light upon an opening for her questions.

"… It was then that I decided, once and for all, never to marry." Miss Nora laughed as she finished her tale about how one local lordling, when they were children, had told Nora that she had better learn to behave like a lady for no man would ever willingly put up with her mischief without taking a switch to her.

"Well, that is no gentleman surely," Peggy said. "How would he, a child himself, know whether or not a man might find you perfect exactly as you are?"

"For one," Miss Nora giggled. "He was seven and ten, a man, close enough, so he told me. While I was no more than four and ten. Secondly," she sighed with great exaggeration, "he seems to have been right all along."

"So, you've put aside all thoughts of matrimony?" Peggy grinned over her teacup. Miss Nora seemed to have no need for a man to take care of her. She had wealth and position enough. Her family loved her, and her brother had given her effective duties of lady of the house. Nora did not seem worried that he might marry and she would lose her position as mistress of the house. In fact, she seemed to encourage it despite her brother's efforts to thwart her. No, Nora was satisfied with her lot and happy in it, and why wouldn't she be, Peggy thought. She had food to eat and a warm bed in which to sleep. She would never know want.

Suddenly, Peggy was glad to see it because she felt much the same. The times of hardship were behind her. She was sure of it. Furthermore, it was nice to have a friend who might be mutually single in their old age. Spinsters through and through. Peggy was taken aback when she realized that she was considering Miss Nora as a potential long-term acquaintance. Yes, she decided. Even after she was removed from Riversbend, she would enjoy to maintain a correspondence with the delightful lady.

"I have given up. Although Father does want to give me a Season. I cannot see the point, parading about looking for a husband. No. I do not think I shall make the effort." Miss Nora nodded as she nibbled a biscuit. "And rightfully so. Men can be so dull these days. No sense of adventure at all. It can be very dreary for those poor ladies who are forced to submit."

Now, Peggy laughed outright. Miss Nora was such a striking personality that no one in their right mind would call her dull. Perhaps it was the result of remaining unattached. Still, Peggy pitied any man who tried to trap her.

"Oh look, Nash is covered in muck," Nora observed without warning.

Peggy turned her head to see the lord of the estate tromping across the grounds looking a strange mixture of focused and cross at the same time. He was, indeed, covered in muck from the waist downward, and his trousers clung most scandalously to his manly form. She drew her eyes upward with some embarrassment. His shirtsleeves and breeches would be the devil to wash, she thought idly. She ought to know, having labored at the laundry for years. His man carried his jacket and waistcoat as his shirt was also splattered with mud, which meant he was in his shirtsleeves, and the fine white fabric was nearly see-through with the damp, either from the misadventure or from perspiration. Her eyes went back to the clearly visible muscles of his chest, and she felt a flush of liquid heat go through her core before she got her thoughts under control.

Peggy could not help but think that keeping the jacket and waistcoat from the dirt was a blessing for his laundress. If he had donned it, the lining of the jacket sleeves would have been soiled. Whatever had happened, willingly or no, it appeared he had gone into some murky water fully clothed save for his jacket and waistcoat.

Miss Nora waved him over to the table, drawing the gentleman from his reverie. When he came to and recognized the ladies on the lawn, he adjusted his course to pause at their side.

"Whatever happened, Nash?" Miss Nora grinned. "Did old Mr. Jeorgie's bull chase you into the pond again?"

He rolled his eyes and flicked a spattering of mud in his sister's direction. She squealed but it fell just short, saving her frock. "I was nine when that happened and you weren't even old enough to remember if Father did not tell the story at every chance. He loves embarrassing me."

"You do well enough at embarrassing yourself," Nora quipped gesturing at his disheveled form. "All the same, you were just as muddied as this," Miss Nora pointed out, wagging a finger under her brother's nose. "I have it on good authority."

"The beavers dammed the south creek again and it flooded Mr. Bowson's field for the second time this year. He's blaming Jemmy for not handling it the first time, so I went with the boy and several footmen to take it apart for good, and so we have it." He gestured at his person indicating the muck as a result of the efforts.

"Surely, there was a better way?" Miss Nora asked. "Especially since you brought footmen with you. You do understand, Nash, you did not have to undertake the actual task yourself."

"Sure." Lord Belton grinned. "I could have sent you."

His sister threw an apple slice at her brother who, rather than being pelted by the fruit, caught it and popped it into his mouth.

"How is Jemmy?" Miss Nora asked before turning to Peggy and explaining further. "He's the eldest boy of our gamekeeper. He's learning but still ripe with youth. Mr. Bowson has had an unfortunate string of luck with his field, but it's not Jemmy's fault." She turned back to her brother.

"He's a young man facing off with the forces of nature." Lord Belton shrugged.

"Bested by the beavers," Peggy supplied.

"Who hasn't been?" Lord Benson laughed. "They'll be building dams long after we're gone."

"Someone ought to tell Mr. Bowson that," Miss Nora quipped.

"I have," her brother replied. Then, he ran a hand through his golden brown hair, mussing it and streaking it with mud in a way that made him seem less a future viscount and more just a hardworking man. He released a long breath. "He's just worried about his crop. I told him not to fret about the harvest. We'll make sure they have plenty to get through the winter. Father's crop is on higher ground and won't be bothered by the flooding."

Miss Nora offered her brother her hand and allowed him to pull her to her feet.

"I'm proud of you," she said, pressing a kiss to her brother's cheek while leaning clear of his mess. "Our father raised you well."

"It's a shame he never figured out how to set you straight," he teased, plucking at one of Miss Nora's pin curls.

She rolled her eyes but grinned up at him. "He knew perfection when he saw it," Miss Nora countered. "Now, off with you. Go and dress, and when you return you can share what is left of our luncheon."

"All of the tarts are gone. Need I ask who ate them?" He raised an eyebrow at his sister. "There are more in the kitchen," she retorted. "But it would serve you right if I did eat them all. You should endeavor to be on time and properly attired for these things, you know."

At his sister's censure, Lord Belton eyes met Peggy's, and he just seemed to notice how improperly he was attired in only his shirt sleeves. Peggy didn't mind. In fact, she was quite enjoying the view, but now that Nora mentioned his state of undress, she felt the heat of a blush fill her face.

It was ridiculous. Having been a laundress, she had seen her fair share of shirtless men in the last few years. She had literally cleaned some spill of sauce and gravy from a random footman's shirt while the man wore it, and she thought only of the stain and the shirt. In that world, a gentleman did not mind a maid in their presence. Servants were invisible. At least, good servants were.

But now, somehow, things had changed. Ladies must be protected from the scandalous view of bare arms and jacketless men, but she was no lady. Indeed, Peggy thought that her time in the laundry had made her immune to the sight of the male body, but she realized that was not so. None set her heart racing like the one in front of her. None was quite so perfect. The symmetry of the muscles beneath the shirt seemed to call to her. A part of her wanted to reach out to touch him and wipe the spots of mud from his torso with only the fine lawn between them. She knew how thin the material was. She knew how it would feel under her fingertips, and she shivered with sudden heat.

Lord Belton, obviously oblivious to her perusal, had snatched up a few of the tiny sandwiches and was already moving toward the great house. "I promised that I would take Jemmy home," Lord Belton called over his shoulder before he crossed through an open set of doors.

"Oh," Nora said, disappointed. "But you will stay, won't you?" she asked of Peggy. "In fact, spend the night."

"I'm sorry, I should be going back to the inn before dark. I promised Mrs. Banning I would help her with the boys tonight," she replied with honest regret. It would have been nice to have remained longer so that she might have posed the questions about Adam that were burning inside of her. Still, she had been far too hesitant to broach the topic with so new an acquaintance.

"The Finch's home is on the way to town. I can escort you back to the inn if you don't mind traveling in the tax cart."

Peggy's heart stopped. In an instant, her thoughts became maternal. The Finch's. As in… the household that had at one point, possibly still, housed her son. She forced herself to take a steadying breath and focus on what she had heard. This Jemmy was the oldest boy of the gamekeeper. Boy, not necessarily a son. And eldest, meaning that there were more. If the Finch family was in charge of the game throughout the Whitefall estate, they would likely need several sets of hands to monitor and track the animal trails and populations.

She had to know more.

Peggy nodded and accepted the offer with gratitude, but Nora protested. "You cannot possibly expect a lady to ride in a cart," she said. "Send Bix to have the gig made ready."

"Oh no," Peggy said. "I don't want to be any trouble."

"It is no trouble at all," Nora declared, reaching for the bell which brought one of the maids—Molly she remembered. Nora gave her directions for the stable lads and told her to pack up some of the leftovers from luncheon to give to the Finches.

Peggy could hardly believe that she was only moments away from meeting the people who cared for her son. For the first time in as long as she could recall, fortune had seemed to smile upon her. She would soon find her son. It was a day to celebrate. Why then was her stomach roiling with fear?

# CHAPTER 7

THE GIG WAS SOMEWHAT LESS OSTENTATIOUS THAN THE
one that brought her to the manor, but in some ways, it
fitted the personality of Lord Belton. He drove the handsome curricle himself. The upholstery was of a more
durable nature, buff leather to match, cushion, dasher, and
all with a single bay mare to pull it.

Peggy and Lord Belton took the seat, and Jemmy rode
tiger, on the back of the gig. He was quite pleased with
himself, holding the strap like a proper groomsman,
although Peggy had suggested the boy sit between Lord
Belton and herself. She wasn't sure if the suggestion was
entirely for Jemmy's benefit or her own.

One would have thought the boy would be occupied
with keeping his balance, but he prattled on about the wily
ways of the beaver and how he was going to make a fine
cap of the pelt when he confronted the irksome beast. She
reveled at the beauty of the narrow path that they took
through the grounds that would lead to the gamekeeper's

home. Adam's home, she prayed and feared at the same time.

If her companions noted her silence, they did not comment upon it. Her heart had filled her throat, and she was too overcome with thoughts and worry to be much use in conversation. Jemmy required little help on that front. He waxed long about the hunting excursions that his father had planned for the cooler months, in preparation for a long winter.

He also spoke, quite informally she thought, of a local girl who had caught his eye and he was certain fancied him in turn. Peggy found herself smiling that the young boy seemed so comfortable with his lordship as to share his personal whims. In fact, Jemmy looked up at Lord Belton with nothing short of pure adoration, and it was clear the gentleman cared for the boy as well. He teased and instructed in turn, both providing sound advice and a listening ear. She noted that Jemmy spoke without formality as if they had known one another all their lives and were beyond such trappings as titles and station. Peggy found the novelty of the practice intriguing. Few enough of the noble class that she had encountered that would allow such informal address. The constant reminder of one's position, particularly over those beneath them, seemed something of an addiction in her opinion. Her own father, a notorious social climber, would have railed over anybody who had dared show him less than an ounce of the deference that he thought his due. Even Lord Sterling, Adam's father, had taken pleasure in touting his rank. How she had been so blind as to think he would have ever lowered himself to...

She shook her head to dislodge the comparison before

it could take further root in her mind. She had perfected the art of not thinking about her past. Not thinking about *him*. Perhaps that was because her days had been so utterly filled with work and her nights with exhaustion. Now, she had time to herself, but she would not fall back into that habit after all of these years. Still, she had too many examples of the peerage viewing their birthrights as reason enough to stomp on those of the middling and lower classes. She huffed in annoyance. The past four years of her life had been testament enough to that.

"Adam said you're takin' him fishing," Jemmy added without stopping for a breath. "Can I come?"

Peggy gasped but quickly recovered, her attention now firmly back on the boy. Lord Belton did not credit her woolgathering or her swift intake of breath, although she caught a short tilt of the head from Lord Belton before he continued the conversation as if he had not at all noticed her reaction. He had the grace not to draw attention to the slip, and she hoped the moment would be forgotten.

So, Adam *was* at the gamekeeper's house. She knew that now as a fact. Her hands worried a loose thread on her glove, and she forced herself to stillness before she pulled it and made a hole in the finger of the glove. She could hardly believe that after all this time she was going to see her son. Adam was there, *and* her new acquaintances were familiar with him. More than familiar, close, as a keeper of the game's household ought to be with the main house.

She tried to steady her heart, tried to prepare herself for what was to come. The rest of the ride was lost to her view as all her thoughts had drawn inward.

She would go to the house and introduce herself. Mr. and Mrs. Finch would welcome her with trepidation. That, of course, was to be expected. She would explain her tale, so much as they needed to know. Reveal her relationship to the boy. They might be surprised, but she would make them understand. He was her son, after all. Then, this Mr. and Mrs. Finch would call Adam inside and explain to him that his mother had returned to collect him. She would take him back to the inn this very night. It was all so very simple. In a matter of hours, they would be reunited.

The gig rolled along beside a sturdy fence that kept two plump dairy cows and a dozen chickens, so much as those could be contained. Peggy allowed herself several deep breaths.

She had prepared for this for months, nay years. She was ready.

The house was small but well kept, worn and repaired in several places. An array of tools and toys were lined with care beneath an overhang that served as a shed. It gave one the impression of a simple life, but one filled with purpose.

When the carriage came to a stop, Jemmy gave a shout, and two other children came bursting from the house—one boy, the one from the pond, and a girl who was perhaps a year or two older than the boys.

Peggy's heart skipped a beat. Had she expected seven or eight children from which to choose? There was only one other boy, and when Jemmy clapped him on the shoulder and declared his name, she froze.

Adam.

It was her son. She now knew it now beyond a doubt.

He barreled at the Baron in an attempt to catch him

unawares but stopped, skidding to a halt in front of the man. He gave a smart bow. "Milord," he said, but the Baron met his manners with a grin.

Before she could stop herself, Peggy's hand flew to her mouth, covering the cry that threatened to break forth. All her preparation had gone out the window when faced with one thing in this world that she truly loved, her son. She had remained in the gig, unobserved by the children who had eyes only for Lord Belton, who pulled candies from his pockets and gave one to each youth. The girl, Martha, Peggy recalled, stood slightly away and stared up at the gentleman with the blush of one in her early years of infatuation. Peggy might have laughed, so unaware was the Baron of the look from the girl, maybe two and ten at best. He likely still saw a babe, but she was in the first blush of a heartbreak.

Peggy had eyes only for Adam. Of course, his hair had darkened over the years, she chided herself. Though he had been light in feature as a babe, was she not, herself, a darker hued brunette now than she was a child? He had her mother's nose and his own father's proud chin. He was thin and tall for his age, perhaps to her chin if she had stood beside him, but the gangly form of his limbs gave him away as far younger than his height would permit. And oh, how she loved him. She wanted to rush forward and swoop him up in a hug, but that would not do.

Peggy clenched her eyes shut for an instant, only an instant, willing her emotions to be held at bay. She had a plan. A plan that included a rational exchange of information that would ease all involved into the revelation without cause for a shock or disagreement. That plan, fantasies aside, had not included revealing herself to Adam first. The last thing that she wanted was to upset him or cause a scene. She had been over the scenario with Mr. Crowley. If Adam recognized her and was determined to be with her, but his caretakers resisted, it would be a traumatic and possibly dangerous experience for the boy. She needed to talk to his keepers first. Needed to make her point and get them to understand, to comply with his release. She had the papers from Mr. Crowley proving her parentage, but the boy had been given over according to the abbey and now belonged to them. She needed the Finch's signatures, and rushing in with a dramatic display of exuberance from Adam was not the way to get in their good graces. She would hate to have to leave her son, even for a night, especially if he felt restricted by the Finch's refusal.

Imprisoned, she thought.

A chill ran over her skin. She knew what it was to be trapped in a place from which one wanted nothing more than to be free. She would not wish such a thing upon her son, not with the hope of freedom that her presence must bring. He had been stuck in this place long enough.

It was then that the wave of dismay hit her. Only the day before, she had eliminated him as a prospect when he had called the woman fussing over him "Mum."

He had called her Mum.

Peggy's heart sank. She looked at him once more. Full, rosy cheeks. A healthy frame and body vibrant with energy. A boy who had been raised in a home full of love. A boy who was part of a family. A boy who called those who had taken him in "Mum" and "Papa."

A boy who, as far as she could tell, did not remember her in the least. Who, perhaps, did not need her. No. It was clear in this moment that it was she who needed him. A sinking feeling filled her belly.

Shaking, her hands wringing themselves into knots and her mouth quivering with emotions that she had long ago trained to conceal, she forced herself to turn away. She had to collect herself.

His was not the face or the bearing of a child who had suffered or been misused. It was not the face of a boy who needed rescuing. His was the face of a boy who was part of a family, a loving family, and she was the usurper.

Behind her she could hear the merriment of the children as they moved toward the house, and she thanked Lord Belton, more than he would ever know, for the discretion and insight that he had to not make the introduction. Honor would say that he must, but she could sense that he had read that something had disturbed her, or perhaps he saw no reason to introduce his sister's friend to the gamekeeper. For once, Peggy blessed the separation of the classes, although she was rightly more a part of the gamekeeper's class than Lord Belton's. Peggy remained silent in the gig with her back turned until the yard had cleared. She covertly wiped the tears from her cheeks and prayed that her eyes and coloring had not been too reddened by her distress.

Only after she had set her shoulders and squared herself to the back of the gig once more did she feel recovered as Lord Belton returned to his perch.

"You seem upset," he said with a voice both gentle and coaxing.

Peggy released a trembling breath but kept her back to him. She'd never shed a tear in front of anyone and would not start today. "No," she replied with what she hoped was a steady voice. "I am well. Thank you."

He snapped the reins, and she felt the curricle start forward. And... bless whatever grace had raised this lord to hold his tongue, they rode in silence all the way to the village while Peggy did her best not to dissolve into tears. Not yet. She would wait until she was alone, and then she would open the floodgates to her wounded heart.

# PART II

# CHAPTER 8

PEGGY PERMITTED THE LORD BELTON TO HAND HER DOWN from the carriage while he was greeted by the locals and visiting travelers alike. So easily the newcomers had taken to him she noted as the Bannings and their companions clapped him upon the shoulders with good cheer. Riversbend was unlike many of the other towns, an open and friendly place to the newcomers without any of the initial hesitancies or quiet approaches that the travelers had to weather before being welcomed into the fold as more than peddlers of their wares. Perhaps, it had to do with the fact that several had been offered permanent residence and a chance to make new lives for themselves. Or perhaps the locals had been so in need of resupply that they were in immediate celebration of the troupe's arrival. The peddlers had been approached as equals with value rather than being treated as gypsies or even as mere passersby.

The inn was bustling with activity when they arrived just in time for patrons to begin claiming their tables for their evening meals and tankards of ale. After her massive meal at the Belton estate, Peggy thought she would skip her evening meal. Eating now would seem like gluttony to her, but perhaps that was because she had so often been without.

Peggy made her way to Mrs. Banning's side and glanced around for the brood of children that often milled about her.

"Oh, they are off somewhere." Mrs. Banning laughed. "The pastor came through and offered them coin to do some spring cleaning at the vicarage, and they've been collecting their pay in service from house to house ever since."

Peggy could not help but smile. The chance to do odd jobs was always something that fascinated the young boys, as it filled their pockets with coin to spend on trinkets and baubles of their own, often traded or sold in the next village over.

"I meant to send word that you could keep the night to yourself, but I hadn't a clue where to send the message."

Peggy apologized for her lack of foresight. She had not thought to inform her friend of her visit to the nearby estate as she had not expected to have been gone long. Nor was she a child that needed minding. All these months, she had always gone about her own business so long as she returned by the expected hour so that Mrs. Banning would not have need to concern herself with Peggy's safety.

"It's quite all right." Mrs. Banning grinned. "It is good to see you interacting with those of your own age and sort."

My own sort? Peggy thought. It was true that she had hardly interacted with anyone in previous towns, but she had never had reason to do so. Here, she had needed information, connections, and to find Adam, although now that she had found him, she was not sure what to do. Mrs. Banning had never fully accepted Peggy as a member of the working class even though that is exactly what she was. Although her father had been a very wealthy merchant, she was not—and would never be—a member of the nobility despite Mrs. Banning's clear disbelief any time that she assured her of this fact. Peggy had more education than she ought for a woman on her own. She was well read and knew her numbers and had a keen eye for business and a no-nonsense way of interacting with those of any class. She was able to blend in with many of the gentry, and for that Mrs. Banning was convinced, and not entirely wrong, that there was more to Peggy Williams' story than met the eye. Still, she did not pry, and for that Peggy was grateful.

The elder woman clucked her tongue at Peggy and waved at her husband who stood spinning his tales across the street. Mrs. Banning bid her farewell and made her way over to her husband with the mischievous gleam of a wife who possessed the promise of a few hours unbothered. No, Peggy realized, she was certainly not needed this night.

She felt a lump grow in her throat as she found herself standing alone under the creaking sign of the inn. For weeks, she had distracted herself with Mrs. Banning's company, but now she realized that her relationship with the woman was coming to an end, and she had nothing to fill her time. She sorely wished that she could go back to Whitefall Hall and distract herself with Miss Nora's cheerful company. She did not want to be alone tonight with her thoughts. Not after having seen Adam, well and happy, and realizing that she had severely underestimated the difficulty of her task. It was one thing to take him from a place of servitude and obligation but quite another to expect him to want to leave people who made him happy just because she needed him. Yes, she realized, she needed him, much more than he needed her apparently.

She sighed. She had not wanted Adam to be unhappy, but if she were being honest with herself, it would have made things much easier. She had not truly planned for this possibility. She had not wanted to think that he might not want to leave his present environs, might not want to come *with her*. Might not need *her* at all.

Furthermore, she suppressed a groan, what did she have to offer him? A life on the road? Of course, they could find a small village and start anew according to her half-formed plan, but for what? He would have nothing but her and whatever life she could struggle to pull together in their new beginnings. She had thought that would be enough, had convinced herself that their bond would be sufficient, but now she was beginning to doubt. The truth was, they had no bond except the bond of blood, and she did not think it was sufficient to pull him away from a family who loved him. She had money enough for a time but no certainty to offer him. If she failed, they might end up on the streets or worse. Although she had refused to think of that as an option before, it now seemed all the more possible when held in comparison to a warm fire, a roof over his head, and the happy household that he seemed to have found with the Finches. She should have known that the good sisters at Halthaven Abbey would not have sent him to just anyone. They would have vetted the family. They made a good choice for him, perhaps a better choice than she herself was. Emotion clogged her heart and migrated up to her throat as she blinked back tears.

Peggy chided herself for having been so certain that she had known exactly how it would all play out. Now, instead of finding her son and making a life for them, she felt lost and out of her element, more melancholy now than when she was trapped as a laundress in a house not her own.

A gentleman cleared his throat behind her, and Peggy turned to step out of his way. She had been lost in the deep recesses of her own mind and might have been blocking the door.

When she looked, she found Lord Belton standing before her and noted that she had not been, so far as she could tell, in his way.

"I beg your pardon," she said as she raised an eyebrow in question and she was once again struck with the man's handsome features. She did her best to bring her thoughts down to earth. He was a viscount's son and a baron in his own right. He was not a man for her, even if she wanted a man in her life, which she did not.

"Have you found your charges?" Lord Belton asked as he leaned against the fogged window of the crowded inn.

"No." She sighed and cleared the huskiness from her throat. "I am afraid that I have been relieved of my duty." She found herself at sixes and sevens.

"A pity." He grinned a boyish smile himself. "What shall you do with yourself?"

Peggy could not help but laugh. Any other night, she would agree with his suggestion that an evening spared from the chaos would be a relief, but tonight she had craved the distraction, needed the distraction, more than she was willing to admit.

"Well, sir," she mused, pursing her lips to one side as she thought about her answer in earnest. "I have no idea." It was, she realized, a brutally honest answer, although he could have no indication how deeply she meant the words.

"How about a stroll?" He gestured with one long arm down the length of the street which still teemed with activity in the early evening hours. She contemplated the offer. There were more than enough people about for it not to be considered untoward for the pair to be seen walking together. Besides, she was hardly a lady who needed chaperoning. There were a few more hours of daylight left, though the sky had already begun to turn a dusky hue. And lastly, had she not just been wishing for a distraction?

What a handsome distraction he was! Too much so. Still, anything was preferable to sitting in her room alone and mulling over every minute detail that she had learned about her son, or every terrifying possibility of how things might go wrong, or perhaps more askew than presently.

Peggy eyed Lord Belton warily, not because she did not trust him, but because he saw too much, and she knew he had questions. Questions to which she had no answers to give. She prayed he did not ask them.

As if reading her mind, he held up one hand in solemn promise. "Just a stroll." He shrugged. When she still seemed undecided, he added, "We do not even have to talk if you don't wish to do so. Just a walk."

"Who says I do not wish to talk?" Peggy bristled at his acumen.

He eyed her up and down, and she felt a blush fill her face, but his gaze lingered not on her ample form but on the stern set of her shoulders and the proud tilt of her chin. Her guard, her father used to call it. The way she stood when she would not give an inch. "Come," he murmured and held out his hand, still gloved from the carriage ride. "If you had wanted to go to your room, you would have done so already."

When she didn't immediately take his hand, he started walking away. At first, she was annoyed. Did he just expect her to just follow him like a lost puppy? What sort of gentleman was he? But what did it matter? She was not a lady. Why then, was she expecting more consideration than her status deserved? The truth was, he probably did not care what her choice was but had decided not to stand here and waste his time convincing her while he had errands that needed attention. She cast one long glance through the window and saw the crowd packing every available inch of the room. The press of humanity intimidated her. For an instant, she thought of the haven of the laundry. Who would have thought she would ever miss the closet of a room that she shared with only a few women as the laundress?

Finally, she found her mettle. He was right. She had not wanted to enter, but she was not so timid as to cower in a corner, even though in such a crowd she would feel more alone than ever. She would be left with nothing but her own thoughts to make her feel trapped and pressured, helpless and hopeless. At least with a walk, she could look at nature. She could revel in the beauty of the happy little town. She could pretend that she still had hopes of finding a life with her son.

"Very well. I pray you, wait," she called after him as she hurried to catch up.

He paused immediately, and ever the gentleman, offered his arm.

When she drew up to his side, she cast a tentative sideways glance up at him and noted that he was doing the same, though downward. She took a deep breath and laid her hand on his elbow. "Tell me about the town," she said in a quiet voice. The least she could do was find out more about the place where her son had spent the last four years without her.

"I did not think you wished to talk," he teased, and a sudden heat blossomed between them.

"I don't," she quipped in reply. "I want *you* to talk."

The corner of his mouth twitched with amusement, but he quickly schooled his features to a more serious visage. Then, taking the task to heart, he began to tell her more about Riversbend.

# CHAPTER 9

LISTENING TO LORD BELTON SPEAK ABOUT RIVERSBEND gave Peggy a new appreciation for what the town had once been and what he clearly envisioned that it could be once more. As he took her on a tour from building to building, describing the tenants and merchants who had once called this place home, Peggy began to imagine the streets as a bustling center of commerce for the surrounding counties. The town hadn't fallen to ruin but had been split during a time of growth and transition. It was clear to her how much love and care the Baron and his predecessors had for the place and its people. His confidence that it would return to its glory was evident in every word of pride that spilled from his constant stream of explanation. What sort of man was he that he took such pride in his underlings?

Peggy had a picture of the aristocracy gleaned from her father's words and her own experience both with Adam's father and the horrid Lady Blackwell, who held her imprisoned in servitude for years. Lord Belton was turning all those presuppositions on end. She could not credit it. Why would he care for these people? They were nothing to him. Was it all an act? But why? What purpose would there be in deceiving her so? She, too, was a nobody. Her opinion did not matter.

Occasionally, Peggy might offer a question, but mostly she just allowed herself to listen and sink into the images that he described. The story took root, and it were as if she had lived here herself, cared for by him, as if she were a part of his extended family.

He told her of the old physician who had no less than twelve children that had followed his father to the new settlement, an old military keep that the Viscount was transitioning into a beautiful estate at Canton Point. He spoke of the family of sheepherders who had split their flock in two between the holdings, and he told of the sheepherder's eldest daughter and her new husband who were expecting their first child soon and his care that they did not yet have a midwife. He pointed out the mill with its turning wheels that had been rebuilt only a few years prior, and the well that had been dug by his grandfather when his father had been the Baron Whitefall and he, himself, was still in short pants.

She laughed at the thought, and for the first time, perhaps ever, she felt carefree.

He described his plans to have the main road bricked to prevent the rutting that required constant maintenance due to the rains. He laughed and he spoke of his sister's desire to draw more women to the local households which were, in her words, overpopulated with bothersome males.

"But surely, she will marry," Peggy interjected.

He shot her a look that said, *do you know my sister?*

"I mean, she is a lady. Surely, she will leave this area

and have her own household for which she will be responsible."

"Nora insists she will never marry, although Father wants her to have a Season."

"Of course," said Peggy noncommittally. A Season, she thought, where Nora like so many women before her would be auctioned off to the highest bidder. Was her own father so different from those fathers among the Ton, she wondered.

"Isn't that what all women want?" he asked.

"No," she said sharply, and he lifted an eyebrow as he looked at her. The moment extended into eternity. Heat crackled between them regardless of the coolness of the coming evening.

"Do you not wish to marry one day?" he asked softly, so softly she was not sure she heard him, but she answered, nonetheless.

"No," she said again with less force this time. "I will not marry."

"You must have loved very deeply or been hurt very deeply to swear off gentlemen entirely."

"I have not found a gentleman worth my regard," she said honestly.

"Perhaps I shall change your mind," he whispered, leaning close.

She pulled away violently. Did he think he could kiss her, just like that? Just as you please? How like a man to take immediate liberties! Fear and desire bubbled up in equal measure, and she was on the verge of bolting, but his hand on her arm steadied her. He stood like a rock, not expecting anything she was unwilling to give. She felt giddy with the knowledge.

85

"Nora says she will not marry," he said bringing the conversation suddenly back on an even keel. "Of course, of late, she has felt the need of female companionship. I hope you will be her friend."

"I will," Peggy said gaining her equilibrium again.

"She wants to collect more women for the area, so I warn you not to be surprised if she tries to collect you." He laughed, a deep sound of merriment that Peggy found she liked to hear. It was natural and unforced. She wanted more laughter in her own life.

Peggy chuffed at the thought but offered no reply. She had no intention of staying here but did not feel the need to state her position, and he went on describing their surroundings without the requirement.

He told her that the local estates had banded together to ensure that the townsfolk had enough meat and produce to eat in plenty for the entire year, even when certain farmers might have a difficult season.

Peggy found herself in awe. When she looked around, she realized that she had seen no hungry children. No homeless and no beggars. Not overt prosperity, but good, hardy lives. Everyone was given a task and a purpose within their means and abilities, and none were left to suffer. It was so unlike Hampshire, and London, and everywhere else that she had been where the rich only got richer and the poor were left in squalor. She questioned him about this strange occurrence here at Riversbend.

"My father taught me that there is a responsibility due to the aristocracy. We are given much, yes, but success multiplies when shared."

"So, you give to the poor?" she asked, confused. Usually it was the poor who were made to give to the rich.

"Not give so much as open opportunities, like this move my father made," he said, his eyes alight at the thought. Lord Belton was so vibrant, so handsome. He would have kissed her, she thought, and just as quickly, she shoved away the thought. She had no time for such fancies. "Now there are two towns where people can be employed instead of just one," he said. "It is not charity which some may not wish to accept. Instead, it is honest work. That is good for all of us."

Despite the gentleman's verve and vigor, there were shops that were empty and houses that had been vacated when the Viscount had made his call to move. The Baron looked so earnest just now. She suddenly wanted to help him to help the town. If those who could support the town did not fill the voids, how long would the good fortune last, she wondered? They could supplement the lack between the two villages for a time, but the travel between would be a hindrance for any long-term arrangement, especially in the winter this far north. Although the Baron seemed certain that his father's dream would come to fruition, Peggy wondered if it could be done. If he failed, would the village fall to ruin? Would everything that the son and father had known and hoped to achieve be lost? Would good people starve?

Peggy hated that the negative thoughts and worries crept into her mind, but life had proved to her that there was a darkness in the world that often shuttered the light. What Lord Belton described was a dream, and she had seen too many dreams crushed and turned to naught. Still, she held her tongue. Mayhap in this strange little corner of England the good could prevail. Maybe it was a magic land. Who was she to say otherwise?

The gentleman was still speaking with all the excitement of a child who had never known hardship. His eyes were bright as he gestured expansively. For just a moment, she felt the magic of that dream, and she wanted it. She wanted to be a part of something greater than herself, and maybe, for once, build something that didn't fall to ash.

"This was the haberdashery," he explained when they came upon the largest of the empty shops. Six sections of large multi-paned windows sat empty and inside she could see the shelves that lined the walls were covered in dust. "Mr. Drake caught ill two winters ago and passed from influenza," Lord Belton explained with a sigh that indicated a sign of concern.

She did not think she was mistaken. This baron actually cared about his underlings. It was unfathomable. Her heart did a strange little flip, but she ignored it. She liked the man. That was all. Yes. The more she learned about the young lord, the more she liked him, and she could not like him. He was, after all, a member of the aristocracy and completely untrustworthy. And he wanted to kiss her, a traitorous voice whispered, which caused her body to fill with heat and her mind to fill with fluff.

"His wares were taken back to London to cover his brother's debts," the Baron said, "and we have yet to be able to fill the position."

"You haven't a haberdasher in *either* village?" Peggy asked, aghast. It was no wonder Nora had complained. If every trinket and bauble, button or ribbon, had to be sent for to London or some other far-off place, the expense and the inconvenience would be enough to drive residents from the area. The haberdashery was the central shopping hub of any community worth note. Even the small town of Halthaven sported a haberdashery.

"A few merchants have considered it, but they have all of them changed their minds when they realized that the shop is entirely empty and it would take months to get a decent supply this far north," he explained. He sighed, the light of possibility going out of his eyes.

Suddenly, she wanted to put that excitement back. She wanted to give him something about which to smile. She wanted to hear that infectious laugh again.

Peggy was annoyed with her own sudden optimism. Nothing would come of it, she was sure. A new merchant would expect to have something to start with before sinking his fortune into a venture. Many would see the waiting period as a time of loss if the shop had nothing to sell. Those who were looking to start their first shop would not have the means to wait out the dry spell. Peggy knew that a well-seasoned merchant would never bother with a single town which was so small or even pair of towns situated so far to the north. The best money was to be made in the port cities. A greenling might be drawn to such a remote place, but such a person faced the very real risk of failure, both because of his lack of expertise and because of the lack of goods and funds. At the very least, a partially stocked storefront would be a necessity. The initial process would be insurmountable otherwise.

Peggy ran her hand over the window, recalling in her mind's eye how her father would buy one store after another stock full of goods and then turn it into a desirable enterprise all under the name of *Wilhelm's*. It had not been until later in his success that he could open a shop from nothing and fill it from his massive warehouses. Father was an ogre, but he did have a business acumen that was second to none. Mentally, she calculated the probable costs for such a venture. Where to start?

"You haven't a stationer or mercer," she observed. "Tea shops are popular these days for the ladies—"

"So, I'm told," he agreed. "The nearest teashop is in Northwick. They do a brisk business if Brambleton can be believed."

"Brambleton?" she repeated.

"As in, the duke of," he said. "We went to school together."

"Oh," she said. The mention of a duke brought her suddenly down to earth. He was an aristocrat. He wouldn't credit her for one moment. He would rather listen to this Duke of Brambleton. One of his cronies, she thought. Another of the aristocracy. Dash them all to hell. Certainly, he would not credit a woman's opinions.

"Go on," he urged.

She was not sure she should, but he looked so expectant. She wanted to help him, and her nimble mind was fully in merchant mode now. She spoke her thoughts aloud.

"There are catalogs from which items of interest can be ordered," she said before she could help herself. "And merchants on the coast that would be willing to cart goods here in a hurry before winter, I would think. For the right price, of course."

He was watching her with interest, but she was not paying attention. Years of training that she thought that she had forgotten took over as she did the mental calculations in her head, recalling names of prominent tradesmen and listing them off for the Baron. The right merchant with the right contacts could see the stores stocked, she informed him.

"Perhaps rather than several individual stores, you might use this building as a combined front, at least until some other shopkeepers offer to make their stay. Then, they could specialize. This space is certainly large enough," she offered pacing the distance and imagining filled shelves. Then she shrugged, finding her place again. "It's really all the same. The purchase of goods and then sale. So long as you are not providing the service, only the supplies, is does not much matter if you sell a mismatch of items. Common folk won't be so discriminating. You might even draw a dressmaker or milliner more readily if they can browse the catalogs or pick through on hand items. With the right negotiations and guaranteed sales, you could secure a decent price for regular deliveries to the area. After all, you are not far off of the North Road. There is always traffic to and from London."

She found herself pacing in front of the windows and chewing on her bottom lip as she was wont to do when she was deep in thought. All this village really needed was a strong merchant supply chain to find its feet once more. "Your cobbler had to mail order a button for your sister's shoe," she added as an aside. "The man ought to have been able to pop into a shop and get what he needed without delaying for days on end for such a small item. Your overall productivity would increase substantially across the entire village with access to one simple shop of… say… miscellaneous goods."

She came to a grinding halt at the corner of the building and stopped herself from saying anything further. She had forgotten that she could get carried away when it came to matters of business, and she had too late realized that it was not her place to give the Baron instruction.

Lord Belton had stopped several paces behind her, and she clenched her eyes shut, regretting having gone off on her tangent. Such was not the thing that a woman was expected to do, nor was it proper. Had her father not often told her to keep her mind for business behind closed doors and let the men think they were handling things, even if she might be the one pulling the strings from behind the curtain? *That is what your husband will do,* he had said. *A man should handle business, although would an aristocrat dirty his hands with such things? I will train you to support your husband,* her father had said. *But it is men who make the deals. No man wants to shake hands with a woman, so keep your mouth shut.*

Oh, how her father would have loved for Peggy to have been a son, but his infant son died at his mother's breast before he even took his first steps. Her father was left with the poor pickings of a daughter who could not even manage to get herself married properly before she had a child.

She released the breath that she had been holding and spun on her toe, a grimace on her face.

"I apologize," she offered, contrite. "It was not my place."

"No…" He stared in her direction as if she were as mystical as a snowy white stag. "You are exactly right. Go on. Please."

Peggy's mouth opened in shock, but she felt none of the pride that he must have expected. Rather, she felt sheer panic and shame. She had known better and yet had been unable to help herself. She clapped a hand over her mouth and shook her head, unable to speak.

"Please," he pressed, "I would love to hear more about how this works. It is not something in which I am well versed, and it is clear you have experience."

"I don't," she spat before she could help herself.

"Nonsense." He offered a half grin as if to say that she was perfectly safe within his confidence, but she felt like an idiot for having mentioned a single thing. "You've spoken more words, and with more passion, in the last few minutes than I have heard since I met you." Peggy cursed herself for the slip. Her old life was gone, and what did she care about the commerce of Riversbend anyway? It was not her business.

"Goodnight," she said without preamble. Aside, from being a man, he was a lord, and she had forgot her place. She was a fool. This man, this handsome man, made her a fool, and he was looking at her as if she had grown a second head.

Peggy dipped herself into a sharp curtsy befitting a maid before a Baron, and then, before he could process what she had said, and without a proper disengagement, she turned and raced down the street toward the inn. She did not look back or give Lord Belton a chance to ask her why she had reacted in such a strange manner. Twice this day he must have thought her the oddest being that he had ever encountered, and yet she cared not. Instead, she hastened to the inn and up the staircase to her room where she locked herself within the safety of the simple four walls. When she flung herself upon the bed, she grabbed a feathered pillow and allowed herself one moment of weakness wherein she gave a single sharp scream into its muffled form.

Then, she rolled over onto her back and stared up at the ceiling, wondering what would have transpired if she had allowed him to kiss her. "Idiot," she hissed, before giving herself over to what promised to be a fitful night of sleep.

Nash stood for a long moment staring after the enchanting creature who had taken the reins to his life and given him direction. He had acknowledged to himself that she was beautiful, with a maturity and womanliness that filled him with desire, but until this moment, he had not seen her completely. He had wanted to take her in his arms. He had wanted to kiss her, but he sensed she had been hurt. She froze like a frightened deer at his very touch, and then she surprised him. She had stepped into that place beside him as he could expect no silly debutante to do. She had put herself beside him, not just as a pretty face, but as a help-mate. She was everything he needed, but she did not need him at all. She did not want him.

## CHAPTER 10

IN THE ENSUING DAYS, PEGGY HAD DONE A FAIR JOB OF avoiding Lord Belton, and he had not pressed the matter, busy as he was with his own duties. Miss Nora had made a point of stopping in for a visit each day to share tea with her new friend and seemed none the wiser to the awkwardness that had rooted itself between Peggy and her brother. Peggy felt like a heel for the way that she had reacted and wanted to apologize but knew not how without giving the poor man an explanation. At least she would be gone in a few days, and she could put her guilt aside while she and Adam made plans for their future.

*Adam*, she thought.

She had twice now seen Mrs. Finch from a distance and had been too cowardly to go up to the woman and introduce herself. Her days were numbered now, and the inner strength that she had been so sure of had seemed to abandon her when she had needed it most.

The woman was, in a word, good.

Mrs. Finch was like a mother hen to all the children of

the village and especially those under her care. They adored her, and she doted on them all in kind. On the first occasion that Peggy spied her from across the square, she was passing out warm meat pies and apples from the bushel in her cart to any that crossed her path, even those who had only come to village in passing. She refused to accept any payment that was offered by those poorer than she but did trade one of the travelers two fine slabs of cured meat for an embroidered shawl and a pair of winter boots that she gave to the girl at her side, Martha. Peggy had remained well away, convincing herself that she would do better to observe for just a while longer. It was a poor excuse, and she knew it.

The second time, Mrs. Finch had come bearing clothes that her own charges had outgrown. She traded the peddlers for larger sizes and clucked over the tinker's daughter, who had immediately thrown one of Martha's old woolen dresses overtop her own ragged sheath dress and beamed with pride even though the dress was still too large for the young girl. Mrs. Finch had pinched and tucked the fabric here and there beneath a leather belt so that the dress would not drag in the mud as the little girl spun in circles in front of her laughing mother who thanked the gamekeeper's wife with a firm embrace.

She was so very good. How could she take Adam from this life?

Miss Nora had been quick to sing the woman's praises as well when Peggy had steered the conversation in that direction.

"Mrs. Finch is a Godsend," the lady had said with a smile. "It was a shame that she could not have children of her own. She was meant for it. But she has found her happiness in her wards and loves them no different than if she had borne them herself."

Peggy had smiled in return, if a bit tight around the edges. She had arrived to ask this couple to hand over their son, their charge. But according to Miss Nora, Adam was more than a ward; he was like a son to them. She felt her heart break a bit. In order to reclaim her son, she would have to ask this woman to suffer the loss that only a mother could feel. The same loss that Peggy had spent four years burdened beneath.

How could she do such a thing? And how could she not? It was a cruel and unfair world.


With only two full days left before the Bannings and their companions were set to break camp, Peggy could delay no longer. On the third morning, they would have to be prepared to leave if they were to turn south with the troupe and head for the village that she had chosen for their new beginning. Certainly, they could rent a coach to take them if the boy was not prepared to make his exit so soon, but she did not wish to prolong her stay in Riversbend any more than was necessary. One day could easily turn into a week or a fortnight if she did not make her intentions clear. Leaving with the Bannings gave her a distinct timeline that she intended to use to her advantage. She knew that Adam and the Finch family might need time to make arrange- ments and say their farewells, and that meant that today she had no choice but to have the conversation that had weighed so heavily on her mind since her arrival.

She dressed in her best gown, a lilac frock of India muslin with a white fichu about the shoulders and three flounces at the hem. It was too much for the occasion, but she wanted to look her best for the moment that she revealed herself to her son. He was all that mattered in the world, and this moment was more important to Peggy than a grand ball to the highest born ladies. Even as she dressed, she knew that Adam would not care about her clothing. Still, she wore it like armor, as if she were going to battle to win her son.

## CHAPTER 11

When she descended the staircase that separated the boarding rooms of the inn from the dining hall below, she was surprised to be greeted by a flush-faced Miss Nora who was questioning a confused looking Mr. Banning and several of his companions as they sat for their morning meal.

Miss Nora caught Peggy's eye and waved before making her farewell to the men and joining Peggy at the base of the stair.

"Honestly," Miss Nora huffed. "Men are the most insufferable creatures when they wish to keep a secret. Either that or it is as if they know nothing at all about those traveling within their own number."

Peggy furrowed her brow in confusion. What secret would Miss Nora feel the need to discover that the travelers had guarded so dearly?

"It's Nash, really," the lady griped as she led Peggy to a table in the corner and signaled for two cups of tea. "He finds a gem and then lets it slip right through his fingers as if it is no matter at all. Then, he has the gall to refuse me even the slightest hint so that I might retrieve it on my own."

"I am afraid that I do not follow." Peggy laughed. Miss Nora was practically spitting with frustration, and Peggy could make no sense of what upset her.

Miss Nora sank further into her chair, her shoulders bent in defeat. She took a sip of her tea before placing the cup back upon its saucer and pushing it away, too flustered to drink.

"My brother has spent days talking about a plan to bring a merchant into the old haberdashery and to convert one corner to a small tearoom where ladies can gather to talk without having to settle here in the chaos of the inn," Miss Nora began to explain as Peggy felt a knot grow in her stomach. "He said that the proper merchant, with the proper contacts, could get the store running before winter and even draw in other marketable services by offering access to catalogs and an increased inventory of supplies for dressmakers and the like."

"That sounds like a fine plan..." Peggy replied with a tentative murmur.

"Of course, it's a fine plan!" Miss Nora threw her hands up in frustration. "It is a brilliant plan. A teahouse! I wish I had thought of it myself."

"Then what seems to be the problem?" Peggy replied. She was glad that Lord Belton had taken her advice to heart, for it truly was an excellent prospect for such a remote town. Her father had once told her that in the colonies they have such stores that sell all manner of general items, and she had often wondered why the more rural areas of the English countryside had maintained their relegation of many small shops, often falling short, rather than maximizing the availability of goods through one larger merchant's organization. Tradition, she supposed. The haberdashery was the closest thing she had ever seen with its odds and ends, but still, they were often limited to smaller items or trifles. Her own father had thought along those lines as he had expanded his empire, though rather than offering his goods in one building he had chosen to own many small shops of a variety of wares that functioned under one identifiable name.

"The problem is that he did not come up with this plan on his own." Miss Nora sighed. "He admits as much but will not reveal from whom he got the inspiration. I've begged and needled. I have coaxed and even tried to trick him up. To no avail. He will not budge."

"I see," Peggy mused. She was impressed and, admittedly, grateful that Lord Belton had left her name out of his plan. She was glad to see him make use of her knowledge but wanted neither a part in its makeup nor the recognition that might come along with having a strange woman suddenly far too aware of the ways of trade. For all her father knew, she had long been dead. She did not wish for any word to make its way south to Hampshire that there was a woman with the mind of a merchant in the north who resembled his long-lost child. She had abandoned that life, or rather it had abandoned her, and she had no intention of going down that route. No intention at all. "Well, you need not unravel the mystery of this person," she added for good measure. "Your brother has his plan and that ought to be enough."

"It would be enough if we might find someone who would take on such a task in a very short time," Miss Nora replied. "He thinks it can be done by winter and… Oh, how nice that would be for both villages through the rainy months when supplies are hard enough to come by. But that seems nigh on impossible, and…" She pouted. "Why should we have to find another diamond in the rough when there must be one so near already?" She leaned forward and whispered to Peggy as if sharing a great confidence. "Nash told me to stay out of it, but I cannot. I am determined that the source of his knowledge came from one of the traders and tinkers in your wagons. Who better than they to have seen how it can be done? Perhaps, they met such a merchant in another town. Or perhaps it is how they themselves procure their wares, though that seems unlikely, as a delivery would only be lost in chasing their trail from town to town. Nash told me not to pester, but I am sure that is only because he was refused." Her eyes grew bright with excitement. "If I could but locate the individual, I am confident that I could convince them to stay and set up shop here in Riversbend or, at the very least, recommend a contact who could do the job."

"Perhaps, you ought to listen to your brother and leave the matter to him." Peggy hoped that the suggestion would stick, but she could see that it rolled right off Miss Nora without the slightest consideration. Her friend would be chasing her tail for days if she kept this up. The men at the far table had not been keeping a secret; they had been truly unaware. Mrs. Banning would be the only soul who might know that Peggy was the object of Miss Nora's obsession, and the bard's wife would no sooner share Peggy's secret than offer herself up for the job.

"Oh, he shall be cross if he finds out how mettlesome I am being," Miss Nora admitted with a grimace. "He warned me against it and threatened to lock me in the great house until Sunday if I could not behave myself."

"He wouldn't!" Peggy said appalled.

"No. He wouldn't," Nora agreed as she winked. "That was how I deduced it to be one of your group. You shall all have gone by then, so he meant to keep me away, but I slipped out while he was back at the dam with Mr. Finch and the boys." She reached forward to grab Peggy's hand and clasped it between her own. "Please tell me that you know of whom I speak. I am sure that I can make a convincing argument, and if I succeed, then Nash cannot possibly be cross."

Oh, he'll be cross... Peggy wanted to say. His entire purpose of keeping his sister away from her meddling was to protect Peggy's own privacy, which had been a clear cause of distress that early evening when they had gone for a stroll through town. She was grateful for his protection but knew not how to put her friend off. She wished she were better at lying.

"Do you?" Miss Nora begged. "Do you know the man I seek?"

Peggy swallowed deeply. She pulled her hand from the lady's and picked up her teacup, drinking deeply while she gave herself a moment to think.

"I know of whom you speak," she said after a long while, realizing that there was no way around it, "but it is no man."

"A woman!" Miss Nora's mouth dropped open in a mix of shock and pleasure. "All the better, for that only increases my chance of success. Of course, Nash would have bumbled it with a woman. Men just don't have the touch when it comes to us females. Particularly not ones with a solid head upon their shoulders as this one must. Pray tell." She leaned in expectantly with her hands clasped before her and her eyes alight with hope.

"I am sorry to tell you that she cannot be convinced," Peggy said, giving the chance of ending Miss Nora's pursuit one last go. "She loathes that life and will have no part in it save the advice that she has already given."

Nora shook her head. "I just want a chance. If she could only be made to see how wonderful it is here, how much good she could do—"

Peggy held up a hand to stop her friend before she went any further.

"'Tis I," she said abruptly.

Miss Nora chuffed, and her face scrunched in a look of comical disbelief as if she thought that Peggy was toying with her. Then, Peggy watched as Miss Nora began to think on the prospect. As if she were witness to the wheels turning in the young lady's mind, Peggy saw that she believed. Peggy was too well-spoken and well-mannered. It was clear that she was educated. She dressed well and carried herself like one of a moderate, if not upper class. Her father had insisted upon it, and with the duchess' clothing, the ruse was complete.

Miss Nora herself had on first glance thought her a well-bred lady. Daughters of merchants were often mistaken for such, as they were known to live a lavish life even if they were not born to generations of fortune and lineage. The upper class thought that their breeding would tell, but all too often it did not.

"Well, that settles it," Miss Nora grinned. "You have to stay." She explained that Peggy was an additional mark on her list of people to convince to remain in the small village. "How I have dreaded the thought of putting distance between our friendship and had planned to work on you as soon as I had settled my mystery. Knowing that you are one and the same makes it all more fated that you were meant to come to us."

Peggy had been meant to come to this place, she thought, but not for the reasons that Miss Nora thought.

"Why on earth would Nash not have told me?" his sister grumbled. "He needn't have kept it a secret, and he has been quite a bear about it. In fact, he told me it was none of my business and would not discuss it at all. I don't know when I've seen him so out of sorts."

So it was that Peggy decided that she ought to at least explain herself, if only so that Lord Belton did not suffer his sister's wrath for Peggy's protection.

"It was my doing," Peggy began. She explained that her father had been a merchant and that she had given the advice unbidden and quite unintentionally.

Miss Nora's eyes widened as she continued the story.

"The memory of my father, of my previous life…" She wondered how she might put it that gave proper weight to her feeling without revealing more than she ought. "It is painful for me to recall." There, that ought to do, she thought. Let Miss Nora assume what she will, that it was pain for the loss or a tragedy of some sort, since certainly it was a tragedy and the loss of her innocence and her joy.

"It is a part of my life that I no longer live. I try not to think about every day of that past nor dwell upon it. So, when your brother praised my speech, I…" She closed her eyes, still embarrassed that she had been so rude. "I froze. I froze, and I was hurting. And so I behaved abominably. I ran away in such a manner that he must have thought me very angry or perhaps a little daft." Peggy gave a small humorless laugh. "That is why he knew that I would not wish to be pressed. That is why he kept my identity a secret. Because he saw that the issue upset me and that I did not wish to speak on it again. I have avoided him ever since, which must have only reinforced his thought that I was cross with him."

Miss Nora pursed her lips. "Well," she huffed, "I suppose I cannot be annoyed with him for that. I really did think he was just being obstinate because he had failed at making a convincing offer and did not wish me to best him at his own game."

"No," Peggy agreed. "He was doing me a kindness."

Miss Nora's eyes rose to her friend's as if weighing whether or not Peggy really could be turned to her purpose. "All right," she said after a time. "I see, and respect, your desire not to suffer at the hands of painful memories. If not for the shop, can you not still be convinced to stay for some other purpose? I could match you with a lord of a local estate and we could be neighbors for all time! Lord Abernathy is handsome enough, if you can stomach his character." She ended her speech with a wrinkle of her nose, letting Peggy know full well how she felt about the prospect of marriage, particularly to the lord in question.

"I think not," Peggy laughed.

"But, Peggy," she began.

"You are the one who has espoused spinsterhood. How dare you pressure me," Peggy said with mock outrage.

"Fine, marriage is out of the question, but what about taking up residence in one of the houses in town?" Miss Nora was all but pleading.

Peggy clasped the young beauty's hand and smiled at her. "I cannot stay, but I promise to write."

"You cannot leave me in the company of all of these men," Miss Nora complained, stomping a slippered foot. "It has been so nice to have another lady to lunch with and talk to whenever I wish." She gave a dramatic sigh and a wink that promised she was only teasing and that there were no hard feelings. A moment later, she embraced Peggy in a warm hug. "In all honesty, I wish you only the best. And I *do* require that you write, and often."

They finished their tea while Miss Nora waited for her carriage to be called. She wanted to get back to Whitefall Hall before her brother returned home. Lord Belton would be unhappy if he found out that she had disobeyed his direct order.

"If you are found out, I'll be sure to tell him that you were no bother," Peggy had promised as Miss Nora took up the reins of her brother's gig. "Besides, I owe him an apology before I make my departure." She had blown out a long breath while she had watched the horses pull away. It seemed she had more than one difficult conversation to address. She straightened her skirts and decided that it was well past time for the first.

## CHAPTER 12

PEGGY HAD BEEN FORTUNATE ENOUGH TO SECURE HERSELF a ride on a hay cart that delivered her nearly two-thirds of the way to the gamekeeper's cabin on the Whitefall grounds. She had not wanted to beg a ride of Miss Nora as the main lane into the estate took a different path, and she had not wanted to explain why she would be making such a strange excursion to visit people with whom she had no acquaintance. Despite their budding friendship, the truth of the reason for her appearance in Riversbend was not something that she had divulged to Miss Nora.

After it was all settled, and she was leaving with her son at her side, everyone would learn the news. But until that time when Adam had been made aware, she kept her cards close to her chest. She hated the thought that the issue would soon become the talk of the town, but there was little avoiding that in such a close-knit community. People would wonder where the boy had gone, and the truth would be told, gossip likely spread in their wake. So long as she had her son, and so long as the mutterings remained in the remote corner of England, she had little to fear.

It took her one-half hour to walk the final stretch to the cottage. It was easy enough to find as she followed the path along the winding fence through the dense forest until it opened into the clearing that she remembered so vividly from the other day.

The cottage looked the same. It was neat and homely, with smoke coming from the chimney that promised that someone was within. She thanked her fortunes for that.

Peggy rapped her knuckles upon the door thrice and held her breath while she waited for it to be opened. Martha, the young girl who was often seen at her mother's —adoptive or no—side opened the door with a look of confusion.

"What is it child?" a voice called from within.

"It's a lady," Martha called back over her shoulder.

Peggy began to shake her head, but Mrs. Finch was already making her way to the door while wiping her hands upon a stained apron.

"The main house is up the way," Mrs. Finch began. "I'd offer for my husband or sons to drive you, but they are out. If you'd like to wait, Martha can run—"

"I'm not lost," Peggy said before the woman could continue or before she lost her nerve. "I'm here to see you, Mrs. Finch."

The woman narrowed her eyes and looked Peggy up and down, from her fine gown to her trembling hands, and nodded. "Go upstairs, child," she instructed the girl. "Leave us to talk."

Martha scuttled away, but not without casting a curious look over her shoulder.

"Come in," Mrs. Finch said as she turned and headed toward the kitchen. "All the way up, Martha! I can hear you on the stair." A few more steps clomped upward and then a door closed above. Peggy smiled a bit to herself. The women certainly did have a way with mothering.

Peggy followed Mrs. Finch into the kitchen. It was bright and airy with a door thrown open to the back of the house to let out the heat that was billowing from the small stovetop in the corner. There were several cups of flowers on the windowsill in various states of wilting, scraggly bouquets that could only have been plucked by children and placed with pride on display by Mrs. Finch for however long they might last.

"Mrs. Finch, I am sorry for the intrusion," Peggy began, her voice quivering though, and she begged it to hold steady. It would not. "I've come a long way to meet with you. To meet with..." She couldn't speak past the lump in her throat. Mrs. Finch pulled out a chair at the worn wooden table and sat, indicating for Peggy to do the same. She did. "I've come because..." she tried once more.

"You're Adam's mother." Mrs. Finch declared with a face that gave away none of her thoughts. "I see the resemblance." She was assessing Peggy, taking her measure, and Peggy could not tell if she would meet with approval or fall short.

She nodded. "I've... been away." Peggy cleared her throat. "Not by choice." Her words were lost. Her breath escaped her, but Peggy knew she must continue. She had to make it clear that she had not abandoned Adam, even if it meant baring her soul, her traumas, to this woman she did not know. "I was held. Against my will. For four years. It was only after that that I learned that my son, who I love very much, was…" Her voice cracked again and failed her. This was not going as she had imagined. Not at all.

"Was given to me," Mrs. Finch finished for her.

Again, Peggy nodded. "I come here today to ask you, to beg you, to transfer him back into my care."

"That simple, is it?" Mrs. Finch asked crossing her arms over her ample bosom. There was a tone that bristled in her voice. At first Peggy was taken aback, but she reminded herself that Mrs. Finch had come to love and care for the boy as her own. She had every right to be leery, to have concern of the woman before her. In the same way that Peggy had wanted to protect Adam from whatever life might have burdened him with, Mrs. Finch now felt the urge to protect him as well. Even if that meant protection from his own mother.

"No, it could never be that simple," Peggy suppressed a sob. "I know that. I've seen you with him these past days. Seen that you love him and care for him. Seen that he loves you."

"I do. But he's your son," Mrs. Finch stated with cool reality.

"Yes," Peggy whispered.

There were tears in the woman's eyes, though she was too strong to allow them to fall in front of her guest. Right or wrong, whatever happened, someone's heart would break this very day. And Peggy hated that she had to do this to this poor woman who had been unable to bear children of her own, who had taken such care with Peggy's child when she could not. For that, she would forever be thankful, but she wanted Adam at her side, needed him.

"I have a letter from a solicitor in London that explains everything." She pulled the thick envelope from her pocket and slid it across the table to Mrs. Finch, who placed her hand over it but did not open it. Peggy had been hesitant to divulge too much of her sordid tale to people that she did not know for fear that they might use it to tarnish her newly restored reputation or twist it in ways that were not consistent with the truth. But Mr. Crowley had found a way to describe Peggy's imprisonment, release, and the following trials that convicted those responsible in such a way as made the matter clear that she had not abandoned her son and still maintained as much of her treasured privacy as possible.

Finally, the woman flipped the envelope over with aching slowness, as if she knew she had to read the contents but wished it were not so. She cracked the seal.

The sound of a wagon out front and cheerful male voices had both women's heads snapping toward the window. Then, their eyes returned to one another with alarm. It was too soon. There had not been enough time to talk, to explain. To come to an agreement. Peggy felt a cold sweat break out all over her body. She needed more time. As often as she had tried to prepare herself, she did not feel ready.

Oh, how much easier it would have been if she could have hated Mr. and Mrs. Finch. How devastating it was to crush another family just to repair her own. Yet, for Adam, she must. He needed to know how much she loved him. He needed to know that he was the thing that had kept her safe and sane all those years of torment. And she needed him. She had seen little good in this world, save her son. He had been the sole light in her darkness, the one person that she lived for. The one person she loved more than anything else. She could not lose him.

"Martha!" Mrs. Finch shouted up to the ceiling. "Go outside and tell the boys you can all wait out there. And send your father in!"

The sound of the front door slamming meant that Martha had scurried along to do her mother's bidding. A short while later, the slow, heavy sound of grown male boots entered the house, and Mr. Finch made his way to the kitchen.

"George…" Mrs. Finch stood, giving her husband one deep nod. "She's here. This is…" Mrs. Finch turned to Peggy with a furrowed brow, and they both realized that they had not actually been properly introduced.

"Peggy Williams." Peggy stood and offered a nod.

"I see," the gamekeeper said in a voice that was a deep and soothing timbre. He stepped through the doorway but seemed unsure of what to do next. His eyes remained locked on his wife's, and they seemed to be able to speak without talking. For so long they stood in silence, and yet Peggy swore it was as if they had shared an entire conversation that she had not been privy to in that time.

The door to the cabin slammed open, and a small form raced in. Peggy turned to see Adam with tears in his eyes.

"It's not true!" he shouted.

"Adam, deary," Mrs. Finch began, but the boy was too worked up to listen.

"That isn't my mother!" he cried. "You said she was dead! You said so!"

"We thought she was," Mrs. Finch began again, step-

113

ping forward to brush a consoling hand over his hair only to have him jerk away as if scalded.

"It's not true!" he repeated. He turned toward Peggy who was staring, open mouthed and with her heart in her throat. "You can't take me away! I won't go! I'll run away. I'll run away from all of you! My mother is DEAD!"

With that, he spun on his heels and raced out the door without even bothering to close it behind him. They all stood in silence as they heard the weeping boy arguing with the other two children as they chased after him. Mr. Finch slowly left the room, shut the door to the house, and returned without a word.

"Jemmy will bring him back," he said when the women seemed too upset to speak.

"Martha must have been listening." Mrs. Finch groaned. "I'm going to have to have a stern word with that girl, *again*."

Peggy plunked into her chair, crestfallen. Not only had that not gone as expected, but it had been worse than she could have ever imagined. He hated her, thought her an imposter, and there was no way that she could force him to come with her in that condition. It would only traumatize him more.

Mrs. Finch turned around and fiddled on the counter until she turned with three tumblers of amber liquid filled to the brim. She handed one to her husband, who threw it back in one gulp, and slid the other to Peggy. Mrs. Finch took a hearty drink, and Peggy, after some trepidation, did the same. The liquor burned and made her eyes water, but the sensation gave her something to focus on. She could not, would not, lose herself here.

"He thinks I died," Peggy muttered after a long while.

It was a possibility that she had considered. In her mind, however, Adam had been so pleased to find her alive that he had flung himself into her arms in relief. She certainly had not imagined the boy shouting at her as if she were an imposter attempting to steal him away for nefarious reasons.

# CHAPTER 13

"WE WERE TOLD YOU HAD DIED," MR. FINCH ADMITTED. "That's what the abbey said when he came to us."

"It took him two years to believe it," Mrs. Finch added. "But in the end, he did because he was so certain you would never have abandoned him."

"He was right." Peggy sniffled as she wiped a rogue tear from her cheek. "I never would have."

"We had no idea," Mr. Finch promised. "And then… he was doing so well, so happy, that when we found out you were alive, we hadn't known how to break it to him."

"You knew?" Peggy's voice quivered with emotion. Of course, they knew. Hadn't Mrs. Finch greeted her without an ounce of surprise? Almost as if she had been expected.

Mrs. Finch nodded to her husband, who turned and took a box down off the highest shelf. One which none of the children could reach. From within he pulled out a letter, a single page, and handed it to Peggy.

"The abbess wrote to us after having been contacted by your solicitor," Mrs. Finch explained while Peggy read the contents that confirmed her words exactly. "She said that they had been mistaken in your demise and that now that things had been set to rights, we ought to expect a visit, but she wasn't sure when, if even, you would wish to claim your son."

Peggy opened her mouth to speak but could not manage to get the words out. Not claim her own son?

"The abbess also confirmed your parentage and sent the church records of the child's birth." Mr. Finch, stoic though he seemed, was having trouble keeping his eyes in one place. The man was at a loss. It seemed they all were.

"She said you were a good mother," Mrs. Finch added, tears flowing freely now. "And that you had been working very hard to provide a good life for him. That you suffered a terrible tragedy that kept you away, whatever it was. The letter was not very specific."

At the woman's loss of composure, Peggy lost her own. Her body was wracked with sobs, and tears streamed down her cheeks and dotted the paper that she held in her hand. It was a kindness unlike anything she had ever experienced that the abbess had done for her, and she was grateful that her son was cared for—but he was her son. And the Finches had let him think she was dead. Her beleaguered mind latched onto that thought. How could they!?

She stared for a long while, trying to make sense of what they were telling her and what her son had screamed at her only moments before. "But you still let him think that I was dead?" she asked, looking up at them and praying for a valid explanation.

"He had been doing so well," Mrs. Finch sniffed. "He was finally happy and seemed settled. He no longer cried for you at night. I'm sorry." She dabbed at her eyes with the edge of her apron. "I'm so very sorry. I just didn't want to hurt him if you did not come."

"We did not know for sure that you would come," Mr. Finch explained when it seemed that his wife could not. "The abbess only said that you might. It seemed unfair to give him hope and to have him go through all of that again, or worse, if you did not appear. And we love him. We wanted to protect him. Then, the months went by and you hadn't come. We could not bear the thought of him staring at the road waiting every day. We did not want him to hope only to suffer loss once more. He is so young, and it seemed he had already lost so much."

"We did consider telling him," Mrs. Finch finally broke back in. "But we never seemed to find the right time."

"It took me... a *long* time to get here," Peggy said when she finally allowed herself to admit that these people had done right by her son, that they had protected him in the same way she would have done herself if the roles had been reversed. "Not because I wished to delay seeing him. It was my sole purpose." Then, deciding that these were good people. That for once in her life she knew beyond a doubt that someone could be trusted, she decided to jump all the way in. No secrets. "I was too frightened to take the mail coach. I was..." She swallowed, "I was abducted from one and held against my will in servitude, unable to even step foot out of doors—for four years."

Mrs. Finch gasped and covered her mouth with her hands.

"Child," the woman crooned, reaching out as if to rub Peggy's hair, as she had only moments before in the effort to comfort Adam. But she withdrew it before contact, catching herself in the gesture that might not be welcome.

In reply, Peggy reached forward and squeezed her hand, offering a tight smile that revealed her gratitude for the understanding.

"So, I did not want to be confined in a coach. I came the slow way with the peddlers. Town to town. Riding on horseback or in an open wagon. The trip also gave me time to prepare myself, to think about the life I hoped to provide and to choose a place that I thought would make a fresh start for both of us." She released the woman's hand and raised both of hers in a shrug. "To heal in a way. To be sure that I could come to Adam whole and without my burdens. Or as much as I can ever be."

"I can understand that." Mrs. Finch nodded.

"So, I understand now why you did not tell him," Peggy continued. "And as much as this has not gone how I expected, I am grateful that he did not spend those months waiting each day only to be disappointed each day I did not arrive. I can never fully express how thankful I truly am for how much you have cared for him and watched over him. He seems... happy."

"Thank you for saying that." Mr. Finch offered a pursed smile. "Ellie's been worrying over it since we got the letter and certainly would have continued to do so if you hadn't been so understanding."

"But you said you've already chosen another town?" Mrs. Finch cut in, as if her mind had been locked further back in the conversation and she had not heard anything at all since Peggy had mentioned choosing a place to start afresh.

"I have," Peggy confirmed.

"Is it far?" Mr. Finch asked.

"It's… not close," Peggy revealed with a grimace.

"When do you plan to leave?" he continued in his low tones.

"Tomorrow next," she said. "With those with whom I arrived."

"Well, couldn't you stay about this town?" Mrs. Finch asked, a pleading in her eyes. "At least until Adam comes to terms with it all? So we can be close. Just for a little while?" Peggy could see that the woman was begging as much for herself as for Adam. The thought of losing the boy, even though she knew she must, was crushing the gamekeeper's wife. If Peggy had to guess, though her husband was harder to read, he was on unsteady legs as well.

Peggy considered it. The thought would shatter everything that she had planned, and worse, if she lived in the inn for the unknown duration, it would make a substantial dent in her purse. She had wanted to put that money into an investment, a farm of some sort perhaps, so that the money would grow. If she wanted to make a real name for herself, she supposed, she could offer up her services as a laundress, but the thought still bristled. She could not afford to wait around Riversbend for months on end. Not without income.

Then, she recalled Adam's threat to run away. He was just young and tempestuous enough to do it. The shock had been too sudden and too great. Having heard from Martha's eavesdropping and not from the cautious approaches of the adults, he had been given the news in the most shocking manner possible. As much as she hated to admit it, the Finches were right. He needed time.

"I don't suppose that I have a choice." She breathed a dramatic sigh. "We cannot have him running off, and I certainly do not want him to resent me for ripping him away without warning."

Mrs. Finch clapped her hands together with relief.

"You might like it here for good," she offered.

Peggy shook her head, wanting to squash that fantasy before it took root. "No. I will delay my plan but not alter it."

"Just consider," Mrs. Finch pleaded. "Then, maybe we can still see him even after... you know. And he could still see Jemmy and Martha and his friends."

It all sounded like a good solution in theory, Peggy noted. But in reality, she was worried that the constant reminder of the Finches would make it difficult for Adam to fully bond with Peggy as a family of their own. This was *their* home. *Their* village. And she was an interloper. No. She could not see how staying in this place would work. She could remain only while he adjusted to the idea of her being alive and not having abandoned him, but she would not do so forever.

"I cannot chance giving him false hope," she said after a time. "I will make some arrangements for the time being, but they will only be temporary. Beyond that, I make no promises."

"That's fair," Mr. Finch said when his wife opened her mouth to attempt what was likely about to be another effort at convincing. "We won't start with any promises. Now, what do we do?"

Though it crushed Peggy to agree to it, over the next half hour, she and Finches decided that the best course of action would be to allow Adam to remain in the cottage where he was comfortable for the time being. They would give him a few days to calm down and then, when he was ready, Mrs. Finch would bring him to town to meet with Peggy and hear her side of the story, so much as a young boy ought to know. Then, they would work on regular exposure and the development of the relationship between mother and child. They had agreed that no word of Peggy and Adam's true relationship would be shared beyond the Finch family and herself. They did not wish for Adam to have to navigate the awkwardness of questions, rumors, and gossip in what was sure to be any already trying time.

Peggy was so grateful to the Finches that they were willing to work with her through the process. Though she could see that it would be difficult for the couple, they wanted to ensure that the transition was as painless for the boy as possible. All were in agreement on that. In truth, it was more than they were required to permit considering that the convent had signed the boy over to their care. Peggy had hoped for a clean break but could have found herself embroiled in a vicious battle. Instead, she found herself somewhere in the middle. She could only hope that it would all turn out for the best.

When Jemmy had finally managed to coax Adam back to the property, and Martha had been sent firmly to her room to await punishment for her misdeeds, Adam refused to come anywhere near Peggy. She did note, however, that he stared at her with a furrowed brow from afar. Perhaps, she hoped, he was trying to align the woman who stood before him with the one that he remembered. She might have done better to arrive in something like the plain grey shifts that had been provided by the abbey all those years ago. It had not even occurred to her that, though she had spent her early years in finery such as she wore today, he had never seen her in anything but the most basic and modest of attire.

After a quiet word of instruction to his eldest adoptive son about the situation, Mr. Finch instructed Jemmy to drive Peggy back to the inn while he and Mrs. Finch had a word with Adam and then Martha. The young girl seemed truly contrite, not having realized how her actions would be received. The young man handed Peggy up into the ancient but sturdy wagon and then hopped in beside her before flicking the reigns.

"So, you're Adam's mum?" the young man asked after a long leg of uncomfortable silence.

"I am," she said without taking her gaze from the road ahead.

"You know he's still my brother, right?" Jemmy declared, turning to look at her with resolve.

Peggy turned to meet his eyes and held his firm gaze. "I know." She nodded. For she did. She might be Adam's blood, but these people had become his family too. She could never deny that, and taking him from it would be one of the hardest things she would ever do. Maybe they could arrange a visit once a year or so, she considered. Perhaps that would be enough. Though, she suspected that while Martha might come to accept the change in time, Jemmy at least would never forgive the removal of his dearest companion.

"All right." He nodded in return. "So long as that's clear."

She would never be able to erase the boy from her son's mind. He would make a point of remaining in Adam's life, if only in a peripheral sense. He would be more than a memory; the determination was as clear as the summer sun. The awkwardness eased from the ride now that Peggy had accepted Jemmy's terms. She was glad of it, for she was not sure how much he was aware, but if this young man had set his mind against her, he could easily sway her own son to hold a grudge.

"How are you going to explain why you are remaining in town?" he asked with genuine curiosity. "I mean, you came in with the gypsies, right? Won't everyone expect you to leave with them? People will talk."

"Yes," she released a long breath in agreement. "They will. I suppose I have a little over a day to figure that out."

"You're pretty," he observed with a matter-of-fact shrug. "I'm sixteen. If you say you're in town because you're madly in love with me then maybe Marie Harper will get jealous and finally let me kiss her."

Peggy laughed outright. "I don't think that would suit." She chuckled. "I'm a bit over-ripe for your pickings."

Again, he shrugged. "Can't blame a man for trying."

Peggy smiled at his audacious suggestion, and even for the suggestion that he was a man, but she had to give him credit for trying to earn his rakish reputation with a ploy rather than real misbehavior. She was grateful for his teasing and the way that it lightened her mood on the way into town. Today had been difficult. She had a lot to think about and a lot to worry about. But with Jemmy making light of the situation, it gave her a small glimmer of hope that, one day, she could laugh with her own son in much the same way.

One day soon, she prayed.

# CHAPTER 14

She was certain that Adam would not be coming to see her the following day. Mr. and Mrs. Finch had warned that he was a boy who came slowly about change in his emotions, and he would need time to settle his thoughts before he could see her with a clear head. She had the same sort of cautious sentiment herself, so she understood it in her son. The Finches also promised to send Jemmy or Martha with a note before they might make their visit so that she was not caught unawares.

So it was that Peggy had an entire day to figure out what her plan was for remaining in the village without causing a stir. She had one idea, but she did not care for it. Not in the least.

After checking in on the Bannings, who would spend the entire day preparing their carts and animals so that they could be off at first light, she stopped by the stables to take her own mount out for what she decided would be a pleasant ride up to Whitefall Hall. The Bannings had been both sad and hopeful when she had shared her intention to remain behind. Of course, Mrs. Banning and the boys would miss her company, but the woman also understood the importance of Peggy reconnecting with her son.

"Do what you must," she had whispered as she had pulled Peggy in close for a hug. Then, she slipped a small vial into Peggy's palm and closed her hand over it. "I know you always say you aren't looking for love, but if by chance you change your mind or meet a nice gentleman that needs a little helping along, you just use this." Peggy glanced down at her palm to the bottle labeled *Ardor*.

She shook her head and laughed, slipping it into her purse for the herbalist's benefit. Peggy had seen Mrs. Banning make her supposed love potions. They were nothing more than a blend of periwinkle and apple skins, apples as red as a kiss, Mrs. Banning would say, that had been soaked in oil, drained, and then the scented oil was diluted with rosewater. There was nothing magical about it, but Mrs. Banning made quite the steady stream of coin selling such things to foolish girls and lonely wives. Perhaps, just the thought that the potion might work was enough to provide the confidence needed, but Peggy would not be fooled. She was a realist. Love did not come in a bottle. Love, she thought, did not come at all.

"I'm telling you it works." Mrs. Banning chuckled but then turned her back to the crowd behind her and winked for Peggy alone. "Got me three strapping boys out of it, I did."

Peggy chuckled and kissed the herbalist on the cheek. She said farewell to the young mischief-makers and waved to the bard one last time before climbing up onto her horse.

She kicked the mount into motion and settled in for a nice leisurely ride to Whitefall Hall, where she still owed one particular baron an apology.

Peggy was pleased to find both the Baron and his sister in residence when she made her impromptu call. In her distracted state, she had not thought enough ahead to have sent word of her intention. In such isolated parts of the English countryside, she had merely assumed that their calendars would be clear. She was fortunate to find that her assumption proved to be true. Miss Nora was thrilled with the arrival of her friend and called at once for a tray to be brought to the breakfast room.

"I had thought to make my way to town in an hour or two," the lady explained, "to bother you for entertainments." Together they laughed. "However, my dear brother warned me that you would be in preparations for your departure and might not wish to be bothered. I did not want to be a bother or distraction, and yet still I could not bear the thought of your leaving without a proper farewell. I must say, I've been beside myself."

"I certainly would not have wished to leave without having seen you," Peggy assured her friend while looking around the otherwise empty room with a feigned glare, as if she would censure the Baron upon sight. The gentleman had yet to join them. Peggy was glad of that. She needed a few moments to calm her nerves, and the Baron's presence was anything but calming. Speaking to Miss Nora was easy enough; she would accept Peggy's words from the off. Peggy had no inkling of doubt in her mind that Miss

Nora could be won over. It was her sibling to whom Peggy owed an explanation.

"It is my departure about which I have come to speak with you," Peggy began and forced herself to settle her hands neatly within her lap rather than wringing them as she felt inclined to do. Though she had agreed with Mr. and Mrs. Finch on the proposal to remain in Riversbend for a time, she could not help the feeling of overwhelming disappointment that her months of planning had gone awry. She knew somewhere deep inside of her that it was for the best. And yet it still felt like a monumental failure. She felt like a failure. To have been so thoroughly rejected by her own son and to now be stuck in this place while she awaited his understanding brought her no joy. Her only hope was that he could be convinced, and swiftly. For she refused to consider the unthinkable; that he might never agree to take his place at her side.

"Oh?" Miss Nora wondered aloud. "Does the weather not suit for the road? Will there be a delay?" The lady laughed and explained that though she knew it was unkind to have such selfish hope, she had on several occasions wished for just such a thing.

"Not exactly." Peggy laughed with a nervous edge. "The others will be moving on in the morning."

There was a deafening silence as Miss Nora pierced her with a searching gaze. Peggy could not bring herself to say the words, for then it must be real. Then Miss Nora said them for her.

"But not you," Miss Nora stated tentatively. She held her excitement, her hope, at bay with the stoic features of one bred to the well-mannered habits of the Ton. One did not reveal too much of their emotions until they were

128

certain of the company. It was so unlike Miss Nora's natural exuberant tendencies that Peggy wanted to laugh. Instead, she nodded her confirmation. At this, Miss Nora clasped her hands together at her breast and revealed a radiant grin. "Assure me that this is not a jest," she begged.

"No. It is not."

Nora threw her arms around her friend and laughed aloud. "I am so glad."

"I am looking for work," Peggy said.

Miss Nora was shaking her head in the negative. "Nonsense. I'll not hear of it. You will be my guest," she said with all the surety of an aristocrat.

"I cannot," Peggy said. She took a deep breath. "In the past, I was a laundress… It really is the only work I know."

Miss Nora's eyes opened wide in surprise. "That is not true," she blurted. "You obviously know the mercantile business."

"That is a man's job," Peggy said.

"Poppycock," spat Miss Nora. "Here, in this town, it is *your* job. Only say the word."

"Well, I must speak with your brother first," Peggy explained. "If I am to stay, albeit temporarily, I shall need to make accommodations. I believe he might be of help in that matter."

"Nonsense!" Miss Nora exclaimed shaking her head most vigorously. "You shall stay here for as long as you need. As my guest." Peggy was pleased to note that her friend had taken her explanation of a temporary residence to heart and had not begged for something more permanent. Still, if she were to manage this situation with Adam with any chance of privacy, it could not be done from one of the most prominent estates in the county.

Peggy shook her head. "I am afraid I cannot impose," she explained and raised her hand to stop her friend when she opened her mouth to repeat the offer. "I am a solitary creature at heart and used to being on my own. I would like to speak with your brother about arrangements in town as you had once suggested. You are right to think that it would be impractical to remain at the inn, but neither can I stay here so far from town. I need a purpose, and I think I have a plan that would be beneficial to both of us."

Peggy spent the next half hour explaining her intentions to her young friend. Of course, she left out anything that even remotely indicated her involvement with Adam or the Finch family. Instead, she revealed that she would be willing to offer her services to help the town grow by spearheading the reopening of the haberdashery. Then, once the shop was on its feet and a new merchant could be found, she would be free to leave without constraints.

"But..." Miss Nora mused. "Would it not be too trying a task? On your emotions, I mean. The subject seemed to upset you, and while you have my full encouragement in your decision to remain at Riversbend, I would hate for you to be unhappy in the undertaking."

Peggy offered a wan smile. It was not ideal, but she could not admit that to her friend, and truthfully, the mercantile was a better choice than laundry. She hated being a laundress and all the memories that entailed, but she had also sworn long ago that she would give up any involvement that reminded her of her father and his lecherous dealings.

Yet, she had nothing else to offer, no other skill set that

could benefit this small community. This was a chance for her to grow the minor fortune that she had been given and build it into something that could provide Adam with the opportunity to have anything he wanted out of life; to be whatever he wanted. She would give him things of which most bastard sons could never dream. She would give him a successful future. He could study a trade or arrange a tenancy with a prosperous landlord. If she did well enough, she could even afford to send him to get a proper education. To achieve such ends, she could not allow her financial security to dwindle. She would not put her son in a position to live hand to mouth. And more importantly, she refused, resolutely refused, to find herself in a position where she must subjugate herself to another ever again—not to a master—and she would certainly not lower herself to the horrors of taking a husband for the mere sake of providing for herself and her son. That was just a different kind of servitude.

She had learned better than to ever tie herself to a man again. She might be breaking her vow to avoid anything in relation to trade, a petulant decision that had more to do with refusing her father the satisfaction than forsaking her own honor, but it was only a brief and lesser evil, she assured herself. These others were vows on which she must stand firm.

"As it shall only be a short-term arrangement, I think I can manage," she explained. "Besides, as you said, I have the knowledge and might as well use it for good."

Miss Nora leapt up with excitement and embraced Peggy in a most casual way that left her laughing. If all of the peerage possessed even a hint of Miss Nora's pleasant demeanor and kind spirit, England would be a much better place. As it was, Peggy had far more experience with those on the opposite side of the coin. Only a handful could she thus far claim to trust and respect. Still, she was happy to see that number growing. Perhaps one day the good would outweigh the bad.

## CHAPTER 15

THE SOUND OF A DOOR OPENING IN THE MAIN HALL HAD Miss Nora calling for her brother's attention.

When Lord Belton poked his head into the room to spy the females at their leisure, Miss Nora raced over and pulled him within.

"Nash, do come in," she said, nearly bouncing with excitement for the news that she could hardly contain. "Miss Williams has come to make you a proposition, and you must hear it straight away!"

"A proposition?" he asked, amusement raising one eyebrow. Peggy sighed and shook her head. Lady Nora's words had had the unintentional implication of a tawdry offering, and Peggy wondered just how many times the wealthy gentleman had been cornered for the compulsion of marriage by some overeager lady or hopeful mother. She was pleased to see that his response was done so in a laughing manner. She appreciated that the gentleman was neither so rigid as to be unable to make light of the situation, nor so dense as to even consider for a moment that Peggy would be here to do anything of that sort.

"What your sister meant to say is that I would like a word, if you might spare me a moment," Peggy clarified.

"Yes, yes. Just so," Miss Nora replied with a dismissive wave of her hand. "As it is that I am already apprised of the situation," she smirked at her brother with a victorious gleam to her eye, "I shall leave you two to talk while I go gather some necessities."

"Oh, there's no need…" Peggy began to argue, but Miss Nora would hear none of it.

"Nonsense," she said having already made up her mind and with a tone that indicated she would not be swayed. "It is the least that I can do." With that, she made her exit, leaving Peggy shaking her head and the Baron in utter confusion.

"What sort of necessities…" Lord Belton began to wonder aloud, but Peggy simply gestured for the gentleman to take a seat in the chair across from where she herself settled upon a delicate carved couch.

"I have much to explain," she began, "but first, I owe you my sincerest apology."

"For what?" he asked, confusion furrowing his brow.

"Firstly, for my behavior the other day," she stated, her lips pressed together in a rigid line. "It was terribly rude of me to have run off like that. I was upset, but that is no excuse for my behavior."

"No," he disagreed most adamantly. "It is I who should apologize. I was unutterably forward. Not a gentleman at all."

Peggy froze realizing he was speaking of the abortive kiss and not of the business arrangement at all.

With his particular acumen, he realized his mistake and re-worded his apology to include the business matter. "I oughtn't have pressed the issue when you made it clear that you wished to speak no more of the business. It was only that your comments were so insightful, and I wanted to know more. Reforming the town has been my utmost priority, and perhaps I was overzealous in my hope that a solution could be found for our dwindling supply problem. The loss of that shop in particular has been a burden to many in the area, and I have hated to see anyone go without. It was, after all, our doing when my father and I agreed to expand our holdings. The transition has not been as straightforward as I had hoped."

Peggy could not help but find his concern for those in the county endearing. She had expected that a lord would care only for the inability to fulfill his own needs or to maintain his life of luxury. A selfish whim, she would have thought. On the contrary, Lord Belton and his sister seemed to have earnest care for all those affected by the decisions of their own family. She understood that in the long run all those surrounding both estates would be better off, but for now, they felt the burden of having divided the town in two.

"Still, you kept my secret even from your sister," she replied, "despite the fact that I had not formally asked you to do so."

"You made your position clear enough." He shrugged. "I felt horrible for having caused you distress. Any distress. That was not my intent. In any of our dealings."

Peggy released a deep sigh. She had made a scene, caused him to feel guilt and keep her secret, and now, after all of that, she was going to negate everything she had said and ask him to allow her to take up the position. If he refused to forgive the trouble that she had caused, she would not blame him. But she needed that shop. She needed the income and the purpose. She needed to convince him that she had decided to stay in her own right with no ulterior motive, for that secret was her own. After she had reacted so poorly, she was not sure that he would believe her or want to have business dealings with someone so tempestuous, especially a female. What she was about to suggest was uncommon, to say the least. Still, she could only hope that it could be done. Again, she felt her nerves begin to take hold.

"I assure you that it was at no fault of your own," she explained. She owed him at least this much. So, she took a deep breath and decided to trust him as she was asking him to trust her. She would reveal more than she had intended to anyone else since her arrival and hope that the explanation would be enough to redeem whatever poor opinion of her he might have developed. "You were right to suspect that I had in my possession even more knowledge about trade than I cared to reveal. My hesitancy had nothing to do with the questions that you asked and was entirely a fault of my own making."

He waited in silence for her to go on.

"My father is... was... a well-to-do merchant in the South." She cleared her throat finding it hard to reveal even a limited amount of the truth to anyone. "He was raised in poverty and worked hard for his fortunes, but was never satisfied that any amount of success would be enough." Without a title she wanted to add but kept that piece of information to herself. "My mother was never able to provide him with a son, and disappointed though he was to have only a daughter, he raised me to have all the knowledge that a merchant must possess to continue his legacy."

"He wanted you to take over the business?" Lord Belton asked with a note of awe in his voice that she, a female, would be granted so much responsibility. Peggy was taken aback for a moment as she evaluated his expression. It was not filled with censure or revulsion at the prospect of a lady merchant. It was almost as if, though she dared not think it, his voice held a note of respect. She shook off the strange reaction and reminded herself that he must merely be skilled in the social graces of not causing offense. Certainly, even her own Lord Sterling, with all his professions of caring about her, had even mocked the notion as ridiculous.

"Not at all," she revealed. "I was merely another tool to be bartered." She waited, wondering how much she ought to reveal and then decided to throw caution to the wind. "A functioning brain to be sold to the highest bidder, whatever gentleman could link our family with the status that my father so greatly desired but had been unable to obtain through any other means. A husband."

"I see," Lord Belton murmured, and she wondered if he did. Perhaps his own sister's refusal to participate in a marriage contract had enlightened him to the female plight. Miss Nora, however, was in a position to refuse such offers. An upstart merchant's daughter was not.

"I hope that you do," she nodded. "When my father… passed…" She had to hold back a grimace at the bold-faced lie. As far as she knew her father was still hale and hardy and swindling someone out of their fortunes as they spoke, but Lord Belton need not know that. She had no dealings with her father and was unlikely to see him. "In any case, after a time, I was free of such arrangements. Free to forge my own path. And free of the constant pressures of that lifestyle. I had decided that I wanted a simpler life for myself, and so I have set out to find it." She took a deep breath and decided that she had shared enough. He seemed convinced. "So, you can see that I have some aversion to the concept of my purposely-honed skills and knowledge being used for the sole benefit of another."

"I never meant to—" he began, but she cut him off.

"I can see now that your intention was not to use me but rather to collaborate." When he nodded, concern written over his features that she might perhaps have perceived his behavior with such malicious intent, she knew that her estimation had been correct. He had only been curious and for good reason. "That is why I must apologize. My previous experiences have left a sour taste, and I reacted without thinking. I wanted nothing to do with the trade and you could have had no way of knowing that. I am sorry."

"I thank you for your explanation." He nodded. "Though the apology was unnecessary, I assure you."

"You might find it more necessary when you realize that I have used it as a preface to ask a favor," she laughed.

"And what might that be?" he wondered.

"After some thought and a bit of convincing." She grinned with a pointed look toward the door. "I have decided that I could be of some use in Riversbend, on a temporary basis."

He seemed shocked and pleased at her revelation. "Nora got to you," he stated with feigned annoyance but certainly not surprise at his sister's meddling ways. "I cannot say that I am displeased."

Peggy laughed and assured him that her friend had stumbled upon the information quite unknowingly. The manner in which he narrowed his eyes revealed that he suspected she was covering for the lady, but he did not press the matter. Instead, he said, "I am glad you are going to stay."

"There are conditions," she added.

"I'm listening," he said, laying a hand upon hers. A sizzling spark of desire rolled through her, and as she looked into his dark eyes, she was aware he felt it too. Perhaps there was more to consider than the business dealings, but she would not address those feelings. They must not be allowed to come to fruition. She was leaving just as soon as Adam agreed to go with her.

She explained her decision to remain in the town for an undetermined length of time but stressed that the delay would be as short-lived as possible. She offered her services in managing the deliveries that would restock the haberdashery and in opening the shop. Then, she decided to be bold. She explained that it would not do for a lone female to take possession of the property. Her own experiences had shown her that such an action would be ill received and perhaps even boycotted. Additionally, at the point that she decided to make her withdrawal from the town, she did not want to be trapped by a sale of business that might take months or even years to complete. She wished to be able to make a clean exit when the time came.

"It is fortunate then that I already own the building," he explained, as if the matter were settled. "When the previous owner passed, I purchased the store in hopes of selling it as soon as a replacement could be found."

What a blessed circumstance, Peggy thought. If Lord Belton was already in possession of the property, then there would be no time wasted in trying to contact the owner and make an agreement.

"Then that makes my proposition all the easier," she explained. "I had come to beg for your support in convincing the current owner to take me into his employ. As I find myself sitting before him, I ask it of you."

There was a long moment while they looked at one another, dancing around the arrangement of a gentleman setting up a woman in his apartments. Peggy felt her face fill with the blush, and he studied her so resolutely that she had to look down at her hands. Again, he placed a hand over hers.

"We are in this together," he said.

She looked into his eyes, so kind, and yet dark with desire. He squeezed her hand gently and spoke. "Business partners, until you say otherwise."

Peggy nodded. Her heart was in her throat, and she felt that she could barely speak, but she had to make this work, for Adam's sake. And so she set her terms.

Miss Nora disparagingly described to Peggy the small apartment above the store, and although Miss Nora thought that it was terribly primitive and she would have to spend time here at Whitefall, Peggy knew that the private abode would be more than suitable for her to take up residence. It was for this modest home that Nora went to collect supplies that she intended to lend to Peggy during her stay. Peggy was grateful since she had nothing to her name besides the trunks and meager belongings with which she had traveled. A bed and a washbasin would be more than enough, even though she knew that Miss Nora would find comforts far beyond that. She could not help but be grateful.

In exchange for housing, Peggy would spearhead the rehabilitation of the haberdashery. She had been cautious in her negotiations for the purchasing of goods and later sale of those items. While she could afford for a time to carry the cost of the supplies and hopefully reap profit, she had three primary concerns that had caused her hesitation, the first being that gossip would easily fall upon her since she was living in an apartment owned by Lord Belton. Miss Nora glanced from one to the other and then quickly determined that she would be their chaperone. Peggy blushed, and Lord Belton huffed.

Peggy worried that upon her departure she would need to recoup funds that she used for buying goods on short notice. The final concern was that when that point arose, it would fall to Lord Belton to supply her with that money and then arrange for care of the store for the future himself. Peggy was well aware that Lord Belton had neither the knowledge base nor the inclination to maintain the ownership of such an endeavor. She hated to suggest he tie himself into such a financial burden when, had he wished to do so, he would have already undertaken the task months before. It was a risk and although also a potentially successful investment, he had much else on his plate without Peggy adding to his responsibilities. Besides, for all his hands-on approach, he was a gentleman. Gentlemen did not worry themselves over business matters.

Lord Belton mulled over the option for a while. He

even stood up and paced the room, his fingers rubbing his freshly shaven face as if unused to the lack of sideburns that he had recently shaved. It had been a funny thing to see upon a gentleman and gave the impression that he was far removed from the pomp of society despite his elevated status. Now, he had more the look of his station, and Peggy had been surprised to note that beneath his whiskers had been hidden very attractive features.

"I'd offer a counter," he said when she had become anxious that the length of his contemplation might indicate he was preparing for a refusal. Despite her keen business sense, there was still the fact that she was a woman, and not many would be thrilled with the prospect of such an unusual transaction.

"I would expect nothing less," she replied with bated breath. He could not know this, but she would be forced to accept just about anything he offered so long as it gave her a place to stay and the illusion of a reason to be in town. Even if she could not bolster her finances, she would settle for maintaining them. She knew the amount of work that would go into resupplying the haberdashery. It would be filled with long hours and backbreaking work, and she was not in a position to deny even the rawest of deals. She had a sinking feeling in her gut. This was the moment when her father would cut his adversary out at the knees. This was the moment that he would make a demand that rose him to glory and left the other with little more than a beggar's bargain. This was where the aristocrat would take advantage.

The town needed Peggy, but Lord Belton had no idea how much Peggy needed the store. For all the gentleman knew, she could press for the king's cut with vicious demands. Such predatory transactions were part of the reason that she had hated Lady Blackwell so fully. There had been something similar in her father, a willingness to take advantage of those who had greater need than he did, acting for his own benefit alone and caring not for whatever ruination was left in his wake. There was never a business transaction of equal benefit. There must always be a winner and a loser. She revealed only her most stoic face, hoping that Lord Belton would have no indication that she was more than prepared to lose. She had already lost just by agreeing to remain. But for Adam, she would do whatever it took.

"My suggestion is this. I will cover whatever expenses are needed for you to fill the shop before the rainy weather makes travel difficult. Rather than pay you a salary, since have no idea what a reasonable amount would be, what say you to splitting the profits? It will motivate you for your effort, and whatever sells will then be a valuable investment for us both." He plunged his hands into his pockets and stared at her as if he felt slightly out of his element. "Would 5000 pounds do to start bringing in goods?"

Peggy's mouth fell open in shock. Five-thousand pounds was an enormous amount of money. If she was prudent about it, it would cover initial stock of both the store in Riversbend and the one at Canton Point. She revealed as much, and he gave a nod of satisfaction.

"Excellent." He nodded. "All the better if you can manage orders for both. I can find someone to merely monitor the sales on my father's behalf and send reports back for your records. Have everything delivered to the shop here and then I shall arrange to have a cart or two sent to my father... shall we say... once per sennight. That will give him time to finish building a warehouse of sorts. Anything with a roof and walls will do to begin."

"Half of the profits seems far too generous considering you are not asking me to make an investment outright," she murmured. She hated to argue with such an offer but was also nearly salivating at the amount that she could save in even a month's time if she made a success of it.

"I find the arrangement more than fair considering how much this community needs to have someone in the shop." His tone was firm and unyielding. "Once there is some measure of stability, others will come."

"I must warn you, I do not know how long I will be here," she explained. The last thing that she wanted to do was start a project and walk out on it. But she did know that, in the very least, her brain had filed away the names of all of her father's contacts, and she could get the deliveries made before the first snowfall. Even if she had abandoned Riversbend by that time, the community would be better off with the goods in stock for the long winter.

# PART III

## CHAPTER 16

THE BARON AGREED WITH PEGGY'S THOUGHTS, AND HE suggested that even having a base of supplies to stock the shelves might be enough to draw a merchant to the area. Part of what had been so off-putting to so many was the idea of starting from scratch. If Peggy were willing to even begin the process it was more than had been done in months, and several months into the future, they would be prepared to weather the cold in some comfort.

"I suppose we are in agreement then." She laughed. "I never thought I would be saying this, but thank you for the opportunity, and I promise to do my best not to let you down."

"Any progress for me is progress for you," he chuckled in response. "And if I am to be perfectly honest, I probably would not notice whether you were the worst Mercer who ever lived until the bill came in at a loss. I suppose I shall have to trust you not to make a failure of my investment. Heaven knows Nora would never let me forget it."

Peggy laughed. "Well then, you shall simply have to remind Nora that it was she that did the convincing."

"You are correct, and she will probably take credit when the town has a boom."

"There is one more thing…" Peggy hesitated, biting her lip as she wondered if she would be able to explain away this request. "When I send out for the purchases, I would prefer to leave my name out of it. If it could be done through your signature, I believe it would be better received, you being a gentleman and all."

He seemed to accept her reasoning well enough, and she allowed herself a breath of relief that he asked no further questions about her request for anonymity. She had seen the wheels in his head turning often enough to know that he was probably curious about it, but he had too much foresight and etiquette to press the issue. The truth of the matter was that in order to make a successful go of this endeavor, Peggy would have to reach out to several men that had, in the past and probably still to this day, business dealings with her father. For all her father was aware, she was dead. The last thing that she needed was any suspicion to arise that she was still alive, and worse making use of her father's training.

Oh, two small shops in the obscure north were no threat to her father's holdings. There would be no competition. Peggy's shops would be little more than a fly at the ear of a horse. An annoyance perhaps, but nothing that could not be stomped out if he set his mind to it. That was the real concern. If her father found out what she was doing, he might set a boycott to these two necessary, but remote, haberdasheries.

Or worse—she felt a chill run down her spine—he

might come for her. Though many years had passed since she had been thrown out, her father was not one to accept a loss. She could fail and he would wash his hands of her. But if she were successful, he might attempt to stake his claim and use her for all she was worth. As always, a tool and nothing more.

# CHAPTER 17

PEGGY SPENT THE REMAINDER OF THE DAY OVERWHELMED by Miss Nora's generosity. In the time that it had taken Peggy and the Baron to come to an arrangement, Miss Nora had commanded an army of servants to collect spare furnishings from the storage room. A wagon was already loaded in the circular drive and heaped with rugs and bedding, tables and chairs, lacy curtains, and even a small bath that Peggy could fill and move about herself without too much effort.

Two maids were seated in the back of the wagon surrounded by supplies for cleaning the living quarters, which were likely to have been overtaken by dust in their months of disuse. Peggy knew not what to say but was shocked by the kindness of it all. In the matter of an hour, Miss Nora had pulled together a collection of odds and ends greater than anything Peggy had owned in over a decade. She had imagined herself scraping through and suffering during this trying time that she waited for Adam to come to terms with her arrival. She had considered the hard work it would take to get the haberdashery on its feet. She had even resolved herself to living with only the barest of supplies and amenities as she saved every bit of her earnings for their future. At Blackwell House, she had had nothing more than a single dress and a lumpy bed in a shared dormitory. From what she could spy in the pile of mismatched items, she knew that she would feel as well kept as a queen. She hoped that did not cause the gossips to twitter.

Peggy expressed her heartfelt thanks as Miss Nora bemoaned not having more.

"Mama took most of the spares to the new estate," the lady explained. "On the morrow, I will sort through the guest rooms to see if there are items more in line with the current fashions."

"Oh, please don't," Peggy begged. "This is far too much as it is."

"Nonsense." Miss Nora wrinkled her nose at the scuffed tables and worn rugs. "I want you to be at ease."

"I assure you that this is more than my ease requires." Peggy laughed. "I have lived out of a trunk for longer than I care to admit."

"She is hoping to entice you to stay by appealing to your comforts." Lord Belton laughed, nudging his sister with an elbow. The lady glared up at him and crossed her arms with a petulant huff.

"So what if I am?" Miss Nora pouted. "It shan't work if you out me at every turn."

At that Peggy laughed outright. "I appreciate the effort, but as I have said, I do not intend to stay for long."

"You must stay at least until the spring," Miss Nora pleaded. "It's a devil to uproot oneself in the winter months. Carriage rides are brutal, stopping at every inn to change out warming bricks, and I must say, some of the inns are not up to standard. Yes, you absolutely must stay."

"All the more time to work at you," Lord Belton said with a laugh.

"Who wouldn't fall in love with Riversbend after several months?" Miss Nora replied. "Even I who have dreamt of being anywhere and everywhere cannot bring myself to quit it."

Peggy shook her head. She knew that Miss Nora's heart was in the right place, but the Lady had no idea what she was asking or why it was that Peggy was so determined to refuse. Miss Nora was not wrong in her statement that would be far too easy to become attached to this place, this simple, collaborative community. Adam certainly had. Peggy would have to be careful to ensure that she maintained an appropriate emotional distance from any connections in the neighborhood. Miss Nora had already grown dear to her, and she knew that when she left, she would do everything in her power to maintain the friendship through letters or inviting her friend to visit. But once she and Adam quit Riversbend, it would be unwise for them ever to return. A clean break was what he needed, and to remove him a second time might be even more difficult than the first.

Again, she thanked her friend for the effort and the kindness. She thanked Lord Belton for having put his trust in her and coming to an agreement. She assured him that on the morrow she would draw up a handful of letters to request contracts with the appropriate merchants. Then, he need only place his signature and seal the document with his crest and send his riders out to make the request. If fate smiled upon them and offers were accepted, they might receive their first parcels upon the riders' return. Then, regular deliveries would be arranged, and the shop may be opened within a fortnight. She knew that she had set her expectations high. Such a speedy arrangement would take nothing less than a miracle and depended entirely on the merchants having the supplies on hand. Yet, she had vowed to have the shop open by the end of the month, and if she had any say in it, she and Adam would be long gone before the last of the autumn leaves fell.

So it was that Peggy climbed into the carriage beside Miss Nora to follow the cart to town. Lord Belton retrieved a set of keys for the storefront and the lodging above which were attached to an iron ring and chain that Peggy could secure to the pocket that she kept tied beneath the folds of her gown. She took them with trembling hands and bid farewell to the Baron as he shut the door between them. All at once, Peggy was overcome with feeling, as if these rusted keys were a monumental symbol of her future. All the bad of the past mattered no longer. This was an opportunity, a chance to do some good and reap good in return. The keys signified hope in the promise that she was doing something right by Adam. Fleeting though it may be, she decided to look at this moment not as a step back in her plan but as a step forward toward protecting her financial freedom.

They arrived at the empty storefront just as the sun reached its peak in the midday sky. The small town was bursting with activity, as towns are like to do during the daylight hours, and all eyes it seemed were on the Lord Belton's carriage and the cart of household items. Eyes peered from windows, and people whispered at the corners all wondering what might be amiss. So long had the towns-folk waited for any sign of activity at the shop that when Peggy opened the creaking door, she could swear she heard exclamations of surprise and excitement as the locals bustled about gossiping about what might be.

Let them gossip, Peggy thought with a grin. Better that they talk about her as a new shopkeeper than as the unwed mother to a supposedly orphaned boy. The ruse would hold. She was sure of it. Adam would be free from censure and gossip, and she would be welcomed into the community with open arms. She hoped that this would allow her son to see her as someone who did good and as worthy of his love once more.

"Good heavens," Miss Nora said with a sneeze. She called to the maids to open all of the windows and let in the fresh air. Then, she led Peggy to the back of the store and with a second key opened the door to a stockroom which led to a stairway that creaked and groaned as they made their way up to the living quarters.

Miss Nora pulled open the curtains to let in the light to the darkened room. She decided immediately that they were not worth salvaging and instructed the maids to discard them. Peggy took a moment to look around the sprawling room. It was large enough to house a small family. She hardly knew what to do with so much space but was grateful that the open air and high-pitched ceilings would keep her from feeling confined. She threw open the window and stuck her head out into the street to take in the fresh air and the wonderment of having something, anything, that resembled a home for the first time in as

154

long as she could remember. Voices on the street called up to her and passersby waved as they asked her if the shop was to be back in business.

Miss Nora squeezed out the window at her side and shouted down to the crowd. "Spread the word! We shall have a grand opening in due time." Her words were met with cheers.

Peggy chuckled, a little nervous. "Let us not put the cart before the horse," she said, pulling her friend back inside and away from any further mischief.

"Well, we must spread the word." Miss Nora giggled. "Customers will come from miles around, from even further estates, to see what you have to sell."

"I can only hope," Peggy replied. "But first I must have something to sell."

"First, you must have some place to sleep," Miss Nora corrected with a wink.

The maids were already scrubbing the floors and the walls. In no time, the room would be spotless if a little worn. It was a blessing that the room was empty, for it made quick work. When the first corner of the room had been cleared, Miss Nora called down to the stable boy and the footman who had driven the vehicles to town. Soon enough the supplies and furnishings were brought up so that the ladies might arrange them in a livable fashion.

In only a few short hours the task was complete, and Peggy could hardly believe her eyes. A large, downy bed had been assembled and sheathed with a flounced coverlet. A sideboard held a washbasin and elegant glass lamp of oil, rather than the tallow candles she had used the past years. Another bedside table held a vase of flowers and a pitcher of water. Peggy touched her fingers to the flowers and felt a lump rise in her throat. Such a simple gesture, and yet it meant the world to her that Miss Nora had thought of it. She had not possessed such a frivolous and beautiful luxury for herself since before Adam had been born. Certainly, she had none of it as a laundress, and the nuns were not ones for such frivolity.

She blinked back the tears and turned to take in the rest of the room. Two large rugs covered the wooden floor and were so faded that she could hardly discern their pattern. Peggy did not care. She crouched down and ran her fingers along their surface, recalling how cold the stone floor at the abbey was without a covering.

There was a small wood-burning stove in the corner across from her bed beside which the small bath basin had been set. Peggy would have to sit in it with her knees to her chest, but she knew that tonight she would bathe in the luxury of warm water and the jars of soaps and oils Miss Nora had lined along the wall at its feet. It had been far too long since she had been permitted such pampering.

There was no armoire, but there were hooks along one wall for Peggy to hang her gowns once she had her things delivered from the inn. Miss Nora arranged for a curtain to be hung in front of the hooks so that Peggy's gowns might be protected from the sunlight that might bleach them.

Lastly, the fine lace curtains were hung to replace those that Miss Nora had deemed unsuitable. It was true that they had been moth-eaten and faded with age—one even appeared to have been set to flame at some point—but Peggy had thought she could not be choosey. Now, the white lace framed the windows and allowed in the beauty of the daylight while providing Peggy with all the privacy that she might need.

Even in her childhood, when her rooms had been filled with ridiculous displays of wealth and exuberance, Peggy had never loved a room so much as this. For the first time, the room felt like it was hers.

Once news of their arrival had spread throughout the town, Mrs. Banning made her appearance to see how Peggy had settled in. She tucked a sachet of herbs behind the door frame, "for good luck," she said. Then, never one to observe the rules of society, she turned to Miss Nora with a motherly scowl and made her promise to "take care of my duckling, you hear?"

Miss Nora assured her that she would, as she prepared to leave Peggy to her work.

Peggy bid her friend adieu as she confirmed to Mrs. Banning that she was being cared for quite well by her new friends.

"Well, we must be off too," Mrs. Banning added as Nora took her leave. "We want to be far south before the weather turns."

"Are you stopping at Northwick or Halthaven?" Peggy asked.

"I leave the particulars to Mr. Banning," she confessed, "but Halthaven is off the wayside, so probably not."

"I wanted to give the good sisters the news that I have found my son but do not want to turn you from your route."

Mrs. Banning nodded. "I will keep it in mind if we decide to tarry at the abbey or thereabouts, but do not expect it. Last time we stopped, the Lady abbess managed to convert two of our young girls, much to the dismay of their prospective beaus."

Peggy and Miss Nora chuckled at the thought of their consternation.

Mrs. Banning pulled Peggy into an all-encompassing hug and held her for a long moment, patting her back affectionately. Then, she kissed Peggy upon the cheek before turning to make her exit. "Take care," she said over her shoulder. Peggy thought she saw the woman wipe a rogue tear from her eye as she descended the stair.

# CHAPTER 18

WHEN PEGGY'S NEW HOME WAS FURNISHED AND MOST OF the items except for a few odds and ends were delivered, the ladies made their way to the inn and requested that the last of Peggy's things be delivered while the pair sat down to enjoy their tea.

"I cannot tell you how pleased I am with the arrangement," Miss Nora declared. "I must warn you, I intend to make a standing appointment for tea every day."

"Then you'll have to drink at the shop." Peggy laughed. "I will be busy." She knew that running the storefront was going to take up a large portion of her day. She was worried that it would keep her from Adam, but she knew that she must find a way to make time for him, for him to get to know her. Beyond that, she did not intend to leave much time for socialization, but she would like to see Miss Nora if the other would come to visit.

"Nash said you might put up some tables near the window so that we ladies might have a space of our own." Miss Nora grinned and promised to be a regular. "There are few enough ladies in the area, unless you count old crones and mothers looking to marry off their sons. Still, I think you shall have plenty of patrons mulling about soon enough. Besides, the more they sip, the more they shall be inclined to browse and purchase!"

"That is the secret to profit." Peggy leaned forward as if revealing a secret. "Don't tell or I'll have to draw them in some other way."

Miss Nora giggled. "Have no worry. I intend to make your little venture the talk of the town!"

"Are you always this scheming?" Peggy asked with wonderment. She found Miss Nora such an amusing combination of mischief and pure goodness that it was hard to find fault with her plotting.

"What else am I to do?" she replied with a shrug. "I could use my methods for much worse, I assure you."

Peggy could not help but agree. She pitied anyone who got in Miss Nora's way, including her brother. It was a wonder that the young lady had set herself against the institution of marriage. No gentleman would stand a chance if she set her cap for him. Peggy almost shivered at the thought. A pity on anyone who thought to go up against the lady. Then, she realized with a start that she herself was going to have to do her best to resist the woman's charming ploys. Miss Nora had already made her intentions to convince Peggy to stay on a permanent basis more than clear. Peggy had refused, but she knew well enough that she had not heard the end of it. She found herself smiling. Well, this time Miss Nora would not achieve her ends. Still, it would be amusing to watch her try.

. . .

The following day, the troop of peddlers were off before the dawn, and Peggy woke to find the town much less crowded than previously. She pulled back the curtain and glanced down at the street to see the townsfolk about their tasks and a few mothers shepherding their children down the lane. There was no sign of Adam, and something in her gut told her that today he would not appear.

She wanted to wallow in her dismay but recognized that there was no good in that. Rather, she would distract herself with work. She reached into her trunk and pulled out a small box that was filled with writing supplies. Beyond the letters that she would need to present to the Baron, it was about time that she wrote to both Marilee and the Duchess of Manchester to inform them of her current situation.

She took the box of supplies below stairs and settled herself at a built-in counter that boasted a single stool. A quick wipe of the surfaces made it suitable for her task.

First, she needed to order supplies. For the next several hours, she crafted her letters, taking the time to offer fair compensation for all of the items that she was requesting. She needed to find the perfect balance to ensure that the offer was accepted outright, and the goods were sent with haste all without sinking an exorbitant amount of the Baron's funds into products that would be unable to be sold at a profit. It had been several years since she had memorized the values of different goods, and she hoped that they had not changed so very much in that time.

After several drafts that left a crumpled pile of stationary at her side, Peggy reached her arms above her head to stretch and felt satisfied with her work. She blotted the pages and set them out to dry before they could be folded. Then, after allowing herself a few moments to stretch her legs, she ascended the staircase, changed into a less crumpled day dress, and pinched her cheeks to give the illusion that she was less tired and drawn than she felt. With renewed spirit, Peggy settled to the task of writing to her friends.

Just as she had folded the completed draft of her letter to Marilee, there was a knock at the door. Miss Nora's doll-like features smiled at her through the glass. Peggy let her into the shop, whose lower level was still dusty and echoed with emptiness. The cleanup could wait for another day. Her top priority was to get the requests for products sent out as soon as possible.

"How long have you been at it?" Miss Nora wondered aloud, looking at the stack of correspondence. It was midafternoon, and Peggy doubted that her friend had been awake for more than a few hours.

"All morning," Peggy admitted. She had grown accustomed to little sleep and found that she accomplished more in the early hours of the day.

"Nash drove me to town," Miss Nora revealed. "I doubt that he expected you to have the letters done so soon."

"I assured him that I would, and I keep my word." Peggy shrugged and gathered the papers together to hand them to her friend.

"You can give them to him yourself." The lady grinned. "He's making arrangements for the riders to be prepared to leave as soon as you might be finished. He'll be pleased to know that they shall get a good start on the journey. He brought our fastest horses to town tied up behind the curricle."

"I am relieved to hear that he does not intend to send the missives by post," Peggy said with relief. It would be a great waste of time, but it had occurred to her early that morning the nobility was not often in a rush when it came to their communications. They could afford to take all the time they needed.

"He declared that time was of the essence, and I quite agree," Miss Nora said with a curt nod. "Travel will only get more difficult with the rain. Come, we shall meet with Nash at the stables and then you can come back to the estate with me for a celebratory nuncheon."

"Didn't you break your fast just a few hours ago?" Peggy asked.

"I did, but I venture you did not, so nuncheon it is."

Peggy felt it was a bit early for celebration but realized that until the goods arrived, she had nothing to do but wait. That and the fact that Adam had still given no indication of wanting to see her, she supposed the distraction would be welcome. She agreed and locked up the store behind her. The pair of ladies made their way out into the town.

It would have taken several hours to reach the stables had they stopped to talk to every person who wanted to ask them questions and find out the latest news about the haberdashery. Thankfully, Miss Nora was able to express their need for haste in such a polite manner that they offended no one as they ducked from one conversation to another. At least in the stable, they were sheltered from the wind.

As predicted, Lord Belton was at the stables and had with him three sturdy riders and steeds that looked strong enough to run for long miles without rest. Each rider would be given a handful of letters grouped by region.

Though she wanted the letters to be delivered with haste, Peggy hoped that the horses would not be overtaxed. She ran her fingers through the coarse mane of one prime bit of blood. The animal, keen on affection, leaned into the gesture.

"Brimmer is one of Nash's favorite stallions," Miss Nora said as she joined Peggy, who leaned in and patted the monstrous beast on his strong neck. The horse turned towards her, nuzzling for a treat, and Peggy showed her flat empty hand. The stallion nosed her glove curiously. "Nash says he's a good judge of character."

"He'll either take to you at once or bite you," said a masculine voice from behind her that made Peggy jump. "There can be no in between."

"I suppose it is a good thing then that I did not get bitten," Peggy said as she stepped away from the horse and turned to face the Baron with wide, shocked eyes. "A creature like that should come with a warning."

"He would not have let you near him if he had even considered biting," he said in reply. "His ears would have been plastered to his head as soon as he saw you."

"I always trust Brimmer's instincts." Miss Nora grinned. "He bit Lord Abernathy straight after the lout called me a pest, and I was ever so pleased with it. Took quite a mouthful from the man's sleeve. He was utterly vexed."

"James was an unruly lad when that happened." Lord Belton shook his head. "I'm sorry to inform you, sister, but Brimmer has since altered his opinion of the gentleman."

"Only because the man bribed him with sugar cubes." Miss Nora harrumphed and gave the stallion a chastising glare. "Turncoat," she hissed. The horse lipped Nash's coat, and the man shoved the stallion's curious nose away. "No treats for you," he said. "You have work to do."

Despite the betrayal, the lady went back to scratching the hollow beneath his long muzzle, and the stallion looked quite pleased with himself.

Peggy brought forth her pile of folded letters and offered them to Lord Belton for perusal. "Feel free to make alterations, but these would be my suggestions to begin."

Lord Belton flipped through the pages, reading them swiftly and with occasional hums or nods of agreement.

"Excellent," he declared when he had finished the task. "I shall sign, seal, and send them off at once. Do you have wax?"

"At the store," she said as they began walking back from the stable.

"Bix, come with us," the Baron called to one of the men who stood with the horses.

"Is there anything else?" the Baron asked Peggy as they began to make their way back to the store.

Peggy shook her head. "Then we have only to wait."

"I do hate the waiting part," Miss Nora grumbled. Then, her face broke out into a grin. "Though, there is the benefit of it leaving you with an empty schedule so that we might have all sorts of fun!"

"Use the time wisely while you can, sister," Lord Belton teased. "For once the deliveries arrive, I doubt Miss Williams will have much time for you at all."

"What an awful thing to say!" Miss Nora released an exaggerated gasp and held her hand to her heart as if she had been mortally wounded. "Don't you know that I am to be a prime patron of the teahouse?"

"Tea *corner.*" Peggy laughed as she unlocked the door

and ushered them into the store. "I do not suppose that we shall be able to boast a proper tea house, but I did ask for Twinning on the Strand to send us some tea. I am excited for the new selection to arrive. Right now, I just have the common block of black tea."

"I see that," the Baron said, perusing the letters and holding up the one addressed to Twinings. He gave them his final signature and sealed them with his signet ring.

"No matter what it is, it will still be the finest location for ladies' leisure that Riversbend has seen in an age." Miss Nora tapped her chin in thought. "Perhaps we can have a wall built to keep it separate from the main store and so that we do not have worry of officious gentlemen listening in on our gossip."

So it was that they fell into musings about what could or would be done in the store to bring it up to more modern fashions. Peggy listened to the siblings argue with amusement. Having never had a sibling, she was unused to such constant teasing. Furthermore, her mother and father would never have permitted her to behave with such open affection toward anyone even in the privacy of their own home.

Here they were verbally poking at one another while filling the echoing storeroom with raucous laughter. It was unlike anything she had ever seen, and Peggy found that she quite enjoyed it. Miss Nora stood to evaluate where exactly the wall should be while Nash teased her about her lack of architectural acumen.

Peggy wondered if Adam laughed like that with Jemmy and Martha. The thought struck her suddenly and with pain. What if Adam did have this sort of relationship with his adoptive siblings? Even in her short time in this village, she could hardly imagine the Baron and his sister being parted. Perhaps that was part of the reason why Miss Nora had refused to get married. It seemed impossible to imagine one without the other. Would Adam feel the same burden of separation? The same loss?

All at once, Peggy felt ill and lightheaded, and she excused herself. She walked a short distance away from the sibling pair. She rounded the corner into a hallway that led to a back room and leaned against the wall, forcing herself to take slow calming breaths, and turned her thoughts to anything but the worry and guilt that had over-taken her so suddenly. She was certain that Adam needed to be a part of her life, that he needed her just as much as she needed him. She could not afford to allow doubts to creep in, not when she was so close. Peggy took several deep breaths to regain her composure.

"I shall see the gentlemen off," Bix said, bowing to his lord and heading towards the stable. When the door closed, she knew the servant had gone.

# CHAPTER 19

LORD BELTON APPEARED SEVERAL MINUTES LATER ON silent footsteps, and Peggy knew that he had seen her in distress if only for those last few moments. He offered her a cup filled with cool water that he must have procured from her stores. She was grateful for it and drank deeply.

Without a word, he turned and leaned against the wall so that they were shoulder to shoulder looking out upon the misty snow that was threatening to fall.

"Are you quite well?" he asked after a long silence.

"I am fine," she lied.

He nodded as if accepting her words, but she could tell from the draw of his mouth that he did not believe her. "You know," he began with a calm tentative tone, "if this business is too much for you, I would understand. You would still be welcome to remain in your lodgings for as long as you need. Or I could send you with the carriage ahead to catch up with your friends. It is not too late to change your mind."

"It isn't that," Peggy replied with sincerity. "I know that I said that trade was something I wanted no part of but, if I am being honest, it felt... rewarding. What I did today." Though she had not given it much thought before this moment, what she said was true. There had been something fulfilling in crafting those letters and knowing that she was making prudent decisions. She had not forgotten as much as she had thought, and though it had often grated on her father's nerves primarily because she was not a son, it did come naturally. It still, after all this time, was second nature to her.

He turned his head slightly to look down at her, evaluating her features with that strange and almost unnatural ability to read a person. Then, he nodded, accepting what she had said for the truth that it was.

Still, he would not be fooled. "If it was not of the store, then what?" he asked.

Observant to the end, she mentally cursed his perception and her own weakness.

"It's nothing really," she said as she pushed away from the wall. "I must be tired." She started to make her way back to the main room, not willing to let the conversation go any further. It would not be easy to keep Lord Belton from the truth if he really dug at it, and Peggy did not wish to lie any more than she already had.

But his voice put a pause in her step, so calm and earnest that she felt like the greatest heel for refusing to accept his attempts at kindness.

"Just so you know," he said as he came to stand beside her and looked down upon her with those piercing blue eyes, "if there were anything amiss, anything that troubled you at all, you could tell us. If not me, then my sister." He glanced towards the main room where Miss Nora stood watching with a concerned eye.

"I hope you know that," he said.

She had no need to respond, for as soon as he had finished his statement, he walked by her and took his sister's arm without a backward glance.

"Do you want us to stay?" Miss Nora asked.

Peggy shook her head. "I will be fine," she said, and the sibling pair left on quiet feet.

Peggy stood there for a long while with her eyes closed and drew deep breaths in through her nose and out through her mouth. She was unsettled. Normally so calm and collected, she was well-equipped to deal with wicked people. She knew how to handle anger and brutality. She had survived severe punishments and berating words. She knew how to handle cruelty. She had little preparation, hardly any at all, for how to deal with kindness.

Miss Nora called upon Peggy every day that week, as promised, and left Molly to help her with any tasks that needed done. When Nora arrived, they had all manner of entertainments. They took rides through the grounds of Whitefall estate, played cards, and Miss Nora even worked with Peggy on the pianoforte to help refresh her skill. She had not sat at the instrument since her time at the abbey, and her technique was rusty to say the least. Little by little, it was coming back, but her hands, callused and aching after years submerged in lye, did not flow as freely as the long, beautiful fingers of Miss Nora. She was sorely out of practice.

She saw little of Lord Belton except in passing. He was

busy with his own activities and had no real reason to interact with Peggy while they waited for the results of her letters to become known. The planting season was in full swing and he had much to do in the bustling town as well as the outside farms. Lord Belton joined the women once or twice for tea and conversation, so she knew that there was no discomfort on his end. Nothing seemed to have changed. It was almost as if the conversation outside the barn had never happened except that Peggy recalled the memory with groans of mortification.

These people had been so good to her, and she was still keeping them at arm's length. Such was her way. It had long been her way. It was what had sustained her through so many trials and tribulations. She did not let people close, and that was her sole protection.

If there did exist any discomfort, it was solely on her end and solely the result of her own behavior.

She had been prickly and on edge all week. Adam still had not called upon her. She had written a letter to Mrs. Finch, not wanting to stop by and surprise the boy only to put him off further. She asked if any progress had been made. The reply was brief.

*Give it time.*

Peggy, it appeared, had nothing but time at the moment. It was for that reason alone that she had allowed Miss Nora to occupy her every waking moment. The shop had been scrubbed and waxed and even painted under the watchful eye of her dear friend. Peggy would have completed the tasks herself, but Miss Nora had insisted that it would benefit the community if they paid some local boys to take on the burden. In the end, she was grateful that she had been not been left for hours upon hours to

171

dwell in her own thoughts. With Adam still refusing to see her, her mind was in a dark place.

Jemmy had been one of the boys tasked with white-washing the shelves inside the store. She had been surprised to see him at first. He and three other boys had appeared on her doorstep one morning with buckets of paint and brushes.

"Lord Nash said we've got to do a good job, so the store does well," he said as he introduced his friends. "Don't you worry, miss," he added as if they had never met before. "It'll all be fresh by the time we're done." When the other boys had turned their backs, he had offered her a pitying smile. Perhaps not pitying, she had been forced to amend after a few days of playing the moment over and over in her mind. Perhaps it had been more a look of understanding. Understanding the hurt she must have been feeling as Adam continued to maintain his silence and his absence.

The boys had worked in the shop for two straight days, and Peggy had been glad when they finished. Although she had been out with Miss Nora during most of that time, Peggy made a point of buying meat pies from the inn to serve the toiling workers during midday. She also gave them each an envelope with some coinage inside for her gratitude. She suspected Lord Belton was paying them as well when they tried to refuse the payment, but still, she had insisted. A selfish part of Peggy wanted to pepper Jemmy with questions, to find out how Adam was doing and to know more than those three frustrating words that Mrs. Finch had sent, though she was sure that the note had not been meant with ill will. She knew it would be unfair to put the young man in the position of spy and so she had held her tongue. At the end of the job, when she thanked the young men for their effort and praised the clean look of the shelves, Jemmy had stayed behind and offered her his hand to shake as he would a man.

She grasped it in return and gave a nod of thanks for the sign of respect.

"I appreciate what you're doing here," the young man said when they were fully alone. "For the town and for Adam. All he needs is a little time. He thought you were dead, you see. It's like being asked to believe in a ghost."

"I understand," she replied. She really was trying to understand. It was not easy, but she could only imagine how confused the young boy must feel.

"He asked me a few times if you were nice or mean, and I said *the nicest*, I did."

"Thank you, Jemmy," she had said with barely restrained tears. "That means the world to me."

"I meant it. No one ever gets us meat pies from the inn. They're my favorite. Better than my mum's, but don't tell her I said that." Peggy tried not to laugh at his words. Everyone knew that the way to a young man's good graces was through his stomach. She was not born yesterday. "You know," he continued without noting her amusement, "I like working for Lord Nash, and I liked working for you just now," Jemmy said as he kicked his toe at a loose board on the floor. "If you ever need help again, you just call for me, all right? I can be really helpful. I'm strong now. I can lift bags of grain and anything that's too much for..." he eyed her as if afraid she might take his words as an insult, "... a lady."

She laughed. "You know, I just might take you up on that."

"Really?" he beamed. "Because I could use the extra money. I'm savin' up to rent my own bit of land." Peggy wondered if his motivation had more to do with a certain local girl that had caught his interest. Jemmy was getting to an age where he needed to start thinking about his future if he wanted to be able to provide for a wife and have children of his own. In a few years, he would be old enough to marry if he chose. A small tenancy on the Whitefall holdings would be an excellent start as he helped his father in the role of groundskeeper.

"I'll make you a deal," she offered without needing to give it much thought. "Once my supplies arrive, I might need help setting things up, but more importantly, I could use a swift set of feet to run deliveries. If I get a request, I can't leave the shop unattended, so I'll need someone that I can trust to take the purchases to the customers for me. Do you think you could do that?"

He nodded with enthusiasm. "As long as my da or Lord Nash don't need me, I can be here," he promised. "If not me, I bet any of the other boys would take you up on it. Just don't give them my spot, deal?"

"Deal!" Peggy laughed and offered her hand to him once more. He shook it with vigor, their agreement sealed.

## CHAPTER 20

I<small>T WAS NINE DAYS AFTER THE LETTERS HAD BEEN SENT</small> that the first rider returned to the village, tired but filled with excitement.

"The wagons are only two days behind me at most, and I received word that the other riders are coming packed full of goods not far beyond that." His revelation brought cheers of joy from Peggy and Miss Nora. Lord Belton, who had met the rider at the stables and come with him to the shop to share the news, revealed a wide smile to Peggy. "I rode ahead to give warning, wanted to make sure you were ready."

"As ready as ever," Peggy said with a bolstering breath.

"I can hardly believe that you managed this all!" Miss Nora clasped Peggy by the shoulders as if to embrace her after the rider had gone off to get his rest. "You have achieved what no one else could."

"It's not all that," Peggy laughed. "I was only fortunate to recall the merchants with the largest warehouses and hoped against hope that they had what was needed on hand." The merchants with the largest warehouses, she amended within her mind, without including her father.

"It really was quite impressive," Lord Belton refuted her dismissal. "I would have been pleased had you succeeded before the first snowfall, but it will all arrive before even the harvest is complete. It is more than I could have ever expected. Thank you."

Peggy, unused to such professions of gratitude, did her best not to appear awkward in light of the praise, but she knew that her cheeks burned bright.

"We ought to send for Mama and Papa at once," Miss Nora exclaimed. "They'll arrive just in time for the first delivery, and we can have a fine dinner to celebrate! Maybe a small ball…" She began to pace the room. "We have two days. I think I can manage if invitations go out this evening." Then, she turned on Peggy. "You will be the guest of honor."

Peggy felt all the color that had built in her cheeks drain in an instant. "Oh, please, no," she moaned.

"Whyever not?" the lady protested. "It would be the perfect opportunity to be introduced to all of your new customers and spread the word."

While Peggy could not disagree that it would be good for the haberdashery to mingle with all of the local lords and ladies, but she could not help the feeling of dread that had taken root in her heart. The last thing that she wanted was to be the center of attention. Even less did she wish to attend a ball. She had sworn never, ever again would she subject herself to the flamboyant rules and expectations of societal gatherings. Balls were where her father had put her on display. Where she had been paraded around like some exotic bird trying to attract the highest bidder. A ball was where she had met Lord Sterling Pentworth, the Baron Banbury. A ball was where he had informed her that she had been nothing more than a temporary distraction, and he would instead make his offer to one very wealthy Lady Clementina Newton even though Peggy carried his child. Peggy's father had money, but Lord Sterling had laughed and said regardless to what her father thought, his money could not buy a title for his daughter, or apparently, even a respectable husband, or a legitimate father for her child.

Peggy had been lost in her own memories and it was not until she realized that Miss Nora was staring at her with confusion that it occurred to her that she had yet to respond. She tried to think of some reasonable excuse but came up short. She had no idea where the conversation had gone while she was woolgathering.

Ever the gentleman, Lord Belton spoke on her behalf. "Perhaps a ball is a bit much, Nora," he said as if the idea also displeased him. "Why not a dinner? A small dinner. Just family."

"It cannot be just family when Peggy is to be the guest of honor," she rebutted. "Besides, if we want the new haberdashery to be known, we cannot just invite Mother and Father. Peggy was glad that Miss Nora had recently dropped the formality of referring to her as Miss Williams or Miss Peggy when in company, but this insistence on a ball was out of her comfort zone. She hadn't even danced in years. She wasn't sure she remembered how to do so.

"I think," Nora's brother replied, "just family and our guest of honor. I am of the opinion that a smaller number will allow us to discuss the details of the endeavor in a

177

way that we could not at an open party. Father will have many questions."

Miss Nora wrinkled her brow and turned her back on her brother to look out the window as she contemplated his suggestion.

Peggy released the breath that she had been holding, and offered Lord Belton an expression that she hoped portrayed her gratitude. His only response was a brief nod of acknowledgment, barely a movement at all, before his attention returned to his sister. He watched Miss Nora as if unsure if she would take the bait.

"Very well," Miss Nora agreed. She turned back to face Peggy and scrunched her nose. "Our father does like to inspect all of Nash's business dealings as, in a way, they are his own. He would simply draw us away from the ball to speak behind closed doors and we would miss out on the fun entirely."

"Half of the supplies will be returning with him." Peggy nodded when she finally regained her breath. "He will want to inspect the load and ensure it is of good quality."

"Not at my dinner," Miss Nora scoffed. "Mother would never allow it, and neither will I. He can inspect his items during the daylight hours. That goes for you too Nashall Belton." The tiny female shook her finger at her brother like a schoolmarm at a naughty boy. "The gentlemen will not sneak off to other matters when there are ladies to entertain."

Lord Belton and his father must have a habit of doing just that, for the gentleman seemed properly chastised but did not argue. "Fine," he grumbled but did not seem all that put out.

"Besides," she grinned. "We are to have a real female guest, and I intend to enjoy every moment of it."

Several weeks passed before the morning of the arrival of the first wagons at the haberdashery. The day was one of celebration throughout the entire village. Children ran alongside the covered cart and begged the drivers to reveal the hidden contents. It seemed that everyone had come out to the main street to witness the momentous arrival, and several had already sent lists of requests to Peggy that they hoped would be filled.

Peggy opened the doors to the shop and could hardly contain her amusement that the Baron and his sister, along with a handful of servants, were already outside shooing the crowds away so that the goods might be brought within and unpacked before the shoppers could buy items.

Piles of paper wrapped packages were unloaded into the center of the room containing all manner of items from bolts of fabric and sewing needles to caps and purses and beads and thread. Another wagon arrived a few hours later boasting crates of books and paper, writing implements, and ink. Sticks of wax in a rainbow of colors were revealed in tissue lined boxes.

Peggy found herself standing in the middle of the room unsure of where to begin. There was so much to do, and it all needed to be catalogued and organized and set for display.

Her companions were still coordinating the gathered crowds and the unloading of the wagons when the door opened, and Peggy looked up in surprise.

Jemmy had entered the shop with a wide grin on his boyish face.

"At your service," he said with a dramatic bow. It was not his bow that stunned her but what was revealed behind him when he had bent at the waist. Adam stood in the doorway behind his adoptive brother with a look of anticipation and discomfort, as if he were unsure whether he would be welcomed. Jemmy seemed to take note that the pair were staring at one another in dumbfounded silence. Neither seemed sure where to begin. "I brought some extra hands, if you have need of them," he explained, his eyes wide with pleasure at the success of what he had accomplished.

"Of course." Peggy nodded and forced herself to snap out of her stupor. "I certainly could."

She was shaking with the surprise of it all, with excitement and a little bit of fear, but her son was here and that was all that mattered. Now was not the time to speak of their situation. Adam had come to be of use and perhaps out of curiosity to see what manner of person she might be. So it was that she set herself to showing him.

In no time at all, they developed a system. Peggy settled herself at the counter with her ledger to take notes and record numbers. Adam unwrapped the parcels, brought them to Peggy to look over for her records, made a count of each item, and then passed the items to Jemmy who placed them upon the shelves according to Peggy's instructions. Jemmy was the tallest of the three and therefore better able to reach the higher shelves, though he still had occasional requirement of the stepstool that Peggy had found at the back of the shop.

Together they labored for several hours without much

conversation save that which pertained to the shop or Jemmy's comments on the items he would like to purchase for his girl of interest. Peggy chuckled to herself every time the young man would point out a bow or trinket that would bring out his fancy's hair or eyes. It was such an innocent, young sense of adoration. He was smitten.

After a while, Adam began to open up too. He had a thousand questions, something she thought had not changed in all of these years. He had always been precocious and inquisitive.

He asked her about everything that he unpacked. He wanted to know why a lady would want this bauble or that lace. He scrunched his nose at the feathers and claimed that they were *fussy,* and he did not care for them. Rather than laugh, she nodded, for she quite agreed.

He was fascinated at the spinning tops and toys that she had ordered with young boys such as himself in mind. He refused to hand over a painted wooden soldier for Jemmy to place on the shelf and instead set it on the counter so that he could look at it while he worked. It was endearing that he was still young enough to care for such things. With tears in her eyes, Peggy realized she hadn't missed the entirety of his childhood.

When the crowd had dispersed and the wagons were empty, Miss Nora and Lord Belton joined them in the task. Lord Belton took over the ledger work while his sister addressed the empty parcel wrappings that Adam had been piling in the corner.

Peggy settled herself to pricing the items, which she marked directly on the shelf with a stick of charcoal that could be wiped clean and changed as needed.

Soon enough, the boys had forgotten all about the

ladies and were vying for the lord's attentions. Their idol, it seemed. He was a good sport about it as they constantly distracted him from his work to show him some thing or other. Jemmy wanted to ask his advice on the best gift to woo a lady, to which he replied in all honesty that it depended upon the lady, and the boy's idea would probably be better than his own. Adam was determined to prove that he was a good worker. He felt that he was now old enough to do work on the estate on his own, without supervision, and would not rest until the gentleman agreed that, if Mr. Finch permitted it, he could help choose the tree for the hall this winter. Peggy bit her lip as she wondered if the boy would even be here in a few months to have the promise fulfilled.

In the matter of a half a day they were all of them exhausted, but the chore was complete, at least for a few days until the next arrival. Peggy looked around the room and was amazed with how many things had been placed on the shelves or stowed in the corners. The shop still looked empty for such a large room, but it was a start, and soon enough it would be full to bursting. For a mad moment she thought that her father would have been proud of her. She managed with the aplomb of any male.

Miss Nora and the Baron disappeared to retrieve sustenance from the inn. The boys sat on the counter with their legs swinging back and forth and wide grins of satisfaction as they waited for the arrival of the meat pies.

"I told you!" Jemmy punched Adam in the arm. "Meat pies every time."

Adam looked a little abashed at having been outed with the knowledge that meat pies might have been his true motivation for joining the older boy at the shop.

Peggy did not care. She was just glad that she had spent almost an entire day in the presence of her son. And it had been a good day.

"Now there is only the matter of your payment," she said crossing her arms before her and looking at the pair as if they had a very serious matter to discuss. The boys perked up at the thought of their reward. "It is your choice," she began. "You can take your value in coin or we can barter."

"What you mean barter?" Adam asked, his eyes unconsciously going to the painted toy soldier sitting on the shelf and then back to a folding utility knife from Sheffield. She could see the debate between childhood and manhood happening as the expressions passed across his face.

"Just that," she grinned. "Your value in coin or the equivalent value in an item or items from my shop." The boys' mouths fell open with amazement at the offer. Really, it was no different for Peggy. She would simply pay the due to the boys for their services or pay the amount to the shop for the replacement of inventory. They could take it as they pleased.

Without hesitation, Adam's hands snaked out and he pulled the toy soldier to his chest. "How many more days do I have to work for this?" he asked. "Because I'll come back if it is not enough."

"It is enough," Peggy giggled.

"And this?" he asked, picking up the knife as well. It was a common model, a penny knife carried by most men. She did not want him to leave childhood so soon, but like every mother the world over, she was helpless to stop the march of time.

She nodded and plucked a candy from a glass jar on the counter and tossed it to him. "Enough for this as well."

He grinned widely as he popped the candy into his mouth.

Jemmy had crossed to the other side of the shop and was looking through a set of ribbons that might pique his lady's fancy.

"Does that mean..." Adam drew her attention back with a sadness in his little voice that had her turning with concern. "Does that mean you don't need me anymore?"

"Oh, heavens no!" Peggy wanted to run to him and tell him that she would always need him, but she knew that that was not what he meant. "You can come back any time," she promised. "You are always welcome to come help or..." She did not know if she dared at first, but the day had gone so well that she could not help herself. "Or just to pay a visit."

Adam bit his lip as he considered her words and then he nodded. If Peggy's heart could have burst with joy it would have done so. The door had been opened, if only a crack. It was more than she could have dared hope for on this day.

The siblings bearing the meat pies made their appearance a moment later, and upon their arrival both boys' focus became devoted solely to their stomachs. With mouths full of their savory meal they said their farewells and made for the door. Before they left, Jemmy pulled a set of ribbons from the shelf and waved them at Peggy in question. She nodded and they were off.

"Thank the heavens for those boys," Miss Nora said with a sigh as she sank down onto the stool. "We might never have finished had it been left to we three."

"They certainly have a lot of energy," Lord Belton agreed with a deep chuckle.

"They earned their keep, and I am thankful for it," Peggy agreed. Her feet were sore, and her eyes were tired, but she was satisfied in a way that she had not been in a long time. "I hope to see them again soon," she said. And she meant it with every fiber of her being.

## CHAPTER 21

P<small>EGGY</small> <small>MADE THE MISTAKE OF GIVING IN TO</small> M<small>ISS</small> N<small>ORA</small> when she suggested that Peggy return with her to Whitefall Hall to get dressed for their dinner. She could have done well enough on her own above the shop, but Miss Nora had made the astute point that it would save a trip of the carriage having to come back for her.

Had she been left to her own devices, Peggy would have merely washed her face, combed out her hair, pinned it back to the top of her head, and pulled out a fresh gown. Instead, Miss Nora insisted on looking through all of Peggy's dresses to find *just the right thing.* If they had not been so differing in height, she suspected that her friend might have considered suggesting that she borrow one of her gowns. As it was, Miss Nora was more than pleased with the selection.

"You have very fine things," she said as she held out a brilliant turquoise empire cut dress with a sheer overlay that glittered with silver thread. "Are you sure you are not secretly from a noble house?"

"You have my word," Peggy laughed. "I have a friend of a friend who is a Duchess and is kind enough to pass on her castoffs."

Miss Nora pursed her lips and sighed as she accepted the explanation. "What a shame," she mused. "You really do make a finer lady than half of those I have had the odious misfortune of making acquaintance. Oh, plenty of them are just fine, excellent even, but *some*." She shivered at the thought. "I met one lady, Blackwell I think was her name, the year that I came out, and she threw herself all over Nash and then tried to befriend me when he would have nothing to do with her! I told him I thought she was a snake in beautiful skin, and lo and behold, just last year it became known that she had done some horrendous things! No one has heard from her since and good riddance!"

Peggy felt as if she were going to be sick. She had known that Lady Blackwell, her very own devilish captor, had made news all across England for the terrible ring of indentured females that she had bought and sold at her whim. Still, hearing the name so far from London had been unexpected. Peggy had hoped never to hear that name again.

"Yes," she said with every attempt to keep her voice from trembling. "I believe I heard about that. Let us not speak of such things when we have much happier thoughts this day."

"You are absolutely right. She does not deserve mention." At that, Miss Nora spun around and held out another gown, far too much for a simple dinner, that was a shocking white satin with black Brussels lace.

"I think not," Peggy laughed. She reached around her friend and grabbed a simple satin visiting gown in emerald green. Miss Nora held the dress up to Peggy's form as she tried to imagine what it would look like on and then nodded her approval.

"My Lily will do your hair, and you can borrow some of my jewelry, perhaps the emeralds.

"Absolutely not," Peggy protested, and Nora relented. "Very well. We shall have to make do with a nice ribbon tied about your neck. It will be just the thing."

Peggy grabbed her belongings and shoved them into a carpet bag with a pair of crème slippers before she pushed Miss Nora out the door. She would attend this dinner as the supposed guest of honor, but she would not make a fool of herself by dressing to the nines. Other than the Viscount and his wife, whom she had yet to meet, there was no one to impress. Her heart fluttered for a moment as she thought of Lord Belton, but she firmly suppressed the thought. Miss Nora and her brother were well accustomed to Peggy's attire and though her gowns were fine, they were cast-offs, and she was not prone to embellishments.

Upon their arrival at Whitefall Hall, the women learned that the Viscount and the Viscountess had yet to make their arrival. Peggy was hoping to delay their primping by making introductions but instead found herself spirited to the second floor and into Miss Nora's chambers.

For the next two hours, she was plucked and pinched and curled and then shoved into her gown without ceremony until finally the pair were declared by the meticulous maid to be suitable for the evening's events.

Peggy could not recall the last time she had done anything more than stick a few pins in her hair to keep it from falling in her face. Tonight, she had to have no less than several dozen pins holding each curled section just so. They framed her face and tickled her ears. Lily had also pulled a few free so that they were made to casually trail down her neck. Peggy's hair was quite long and with the delicate pieces had surpassed what the maid had considered an appropriate length, and she had cut them off without warning. Now, they hung just above her shoulders and would not dare to get tucked into the edges of her low-cut gown. Peggy had attempted to secure a Fichu about her shoulders, but neither the Lady nor the maid would hear of it.

"You would wear it perhaps in the morning," the maid said, "but in the evening, no."

Peggy had sighed and decided not to argue, but she felt self-conscious with her shoulders bare. Miss Nora had waited ages to have any female to dinner that was not her relation or multiple decades her senior and so she would allow her friend her small excitements.

"Can there really be no other ladies in the area?" Peggy asked with incredulity. "Certainly, you must have some companions in the neighborhood."

"I had at one time," Miss Nora explained. "Now they are all married off or spend most of the year in London. Of course, by now, it is unbearable in London. Most of the fashionable ladies are in Bath or Brighton by the Sea, although I'm sure a few of them are at their country homes. Not many are so far north. I see them all here and there, or we write, but it is not the same as when we were girls at school."

Peggy could understand that. With adulthood came certain changes in behavior that Miss Nora had on several

189

occasions condemned with dissatisfaction. Peggy could also understand why her friend did not wish for anything to change. Having witnessed her relationship with her brother these past few weeks and the lighthearted playfulness that still existed between them, she could see how Miss Nora would mourn that same sense of loss with her friends. She only hoped that if, or when, Lord Belton chose to take a wife for himself, his sister would not be excluded from his affections.

When the ladies descended the staircase, it was to be greeted by a petite woman that showed a striking resemblance to Miss Nora, save for the possession of several additional decades. Her dress was ice blue with silver embellishments. Diamonds surrounded her neck. Peggy could have determined even in a crowd that this woman could only be Miss Nora's mother. They possessed the same delicate stature and bright green eyes filled with merriment, and although the Viscountess's hair was streaked with silver, it was clear that it was once as golden as her daughter's.

"Darling!" the Viscountess of Umberly greeted her daughter with open arms. Miss Nora fell into the embrace and clasped her mother's hand as she pulled her forward to make Peggy's acquaintance. Greetings were exchanged, and Lady Umberly insisted at once that Peggy call her Augusta.

"Lady Umberly makes me feel old," she had complained. "It was all well when I was Lady Whitefall, but Umberly was always Peter's father. When the late Duke died and we all moved up, that's when I really began to feel my age. So, spare me the horror and just call me Augusta, my dear."

Peggy laughed and promised to do as requested, even if it went against everything her father had taught her about titles and circumstance. In fact, even the lady's age demanded that she be given some deference, but Peggy nodded, agreeing to adhere to the lady's wishes.

"Good. Good." The Viscountess nodded. "I could tell you had sense when I first saw you. Not like my Nora; she's all trouble and misadventure. But I told her she has to remember that she is a lady regardless to the fact that she has allowed half the town to call her by her given name. I have so tried to keep her from becoming entirely feral."

"Mama!" Miss Nora exclaimed. "How can you fault me when you do exactly the same thing?"

"Only teasing, love." Augusta grinned as she patted her daughter upon the cheek. "I'm sure you will have the right of it once we arrive at London for your Season."

"Oh Mama, no!" cried Nora.

"Tut, tut," her mother said, forestalling an argument.

Peggy could not imagine why a young lady would not want a Season. At the very least, it was a succession of parties and outings to see the world, but she had no time to express her opinion.

"Oh my!" a deep male voice boomed from the doorway to the parlor. He was an attractive man with greyed hair that was pulled into a ribbon at his neck and a great booming laugh that was not unlike his son's. "A finer picture of ladies I have never seen. Nash, do you think that beauty in blue and silver has an eye for me?"

Lord Belton poked his head out into the hall, declared that his mother certainly did not, and then returned to the

191

parlor. Peggy could not help but laugh. It was all so unlike anything she had ever witnessed among the gentry.

As she listened to the family banter, it all began to make sense. The apples, it seemed, had not fallen far from the tree, and the affection that was shared between the siblings seemed to run throughout the family. Peggy thought of her own parents who had barely shared a handful of kind words to one another each day. They certainly had not laughed and teased and touched one another in the easy manner in which the Viscount and the Viscountess seemed to do as if by instinct alone. She could never, not once, recall her parents... flirting in so obvious a fashion. If she really thought about it, she did not much think her makers had even liked each other. Theirs had been an arrangement of practicality. This couple, she realized with awe, were truly and undoubtedly in love even after all of these years.

No wonder Miss Nora had refused to give up playfulness for marriage. Her own parents were the prime example that she could have both, if she ever found it. The prospect seemed rare enough, and their daughter had decided never to settle for anything less.

A moment later, the party removed to the dining hall where a feast had been set capable of feeding a number much greater than their five.

"Not to worry, child," Augusta explained when she saw Peggy frowning at the piles of food. "We intend for there to be plenty left over to nourish the servants and their families."

Peggy opened her mouth in surprise, and Augusta laughed, the same light sound as Nora's levity. "My daughter told me about your penchant to eliminate waste," she said with a raised eyebrow.

Peggy blushed and settled into a chair that was held out for her by Lord Belton. She was surprised to see Lord Umberly hold out the chair at the side of the table for his wife. Rather than observe the protocols of the Viscount and his wife securing opposite heads of the table, the Lord had seated his wife beside Peggy while he took one head and left the other empty. At first, Peggy had wondered at what many would consider an insulting arrangement, but then she saw Lord Umberly grasp his wife's hand at his side and she realized that they merely wished to be close. Lord Belton seated himself between Peggy and Nora, across from his father. She caught of whiff of his cologne and was immediately entranced. She tried to keep her composure, and yet, she was glad that he was close by. His nearness made a flutter of nervousness fill the pit of her stomach, but in some way the feeling was pleasant. How silly, she thought. Hadn't they been doing books and talking business all week? Why was she nervous now? Could it be that he looked such the gentleman dressed in his fine clothing?

"What news of the neighborhood?" Lady Umberly asked as she began to pick at the food which had been served to her by the footman.

"Missy Pekering had another baby," Miss Nora offered without much interest.

"Oh, how nice," her mother replied. "When are one of you two going to give me a grandchild?"

Peggy nearly spat out the carrot that she had just placed in her mouth, but she covered her surprise with a cough instead.

"Lady Abernathy informs me at least once a week that her son is in need of a bride," Lord Belton mused. "I've decided to offer up Nora, so you may speak to my sister."

Peggy grunted and gasped as she received a swift kick to the shin.

"Oh! Sorry!" Miss Nora exclaimed. "I thought that was Nash."

Nash chuckled as Peggy reached down to rub the aching limb only to find another leg shift so as to press up against her own. Her eyes shifted to Lord Belton in question, but he merely blinked innocently. A moment later, his sister cried out in pain as her second attempt at an attack was met by the wood of his chair. Having cleared his own limbs from his sister's reach, the pressure against Peggy's leg was removed and she regained her space.

"Honora Rose, you brought that upon yourself," Lady Umberly scolded. "Do not make a third attempt. If you cannot sit at table with the adults, I shall send you from the table with no supper as I did when you were still in the nursery."

"Yes, mother," Miss Nora grumbled.

"Speaking of Lord Abernathy," her brother continued as if nothing had occurred, "why shouldn't you marry him, Nora? He adores you."

"He does not," Nora spat.

"His property borders ours," the Viscount said, "and he has grown into a fine gentleman with many accolades. Quite the soldier I am told. Although I believe he has sold his commission now, much to his father's relief. He is home for good now."

Miss Nora huffed and crossed her arms. "Lord James Abernathy is the bane of my existence. Has been since I was ten," She directed her explanation at Peggy who seemed to be the only one at the table who did not know the history. "He was the terror of my childhood and," she turned to her father and brother in turn, "I don't care what kind of gentleman he's grown into. Accolades or no, I wouldn't have him if he came with a crown."

"You hardly had the chance to meet with him more than a handful of times in the of years while he has been away," Lord Belton continued, grinning that his sister had been put so out of sorts by his suggestion. "He's only been back for a month."

Jesting or no, Miss Nora would not tolerate the suggestion. "I have met him enough for a lifetime, thank you very much," his sister replied.

"Ah well," Lord Belton feigned resignation, "I suppose he will just have to suffer the dozen ladies his mother has invited to catch his eye for the Christmas season. From what he tells me, they will be hosting a Christmas Ball."

Miss Nora seemed to take sordid pleasure at the news. "Good. He deserves all of them," she declared.

"Of course, we will be invited," Lord Belton continued.

"Father said I am to have a Season," Nora said, looking towards the Viscount. "Perhaps we will still be in London."

"Not at Christmas, surely," her mother said.

"Oh, so you have decided to have a Season," the Viscount added, trapping Nora in the proverbial corner.

"I don't know," she said petulantly.

"Well, we do not need to decide right now," the Viscount said, smoothing his daughter's ruffled feathers. "There is plenty of time."

"Speaking of the Christmas season," Peggy butted in with a change of subject that she hoped would ease her friend's distress, "I expect the haberdashery will be in full swing in time for everyone to do their holiday shopping." And with that the conversation turned to matters of business. As promised, the Viscount had innumerable questions that kept the party busy for the duration of the meal.

When they had finished their desserts and Peggy was full near to bursting, Lady Umberly declared that there would be no more talk of anything so gauche as business for the remainder of the evening.

"On the morrow you can visit the store and see for yourself, darling," she said with a gentle smile for her husband. "Tonight, I would like to enjoy my time with the children."

Together they retired to an elegant parlor big enough to house dozens and dozens of guests. It was only slightly smaller than a ballroom in Peggy's estimation.

For an hour, they sat about laughing and reminiscing. Peggy enjoyed hearing tales of happy childhoods so different from her own. She wondered what it would have been like to have grown up in such a place. She wondered if this was what Adam had enjoyed in the Finch house. She must have been lost in her musings since it was not until Lord Belton strolled past her chair and tapped his fountain pen beside her head that she snapped to attention.

"Hmm?"

"I asked if your siblings were as poorly behaved as my children?" Lady Umberly repeated the question with amusement, and Peggy turned her attention to Lord Belton's mother.

"No, not at all," Peggy replied without thought. Then,

she grimaced as she realized how her words might have landed. "What I mean to say is that I have no siblings. I was a solitary child."

"I am sure that was wonderful." The Viscount laughed. "These two were as much trouble as if we had had a dozen."

"I cannot say that it was," Peggy answered in all honesty. For the first time, she was not filled with bitterness at the recollection of her upbringing. Sadness, perhaps, but it seemed as if she were somehow slowly learning to let go of those years. It was as if having found herself surrounded by good, happy people these many months since she had regained her freedom, her wounds had begun to heal. Not that they did not exist. It was only that she was beginning to feel less burdened by them. She could not say how. She only knew that she felt a change had taken root, and her new friends had certainly been a part of that healing.

"Either way, you seem to have been brought up in good society," the Viscountess observed. "You are well spoken, well mannered, and are clearly educated. What other accomplishments can you boast? Do you play?" She gestured to the pianoforte in the corner of the room, and Peggy's eyes shot to meet Miss Nora's. She suddenly felt trapped in a world where she did not belong. By some miracle, she might have made a good impression thus far, but she was not prepared to make a fool of herself by plunking away at best at a childish tune. She would need months more practice before she was anywhere near her previous level of skill, and even in her past, she had only considered herself a passable pianist.

She began to shake her head to the negative, but Miss

Nora cut in. "She does play, but she is shy in company," her friend explained. "Why do not I play for you, Mama? I do know how much you love to listen, or perhaps dance," she whispered for her mother's ears only. Miss Nora removed herself to the instrument and settled before it. She warmed up her fingers with a few lively pieces before settling in to sultry, romantic number that Peggy recognized but could not name.

Her audience listened with rapt attention as Miss Nora worked her art over them. After a few minutes, as Nora predicted, Lord Umberly stood up and approached his wife with an outstretched hand. Lady Umberly giggled and accepted with a blush as genuine as the first bloom of love. She turned to Peggy with a smile as her husband swept her into his arms.

"You do not mind if we dance, do you?" she asked. "We do love to dance, and Nora plays so beautifully."

"Not at all," Peggy assured her hosts and waved them toward the open floor in front of the hearth.

She watched the couple take their spins for ages with a sort of guilty fascination. No, she had never experienced anything quite like the Belton family. Miss Nora swept from one piece to the next with seamless transitions. Her fingers never seemed to tire. On and on the Viscount and his wife danced. The room could have been full or empty and it would not have mattered. They had eyes only for each other. It occurred to Peggy that she had never seen her parents dance with one another, not even at a ball. In fact, she had never seen them dance with anyone. Her father was always off in some corner making deals or introductions to new business prospects. Her mother, on the other hand, had worked the floor with the sole purpose of shunting Peggy off on some gentleman or other. Peggy had never been without a partner, and every moment of it had felt like a chore. Never had she been so enraptured as the Viscountess appeared to be.

A hand appeared before her face and pulled Peggy from her reverie. Her gaze followed the long arm upward, and she was forced to twist her chin to look over her shoulder to find Lord Belton's face above her own. He had made the gesture from where he stood along the back of the couch in such a casual manner that she had laughed before she thought better of it. She covered her mouth with her hand and apologized for the rude response.

"Now you have to dance with me if only to repair my bruised pride," he teased with a half grin.

"Is that so?" she replied in challenge.

"Mostly, mother will have my neck if I leave you sitting here without an offer." He smiled. "If you decline, she shall say I deserved it for my abominable behavior. Please." He begged as if craving a boon. "You must save me."

"Then allow me to be your knight in shining armor." Peggy laughed as she placed her hand in his. "As a guest, I would not want to upset your mother."

"She'll think you gave me the cut," he added for good measure as he pulled her across the room to an open corner well out of earshot of his parents.

"She would not," Peggy protested. "She would trust my decision absolutely."

"I am afraid you are right." He laughed as he pulled her into his arms.

# CHAPTER 22

Peggy felt her world reel as she was embraced by the gentleman. She had meant to tease him with a hint of flirtation, but all such intentions were forgotten in that moment as waves of heat flooded through her body and the scent of him took her breath away.

His laughter, too, seemed to have dissipated in a flash, and when he drew back, his gaze held an intensity that made her cheeks grow hot.

As the blush crept up Peggy's cheeks, she dared not look at him for fear that he would detect the conflicting emotions that were beginning to rise within her, and so instead, she kept her gaze locked firmly on his shoulder until she could breathe again.

As they whirled about the room, she at last met his gaze—hoping to make some lighthearted comment to excuse her reaction—when she realized that he was looking down upon her with just as much passion as she felt herself. His pupils were dark and dilated, his breathing unsteady, and she wondered if he too had been unprepared for the feelings that their embrace had unleashed.

Peggy forced herself to focus on his shoulder beneath her hand. She had meant to focus on the threads or the pattern of his jacket, but instead all she noted was the heat of her hand against the warmth of him that she was acutely aware of even through the clothing.

How had this happened? When did this happen? She wracked her brain for any moment when she had harbored such shocking feelings for the brother of her friend and could recall none. Yes, she had thought him handsome from the beginning, but she had been too wrapped up in her own affairs to have noticed him in the way that a woman might notice a man, and yet, some subconscious part of her must have been doing so all along to have been struck by such a sudden wave of heat. For years, she had been bereft of such sensations, and she had been determined to keep them away. This, however, had been unavoidable and caught her completely off guard.

His fingers flexed against her back, and she startled.

"I am sorry," he muttered, stopping their movements. "We do not have to continue."

The piano skipped a beat, and Peggy looked over to discover Miss Nora watching with keen interest. Upon being caught, the pianist's eyes returned to the keys.

"We have an audience," Peggy replied with shaken breath.

"I see," he replied with a voice nearly as unsteady. He cleared his throat.

"It is fine." Peggy shook her head as if she could free it of the cobwebs that had taken over. She stepped back into his arms, this time prepared for the flush and the rapid increase of her heartbeat.

They finished the song without incident even though Peggy suspected that Miss Nora had doubled back to add length to the piece. She was glad that Lord Belton had chosen a spot away from his mother and father who would have though it strange that the pair had uttered not a single word once they had resumed their dance.

Peggy was glad that she was not the only one who was off kilter. She would have been mortified if she had been alone in her discomfort. If only for the reason that if it seemed like she harbored unwanted affections, he might be put off from their friendship. As it was, Lord Belton seemed to be just as disconcerted as she.

They pulled apart and Peggy returned to her seat, while Lord Belton remained on the far side of the room seemingly to peruse the bookcase. Peggy was glad that Miss Nora was trapped at the pianoforte while her parents continued to dance. It allowed her to keep her back to her friend while the color that she was well aware had risen to her cheeks faded. Eventually, Lord Belton returned to the cluster of seats where he took his place across from her. She could feel his questioning gaze upon her, narrowed blue eyes that tore at her periphery, but she refused to return the look, instead focusing with determination upon the dancing pair. Perhaps he too was wondering if it had all been imagined. Perhaps, like her, he wondered if the sudden heat had just been a strange occurrence brought on by the wine from dinner.

# PART IV

# CHAPTER 23

W<small>HEN THE</small> V<small>ISCOUNT AND HIS WIFE HAD FINALLY HAD</small> enough dancing, they all gathered for a customary end-of-the-evening cup of tea and trivial conversation. It took no time at all for Lord Belton to appear to have recovered from the awkward encounter, and so Peggy felt sure that the moment had passed, and they could both be free of it.

She allowed herself to sink into her chair with relief. The last thing that she wanted to deal with were unwanted emotions. She had no time for such things. She needed to focus on her son, not this strange attraction that had likely only developed as a result of some misinterpretation of his consistent kindness and would likely fade after a few hours of rational thought. The initial jolt could not have been controlled, but the ability to ignore it was within her power. Feelings were sometimes surprising but often not worth a second thought, she reminded herself.

When Peggy struggled to suppress a yawn, she stood and expressed that it was time for her to return home.

"Oh," Lady Umberly exclaimed, "I sent the servants to bed ages ago. I was sure you would be staying the night."

But Peggy could not. Tomorrow the shop would open for the first time, and customers would be waiting as soon as the dawn.

"Of course." the Viscountess nodded. "I shall call to wake a driver."

"There is no need to bother, Mama," Miss Nora chimed in with a grin. "I'm sure Nash can take her home. He likes to drive the curricle." Both Peggy and Lord Belton began to shake their heads, but the lady went on without pause. "I cannot say the number the times he has taken Lady Rose home when she has been unable to stay the night."

"Lady Rose is married," her mother replied. Then, she pursed her lips in consideration. "Though it is true that she was not always... and the ways of the country are not so rigid as that of London."

"And Nash is entirely trustworthy," Nora said. "It's not like he's a rake."

"Of course not," the Viscount snapped.

Besides, he has already taken Peggy home once before in the curricle," Nora said.

With Jemmy, save for the last short stint, Peggy thought with a grumble, but she did not protest. In truth, a part of her wanted a moment alone with the man.

"It is not very far," Nash added, and Peggy realized that he wanted a chance to speak with her privately too. The thought excited her, and yet, she thought, such a thing was dangerous. She should insist that Nora accompany them, but for some reason, she did not.

"It's settled then. Nash is already here, and there is no

need to wake the others only to have to wait another hour at least for them to dress and be ready to set off," Nora added.

"You could ride with your friend," suggested the Viscountess to her daughter.

"I could…" Nora said consideringly.

Peggy found it amusing that the females were making considerations as if her virtue were at all in question. Little did they know that Peggy had lost her virtue ages ago. If anything, her reputation might corrupt the good name of the Baron. Furthermore, she had no fear of being alone with a man on the ride to town, rather she feared her own leaping pulse being sent into another round of spasms at the prospect of that man being Lord Belton. She had not quite purged the recent shock from her mind.

"Come along then, Augusta," said the Viscount to his wife, as if the matter was settled.

"I'll go hitch the horse and meet you at the front door," Lord Belton said.

Before there could be a word otherwise, Lord Belton was gone. The Viscount and Viscountess had hurried upstairs, lost in each other, which left Nora and Peggy to get their cloaks, since although the days were still warm, the evenings had begun to cool. However, instead of Nora donning her cloak, she helped Peggy with hers and then embraced her friend with a curt goodnight.

Miss Nora raised one shoulder in mock innocence, her eyes twinkling with mischief, and then she opened the door. Peggy stepped out into the night just as the curricle rounded the corner and came to a stop at the bottom of the stair.

"Goodnight," Nora said again in a sing-song voice as

she shut the door behind her friend.

Lord Belton abandoned his perch to hand her up. Careful to tuck the folds of her skirts away from the wheels, she pressed herself as far away from the gentleman as the narrow bench would allow. Still, they were hip to hip, and his broad shoulder bumped her whenever the vehicle jostled. This was madness!

The lanterns that hung from the front of the vehicle had gone unlit and for good reason because the moon had risen full and bright in the harvest sky. Peggy gazed out upon the open fields and pastures with awe. It seemed a distant memory, those years that had gone by when she had only seen the moon through the dirty panes of a London window. Those days now seemed far off though only a year had passed since her rescue.

They rode for a while without speaking. It was a pleasant silence, not at all undercut with the agonizing thoughts or nervous sensations that she had anticipated. Peggy lavished in the crisp scent of the fresh air and the gentle breeze that tickled her cheeks. She wanted to soak it into her soul. Cities were made for pressing down upon you. This was something quite different. It was as if the countryside was made to heal.

She caught a flash of movement across a silvery field and squinted her eyes to better ascertain what she had seen. The creature turned and froze.

"Look!" she gasped, and her hand landed upon Lord Belton's forearm and pulled, forcing the reins to draw the horses to a halt. Her other hand shot out to point across his vision so that he was forced to turn his back to her to follow her gaze.

There stood an enormous stag with a pale white chest

and tail. It moved not an inch as if frozen by the moonlight. The animal and the humans watched one another for what felt like ages. Peggy had dropped her free hand to her lap but the other remained upon Lord Belton's arm, for she was afraid that if she moved again the creature would bolt.

"Well, I'll be," Lord Belton whispered. "Finch has been swearing up and down for years that he has seen a beast of monstrous size, and no one would believe him."

"Now, you must," she mouthed at his side.

The horse tossed his head and snorted, annoyed at having been stopped in the middle of the lane. The sound jolted the stag into action, and three bounds later it had disappeared into the wood.

Lord Belton returned to face the front of the curricle. The action brought the length of his arm within inches of Peggy's front where she still knelt on the bench looking out over the field. Too close.

Her cheeks flushed when he turned to look at her, and she went still, not unlike the stag a moment before. Somehow, this time with little more than a glance, her body had gone all flushed and liquid. She could feel her heart pounding in her chest as she averted her gaze. Her ears rang, and she felt at once as if she were breathing through very thick air. Perhaps if she ignored it, it would stop? She knew that was a false hope when she could practically *feel* him asking the question that neither of them wanted to address.

"Miss Williams…" he said in a voice so quiet that she was not even certain whether he had spoken, or had she imagined her name upon his lips? "Peggy," he said. He had never been so informal, and the thought sent a chill down her spine. No, not a chill… a thrill.

Her mouth opened in surprise as if to speak, but no words came out. Then, before she even realized that he had shifted, his mouth was upon her own. It was a brief kiss. Tender and sweet. A test or a question, or both perhaps. He pulled back, seeming to share in her surprise.

Peggy stared at him, her eyes wide and uncertain. The tilt of his head revealed that he was awaiting her reaction. His blue eyes filled with concern. Would she be cross? Had he been unwelcome in the advance? Her breath came in shivering gasps, but her mind had gone blank in the moment as her trembling hand rose to touch her lips.

"Peggy," he repeated, but this time the word was filled with apology. "I'm sorry." The words broke something within her.

Without taking the time to think about her response she reacted. "No," she said. "Do not be sorry. I wanted to…"

She never finished the sentence. His lips came down upon hers again, this time filled with desire.

Feelings that she cared not to name exploded within her. Their mouths melded together with a strange familiarity, like they had been here before. It was as if their mouths, their bodies, had long known one another. Ages, lifetimes perhaps, longer than their brief acquaintance. She opened to him, surprised that it all felt so natural, so easy, so perfect.

His arms wrapped around her waist and pulled her closer. Peggy cursed the arrangement of the bench for nothing seemed close enough. She threw her arms about his neck, one hand splayed across his back and the other burrowed into his hair. She felt that she could not get close enough, as if she wanted to sink into him and meld their very beings.

Sensations and urges that had long been forgotten raged full force within her, and she was shaken by the pure power of it all. She wanted, and it had been so very long since she had allowed herself to want.

When his mouth moved to the curve where her jaw met her neck, she threw her head back in pleasure, gulping at the cool night air. His hands were clenched in her cloak, and she cursed the damn thing for its thick folds. She felt her body ache for him and tried to press closer, but there was no further to go. Like the slow burn of an ember catching a paper to flame, she felt herself ignite. Her mind was spinning, reeling, and luxuriating in every touch, every sweet press of his mouth to her skin.

His mouth returned to hers, and she met him passion for passion, unable to quench the thirst that had built inside of her. Never before, not even all those years ago, had she been thrust into such blinding ecstasy so quickly and with little more than a kiss.

His hand found its way beneath her cloak and settled at her waist. Even with her corset and gown, she could feel the heat of his palm burning like a brand against her skin as he held tight. It seemed as if the world were spinning around them, unstable, and they had only one another which to cling for support.

She shifted, trying and failing once more to press herself against him in the hope of satiating that need. The movement, through no fault of his, left his hand brushing against her breast, and she released a groan. No, she amended with horror, a moan.

The sound of her own wanton cry brought Peggy crashing back to reality, and she jolted away from him. She knew that her lips must be swollen, and her cheeks flushed with heat, her eyes wide and no longer glazed with passion, but shocked in the horror of her behavior.

"Oh God," she groaned as she turned and would have leapt from the curricle, but he caught her elbow and drew her to a halt. He turned her to face him, and she heard, but mostly ignored, the stream of apologies that he offered.

"It isn't you," she said when she raised a hand to stop his proclamation of guilt.

"I shouldn't have," he repeated, seeming distraught by her response and ready to take full accountability, though Peggy knew very well that the fault was her own. When would she learn?

She shook her head and repeated herself. "This is not your fault," she promised. "Please, just…" She did not know what to say, how to explain that she blamed only herself for what had occurred. For having given in to that terrible side of her that she had so long denied. Passion was a curse, her mother had used to say, and Peggy had learned that lesson far too well. "Just pretend it never happened. That is all I ask."

"Pretend it never happened?" he asked in shock as if such a thing were unthinkable.

Peggy groaned and rubbed at her temples. She had made a mess of things, and if anyone ever discovered this misstep, then her reputation in Riversbend would be ruined. She cared not for her own sake but for Adam's. Would she never learn, she scolded herself for the hundredth time.

"Please," she begged. "It is all that I ask of you. Please let us just go back to the way things were. I beg you."

"Back? No. Why?" He seemed hurt by the prospect, and she nearly laughed in his face. Such a dalliance would do little to a lord, she knew well enough, but nothing could come of it besides her own shame.

"This can *never* happen again," she continued. "Ever. And I beg you, for my sake, to speak of it to no one."

"I wouldn't think of it, but why?" he argued.

"You must trust me," she said with as firm a voice as she could manage despite the fact that her entire body was shaking.

"Peggy, please," he offered in a tone far too gentle, for it made her feel like a heel. "This is my fault."

"No," Peggy said, when he interrupted.

"It is neither of our faults," he proclaimed with surety. "I lay this firmly in my sister's lap. You know Nora maneuvered the drive with this exact hope in mind, and we both fell into her trap."

Peggy had to laugh at the folly of it all, and he joined her in chuckling. Suddenly, they were friends again, although the heat of the moment was still there underneath it all.

If her friend only knew that her meddlesome attempts had thrust her brother into the arms of a completely ruined woman with whom there would be no future. In some ways, she was honored that Miss Nora had even considered Peggy a viable prospect, for she certainly was not the type to have pushed them to drive together for only a tryst.

She sighed and nodded. "All right. Please drive on." She put her hands in her lap and her eyes firmly on the road ahead as he released the brake and urged the horse forward. She feared it would be some time before she felt herself steady once again. They rode on in silence with two sets of eyes focused ahead and not a word between them.

# CHAPTER 24

PEGGY HAD A RESTLESS NIGHT AS HER MIND REPLAYED THE scene over and over no matter what distractions she had offered it. She had taken a bath, attempted to read a book, and made several failed attempts at a letter to Marilee. She could not tell her friend what had happened, and merely writing a superficial update on the shop and her interactions with Adam seemed too cold and impersonal for the turmoil that she could not abate. Eventually, she wrote it all down, every last detail, before promptly burning the false letter. Afterward, she told herself she felt more settled, having purged the unwanted desire from her system. By that time the sun was beginning to rise, and there was no time for sleep.

She went below to open the shop, brewed herself a strong cup of tea, and braced for what promised to be a distracting day.

The boys showed up just as the first customers began to browse the shop. Peggy had already pulled the list of items that had been requested by several locals for delivery and sent them off to run. Each time, Adam returned with a grin. Everyone was so pleased with the opening that the boys had been well tipped and thanked for their efforts.

She had hoped to close up for a midday meal, but there were far too many interested visitors. Most made purchases. Others made requests for future items or asked when Peggy intended to allow ladies to settle in for tea and conversation. She had informed them that a wide selection of tea would be arriving shortly, and they could make their arrangements to begin the week next.

The Viscount and Lady Umberly made their appearance in the late afternoon along with their daughter and, to Peggy's discomfort, their son. Of course, he would have to come with them, she reminded herself. It would have been strange had he not. He was, after all, the true owner of the shop. Still, seeing Lord Belton so soon after their embrace left Peggy on trembling legs.

Miss Nora flitted about the shop with excitement as she pointed out one thing after another to her mother.

"We shall hang the curtains here," she said with a sweep of her hand, "to partition off the ladies from the rest of the shoppers. The color could be changed for the season, and with the wide windows to one side, I think it will soon become the place to be."

The Viscountess had nodded and gone off with her daughter to muse about the décor that could be brought over from the manor to make the place more suitable for their patrons.

"A fine thing you've done here," Lord Umberly declared when he had finished his perusal of the ledger. "When the other wagons arrive, you will have a full to bursting shop on your hands."

Peggy nodded and explained that she had already engaged the help of two sprightly boys to keep the shop running.

The Viscount expressed his approval and was soon nearly trampled by those same boys as they came rushing back into the shop.

"I'll show you what we've set aside for you to take back to Canton Point, My Lord," Adam said with pride as he and Jemmy coaxed the elderly gentleman into the storeroom where stacks of parcels had been piled for the secondary storefront. "You'll need a whole cart just for this, and there will be cartloads more within the week!"

Peggy could not help but smile at the boy's exuberance. He had truly taken to the task and claimed the duty as his own. Her heart ached as she watched him.

She caught Lord Belton watching her from the corner of her eye and turned her back to him under the guise of straightening the ledgers. Now, more than ever, she needed to hasten her departure from this place, but she would have to wait for the rest of the stores to arrive. Still, things had become too complicated for her liking.

So it was that two weeks passed while Peggy studiously avoided contact with Lord Belton. The remainder of the deliveries arrived, packing the shelves from floor to ceiling. Peggy found herself busy from sunup to sundown, and she was thankful that the work gave her reason to decline several invitations to dinner with Miss Nora and her family. While she was certain that she could avoid a repeat of the encounter that had shaken her to her core, the fondness for dancing in the house was enough to give her pause. Even with other neighboring guests invited, she was hesitant to risk finding herself in the Baron's arms for any reason. When the Viscount had finally arranged to have his mountain of goods collected and he and his wife returned to their new settlement, she no longer had to fear the invitations and was able to breathe a sigh of relief. Her friend still came for tea a few times a week, and Peggy sat with her when she could be pried from behind the counter. She was, after all, in her element as a merchant's daughter, much as she wished to deny that parentage. She was more the daughter of a merchant by heart than the granddaughter of a baronet.

Adam, who surprised Peggy with his skill and knowledge of numbers, had been a quick study on the ledgers. She treasured the hours they had spent leaning over the pages, laughing and learning about one another as she taught him how to keep the records. So it was that whenever Miss Nora appeared and declared that Peggy must take a break, Adam and Jemmy were entirely competent to watch the store in her stead and keep the books if any purchases were made.

Peggy's heart grew lighter with each day that her son seemed to welcome her more fully into his life. She was given the opportunity to explain where she had been for the last four years, and to her relief, he accepted the tale for the truth that it was and the knowledge that she had not abandoned him of her own volition. He would greet her each morning with a hug about the waist and bid his farewell with a kiss upon the cheek. Several times, when he had come across some flowers, he had brought her the blooms so that she might keep them in a vase on the counter. It was not unlike the collection that she had once noticed upon Mrs. Finch's windowsill. She would look upon them several times a day and allow herself to hope.

Still, whenever the conversation would turn to their leaving, the boy would resist with tear-filled eyes, and she found herself less and less able to bring up the topic. The shop was doing so well, and he begged her to stay, begged her to make a life in Riversbend where she seemed to have fit so well. Peggy wanted to consider it, and in truth, she might have done so if she had not made such a mess of things with a particular local lord, her own business associate no less.

Besides, Adam was still returning to the Finch home every evening with Jemmy and had given no indication of wishing to stay with her. She refused to make a home here only to maintain the current arrangement. It was as if he knew if he took that final step, it would mean that they would make their exit shortly thereafter. He was not wrong.

Peggy was torn with the wish that that day would come and the sadness that she had muddied things so thoroughly that staying seemed an impossibility. But every encounter with the gentleman reminded her of why she needed to leave. Nothing had happened between them. Not since that night. The problem was entirely within herself. He behaved as a perfect gentleman ought to whenever he stopped in to look over the ledgers and see if she was in need of any more funds or repairs to the shop. He had sent a footman to hang the curtain wall and provided three circular tables with four chairs each for the tea room, which had become such a success that Peggy was required to keep no less than three kettles brewing each afternoon.

He had sent another footman to oil the squeaking doors

and even arranged to have the lock replaced to the store-room when Jemmy had misplaced the key. He made no overtures toward her, and it was clear that not the smallest suspicion had arisen, even from his watchful sister. Yet every time she was near him, her blood burned hot. She felt her breath constrict and her thoughts fly away, unable to focus on anything but his nearness. It was infuriating that he could do nothing and yet bother her so. If the Baron felt the same way, he gave no indication of it. He was as steady and controlled as ever, kind and prudent, if a little distant for her own sake.

Peggy found herself enjoying a late cup of tea one afternoon with Miss Nora in the corner of the shop. The other ladies had finished, and there had been just enough hot tea left for the pair to sit down and enjoy. Jemmy and Adam had finished their deliveries, and for the first time since opening day, the shop was blissfully empty. Peggy locked the door with a sly grin.

"I think we can close early for one day," she said with a smile as she settled herself into a chair across from her friend. Then, as if feeling quite bold, she stretched her legs across another chair and sank into the cushions with relief. Her feet were aching, and she declared that she deserved to rest.

"Right you are!" Miss Nora agreed with a crisp nod. "You ought to come to the manor for supper. You haven't been in ages." The complaint was valid, and Peggy had no proper excuse save her own untrustworthy nerves. She must have grimaced or revealed something in her features before covering her mouth with her cup and taking a long draught, for Miss Nora's eyebrows shot upward.

"Unless there is some other reason you have been

avoiding the house…" she mused with a half grin that was so terribly like the one that could often be seen upon her brother's face that Peggy cursed the deep blush she felt race over her cheeks. "I knew it!" Miss Nora threw her napkin down upon the table. She stood up and began to pace, her mouth in a wide grin, until all of a sudden she slammed her hands upon her hips and rounded upon Peggy with a scowl. "Well, what is the matter then? You do not care for him? Well, that cannot be true. I saw it well enough with my own eyes the way you went all rigid and soft at the same time when the two of you danced. And you blushed then as well!"

Miss Nora continued on without need for air or for Peggy to speak as she held a conversation quite with herself. "And he did the same. Looked like he'd seen a ghost. I've never seen my brother so out of sorts. So, then, what is the problem? He is far too well-mannered to have said anything untoward. At least, so far as I am aware, and he is certainly no rake. He works too much. Even Father says so. And I would kill him if he were ever to hurt you so." She twirled a curl about her finger as she continued to try to make sense of the puzzle.

Peggy was still too shocked that she had been outed to be able to speak.

"And you," Nora continued. "You are so kind and gentle that I just know you would make the perfect match. I said as much to mother in my letter that first week."

"Me?" Peggy protested. "I am a merchant's daughter. He is a baron, one day to be viscount."

"Oh, pish posh," Nora said, waving a hand in the air to dispel the difference in their station. "And didn't you say your mother was a baronet's daughter? You are not common."

But Nora did not know the half of it. She was no blushing maid but an unwed woman with a child. "After meeting you, even Mother agreed," Nora said between sips of tea. "We were certain that if we thrust you together enough, some spark would come of it."

Spark? Conflagration, more like, Peggy thought, but kept her peace.

"But no, nothing," Nora continued undaunted. "Not a word. It has been weeks, and we've not had the slightest hint that you are in love. Except of course, for Nash's melancholia."

"That is because we are *not* in love!" Peggy protested, but her cheeks reddened even further, and she felt the traitorous color spread to her neck. "We cannot be."

"Ah-ha!" Miss Nora snapped her fingers. "Denial! The first stage.

"The first stage of what?" Peggy asked, but her mind skittered to her other revelation. Lord Belton was melancholy? Could it be because of her absence? It did not matter. There was no future for them. The future with her own son was more sure than one with Lord Belton, and that was certainly still on shaky ground.

"Mama told me. Well…" Miss Nora flung herself back into her chair and stared at Peggy with anticipation. "Has he kissed you yet? At first, I did not wish to know, his being my brother and all. But if he hasn't at least tried to kiss you then he is a bigger fool than I would have thought, and I shall have to tell him straight out what I think of him dragging his feet."

Peggy merely stammered with terror as the sudden heat of a blush filled her face. "Nora... I..."

"All right... so he has." She looked pleased. "Then why have you two been behaving like you barely know one another?"

Peggy released a slow breath. She could hardly keep up with Miss Nora's path of conversation, and yet the lady seemed to have covered it all in record time.

"Peggy, darling, what went wrong?" Miss Nora's voice calmed, and concern for her friend's feelings took precedence over any plotting. "You can tell me." She reached across the table and grasped Peggy's hands in her own. For a moment, Peggy was transported away as she remembered the Baron's hands—Nash's hands— holding hers in just the same way, pronouncing them partners in a way that meant much more than a business relationship.

Peggy groaned and pulled her hands away. She covered her face with them and felt the heat of her cheeks. She was blushing profusely. She had to give Nora some explanation. "It was me," she admitted. "It *is me*. I put him off, and for good reason. No, nothing he did, I assure you, so you can quit looking like you want to pelt him. There is nothing at all he could have done. I have my reasons and... they shall remain my own."

"But—" Nora began.

"No!" Peggy interrupted sharply.

Miss Nora nodded, understanding at once that Peggy would explain no further.

"Answer me this," she asked in a tone that implied that she would put the conversation to rest as soon as this one question had been answered. "Are you in love with someone else? Is that why you have been traveling? Are you trying to outrace a broken heart?"

At this Peggy offered a soft and sincere smile. This she could answer and with full honesty. "No. There is no one else, and I haven't suffered a broken heart."

Miss Nora appeared relieved but irritated. "Then why?" she began again as if she could not help the questions from bubbling out.

Peggy gave her a look intended to remind her that she had only been permitted one question and she had already received her answer.

"Drat," Miss Nora huffed. "You are right. I need to keep my curiosity at bay. I was just so certain…" She bit her lip. "Just one last. Then I cross my heart that I will not speak of it again. Do you really not like him?"

"I like him just fine," Peggy admitted with sadness. "If my life had been very different or we had met at a different time in my life, I am sure I would have liked your brother… very much indeed." It was the truth, and it saddened her deeply. If things were different… but they were not, and she could not risk her heart for Lord Belton. One lord, an unworthy prat, had wounded her once, but she had mended. She was sure that her heart could not take another such blow, but more than that, Lord Belton deserved better than one such as she. Better than an old maid with a child by another man. She could not tell him of the indiscretion, and she could not keep such a thing secret. Even if they were not divided by class, this divided them. Irrevocably.

They finished their tea, and Peggy let Miss Nora back onto the street with a kiss to her cheek. If the world had been very, very different, this wonderful creature might one day have been her sister. But that world was not kind. The world that Peggy knew was cruel, and this sweet bliss here with her son was not to last. She could feel the impending doom in the air. Never mind the wish that she could make a life with Lord Belton. No. She should gather her child to herself and leave. This instant if she could. Disaster was on the horizon with the coolness of the coming autumn.

# CHAPTER 25

SHE LOCKED THE DOOR BEHIND HER AND LEANED AGAINST it. She felt a bone-deep exhaustion that had less to do with her aching feet than it had to do with her bruised emotions. The conversation had worn her down. Miss Nora's naïve hopefulness had been brutal. If her friend knew who she really was, what she had been through and how she had ruined herself ages before, she would not have pushed for the romance with her brother. In fact, Peggy was quite certain that both Miss Nora and her mother would have warned Lord Belton as far away from Peggy as was possible. On the morrow, she would speak to Adam. She would implore him to come with her. She would somehow explain that they must leave the town before the cooler and rainy weather came to the area. She would make him understand.

On the following morning, she did not speak to Adam about leaving. There was a steady stream of customers,

225

and it never felt like the right time. She hoped to do so at the end of the day, but Adam and Jemmy had hurried away with the words that Mum was baking blueberry pies. Mum, she thought. It was understandable that Jemmy still called Mrs. Finch Mum, but Adam did not correct his friend and almost brother. Did Adam still feel Mrs. Finch was his mother, even after so long in association with her? Would he ever accept her? Love her? She was feeling despondent and sorry for herself. In an effort to dispel the feeling, she took up her broom. Cleaning always seemed to knock away the cobwebs in her mind as well as her environs.

When a knock sounded on the back door of the shop later that evening, she set her broom aside and opened it expecting that Adam or Jemmy had forgotten something and returned to claim it.

Instead, she was faced with an uncomfortable looking Lord Belton on her doorstep.

"I thought we were doing the ledgers tomorrow morning?" she blurted dumbly as she wondered if she had mixed up the days.

"We are." He nodded. "That is not why I am here."

It seemed silly for the gentleman to have to ask permission to enter his own shop, so Peggy stepped out of the way and invited him inside without preamble, although she could not think why he had come. The room was dark save for a few candles. She had pulled the curtains when she locked the doors to keep the local children from pressing their dirty faces to the glass in search of their next treasure. She had not expected any visitors and would have burned every candle and left every curtain open if she had known who was coming. There was something far too intimate about the darkened room, closed off from prying eyes, that sent her pulse racing before he even spoke. She could nearly taste his lips on hers.

She did her best to shake such thoughts from her head. The room was not intimate. It was a wide, cluttered storefront. It was no darker now than it had been when she had been sweeping alone only moments before. It was only that her mind went to sensual places whenever Lord Belton was near, and she had been unable to kick the habit even after weeks of telling herself that she was a fool. She could not love him.

"How can I help you?" she asked in the same tone she used with customers. She moved to put the counter between them. Perhaps then she could think of him in a professional manner and not keep noticing how fine he looked in the exquisite tail coat and Hessians. She wondered where he had been, dressed so, but she did not ask.

He followed her around the back of the counter, and it was only then that she realized she had trapped herself. Now, what was meant to be a wide sprawling room felt impossibly small. He leaned against the counter, leaving her room to press by him if she wished, but she could not have done so without revealing her flustered state. Instead, she begged calm and took several slow breaths.

"I have had a word from my sister," he said as he picked up a tin soldier and began fiddling with it, his gaze devoted entirely to the toy though his words sent a jolt of something, panic perhaps, through Peggy's veins. "A lecture more like," he chuckled.

"Oh?" she mused. Perhaps, she could pretend to misunderstand, and the entire conversation would end right

227

here. She had been agonizing about Lord Belton in the days since her conversation with Miss Nora, dreaming of him even. She was acutely aware of how alone they were. There was no chaperone. No likelihood of anyone stopping by at this late hour. This was even more dangerous than their curricle ride. If he touched her, she did not know if she had it in her at this moment to resist him, nor did she have the strength to tell him the truth about her past that promised to leave him with hatred for her and her secrets.

"Yes, Nora can be quite the brute when she wants to be." He grinned to himself at the memory of whatever it was that his sister had said.

"I see."

"Do you?" He looked up at her, caught off guard that she did not seem at all surprised by the conversation.

"I did not receive a lecture," she explained with a laugh, "but I did experience something between an interrogation and having been subjected to the amusement of observing her talk out some silliness with herself during tea a few days past."

He pressed his lips together in an attempt to suppress a smile as he shook his head. "The audacity," he grumbled.

"She does possess it all," Peggy confirmed with false brightness. "And that is what has brought you here?"

"In a way," he confirmed, "though I'll be damned if I let her know she had any part in this. The nosy little minx. I asked Lord Abernathy if he would call after I left, and I left him sitting in the parlor. She'll stay in her room all night if he's below."

At that Peggy laughed outright. "And he agreed to this?"

Lord Belton nodded. "He's a good friend and not nearly as terrible as she makes him out to be."

"Won't he be cross at being made to wait?" she wondered. The Baron shook his head and explained that the gentleman was well aware of Miss Nora's aversion and had willingly taken up the task if only to vex her.

"He won't budge, and neither will she." He laughed. "They are both stubborn."

"You have set the perfect trap!" Peggy said with approval. It seemed fitting that Miss Nora receive her dues. Without realizing it, Peggy had inched closer, craving the nearness of him and relishing in their shared pleasure at Miss Nora's expense. She could smell his fine cologne on his skin. He really did not come here to work then. No. He had dressed as the gentleman caller. She realized that he had prepared for this meeting as she had not. She was dusty from the sweeping, and her hair was falling from its pins. It was not until his fingers linked with hers that she realized just how near she had drawn to him.

"I had to see if it was all just that one night for you," he whispered, looking down at their hands and then up at her with the bluest of eyes.

"Lord Belton…" she began.

"Nash," he corrected. "I want to hear my given name on your lips."

She sighed. Despite the fact that her fingers were still laced with his, it seemed a step too far to say his name. She was already dangerously close to losing her heart; or perhaps it was already lost.

"It has been constant for me," he continued when she would not speak. "Every time I see you, whenever your name is brought up, even just driving by the shop and knowing you are within, I cannot stop thinking of you."

She pulled her hand free and turned away from him. Perhaps if she could not see the longing in his eyes or the way his body leaned over her as if he wanted to touch her but was afraid that she might run... Perhaps then she could resist despite every piece of her calling out to him. She stepped back to escape him. No. To escape her own desire more than him. She tripped on the edge of the worn carpet, and his arms tightened around her.

"You caught me," she said.

"I will always be there to catch you," he promised, his lips impossibly close to hers.

"You can't." She shook her head. "Be there. I have told you; this cannot be."

"I will always be there," he said. "Always."

Peggy did not know how to answer. She couldn't. The truth would cause problems for her, but mostly for Adam. Adam, who lived on the far edge of Lord Belton's estate. She did not want him to have to escape with her. She wanted Adam to choose her, and it seemed as if he might never do so. Nonetheless, she didn't want to force Adam to her side. She could not be so cruel, not when she herself had been forced into so many things in her own life.

"At first," Lord Belton said, "I convinced myself it was one-sided or just a momentary lapse that you regretted. Then, I resigned myself to the belief that there had to be someone else who held your affections. Someone from your past," he began. She shot around to look at him to condemn the ridiculous notion, but he continued on before she had need to speak. "Nora assured me that there was not."

Peggy wished she had lied to Miss Nora, for it would have made an ironclad excuse, but then she realized that her own reaction in this moment would have disproved that very lie in an instant. She knew her face was flushed with longing.

"I had mistaken everything, but then Nora said there was no one else. I must hear it from you. I must know."

He was talking in circles. Peggy didn't understand what he meant. Know what? The look of confusion must have shown on her face.

"Now, there is only one thing that matters." He took a breath, steeling himself. "Do you love him?"

"Who?" she blurted.

"Adam's father."

"No!" she said immediately. She had not credited where this conversation was going or how he knew about Adam. She was completely out of her depth, but she had no time to consider. She shook her head trying to clear it, trying to make sense of everything.

"There is no one, but that does not change anything," she cried, splaying her hands between them with hopelessness. He caught them up and pulled her to him so that she landed fully against his chest. His strong muscled chest. He was so incredibly warm, and his strong arms wrapped around her sheltering her in a way that was so foreign and so incredible that for a moment she could think of nothing else but the nearness of him.

"That was the only question left that mattered," he replied as his mouth found hers.

# CHAPTER 26

PEGGY WANTED TO REFUSE, WANTED TO TELL HIM THAT there were so many more questions that he could not have known to ask, but all thought fled from her mind as emotion and longing took over. She kissed him back with all of the pent-up agony and frustrations that she had been holding within. She was not naïve. She was not some frail maid. She was a woman grown, but he was still a baron, and she was a nobody. Still, she felt her own desire echoed in him. He had been just as bothered as she. She ought not to have reveled in that knowledge, but she could not help herself. He wanted her still and had been just as struck by the constant need of it. Wanted her as an aristocrat wanted a commoner. The thought popped into her mind, but she did not care. In this moment, there was only him, the strength of him, the scent of him, the feel of his arms around her.

Peggy grasped at his waistcoat, not caring if she left the crisp fabric wrinkled and mussed. For how long they were wrapped in each other's embrace, she could not say.

It could have been moments or hours, and she would not have been able to define the time in which they clung to one another. It was not until he spoke that her mind flitted back to reality. The emotions inspired by the kiss could not be. This happiness was not for her.

"You should stay," he breathed against her. "Don't go."

Peggy felt a sinking feeling grow within her, and she pulled back enough to break the kiss and look up at him, though his arms remained wrapped around her waist, pressing her to him. Desire still strummed through her, reflected in him. Of course, he would think it were as simple as that. He could even visit her here, just as he was. She had a room here at the shop. It could be as she feared and desired in equal measure. She could be his mistress.

In any other town, the temptation would have been too great. If she had not met and loved his sister... But it could not be. She could not do that to Adam. It was then that she realized she had to tell him, and yet, he knew. How did he know about Adam? Surely, that knowledge should have put an end to his affections and ruin what had only just before been a moment of heaven. No. There was nothing heaven blest about their passion.

She swallowed deeply and prepared herself. "There is something that I must explain," she began, already trembling in his arms with preparation for the hurt that must come.

"Adam loves it here," he broke in. "You do not have to go, not on his account."

"What?" she stammered. She had to blink her eyes and shake the distracting sensation of being held in his arms to try to make sense of his words. Had he really just said what she thought?

233

"I am sorry. I held a secret too. I am aware that Adam is your son," he repeated with a sigh, finally releasing her and stepping back. He ran a hand through his hair, leaving it adorably haphazard in his frustration to explain. All Peggy could do was wait in silence with her arms wrapped around herself as if she could physically hold herself together.

He knew? She could hardly fathom how. "How?" she whispered. The word flitting about her mind came to her lips.

"I've known since the beginning." He then explained that when Mr. and Mrs. Finch had received the letter from the abbey months prior to her arrival, the gamekeeper had brought it to his lord for advice about what could be done. Of course, they had wanted to keep the boy, but the letter so clearly described the mother as a victim of horrible circumstances who had loved her child very much. They had no legal right to the child. The letter instructed that they ought to let him go. "They were devastated. I wanted to be angry at you, a woman who would uproot her child…" He shook his head.

Peggy chided herself for a fool. She ought to have considered that the gamekeeper would have consulted his employer. Such was the way of things when legal matters were involved.

Lord Belton went on to explain his feelings. "I had so many suppositions… A woman who bore a child out of wedlock, she must be somehow…"

"Tainted?" Peggy said softly.

"No," he said, but ran his hand through his hair with a nervous gesture. "Yes. I suppose I thought that at first, but then I met you. In that first meeting, I was intrigued by you. Attracted of course, but I had not really identified you as his mother, and Nora liked you so much. I guess, I just didn't connect everything. I should have. Then the day at the Finch's, I realized how wrong I was. When you reacted to the sight of the boy with such agony, I knew you loved him. You did not want to uproot him. You just wanted to love him. I knew that the letter had been about you. That finding your son had been the reason for your arrival here," he revealed. "And the reason for your staying."

Peggy stood glued to the spot, unable to speak or in any way disturb the events that were playing out around her. "I had hoped that you would tell me on your own. That you would offer up your burden so that I could help you. I wanted you to trust me with the most important thing in your life, your son, but I did not want to press. My own feelings were so …" He shook his head.

"Wrong?" Peggy supplied.

"No. Never wrong. Confused, yes. I can only imagine how hard it has been for you. Then, I saw that things were going so well with Adam here, and it was only then that I began to think that you might choose to stay. After we danced… After we kissed, I hoped that you would, but instead you seemed even more set on leaving. I couldn't understand why." He looked at her, a guileless hope in his eyes. "You could, you know. You could stay."

She stared at him unable to believe that he could be so naïve. She could not stay. Only as his mistress, and even then, it was impossible. "You don't care that I have a son?" she snapped with disbelief. "A child. You don't care that I have been ruined in more ways than most women would experience in a lifetime?"

He shook his head. "I know you," he protested. "You

are not ruined. In fact, add in the letter, and I had confirmation of everything that I already knew as to your person, and I would say you are the strongest, most remarkable person I know."

"Then you know about London as well?" She did not know why she was getting so defensive, but she felt anger for some inexplicable reason. She could not, would not, believe that he had known all this time and still chosen to accept her. Such things were not done. It had to be a trick, and she was soon to be the recipient of a poorly timed joke. That was what aristocrats did. Could she believe that of *this* aristocrat? She had come to know him, and nothing in his character was so cruel. Dare she take him at his word?

"I do," he murmured. "It was easy enough to piece together the timing of your captivity and the story that broke all of London last season. A duchess was involved. Unwilling captivity. A court case in which several female witnesses went unnamed and were rewarded with financial security for their suffering. It was no secret. Peggy, I..." he reached out to her, but she flinched away, and he let his hand drop to his side.

"Do not say that you are sorry for me," she snarled. "I do not need your pity. Is that what this all has been? An attempt to make amends because I'd been wronged? Well, I assure you that I do not..."

He cut her off a snap in return. "I have never once pitied you! No one ever could. You are a beautiful and vivacious woman."

"Beautiful?" she said, disbelieving.

Again he raked his hands through his hair as if he wished he could tear it from his head to get through to her.

"You are the strongest, smartest woman that I have ever encountered, and you have never needed pity. If anything, I find myself amazed by your resilience. And I am honored that you would even deign to take the time to help a small village or me…"

She stood staring at him unbelievingly.

"You could have just snatched up your son and went on with your life. You have no need for pity; you deserve a medal."

Peggy was touched by his words despite her best effort to remain cross. She gave a halfhearted scoff. "I tried to snatch him up. He wouldn't come."

"A less kind mother would have forced him," he disagreed. "You gave him the chance to adjust. You put yourself out, altered all of your plans, and took on this enormous project." He gestured at the store around them. "Successfully, I might add, just to give your son the time that he needed. If anything, I loved you more for it. And so does he."

Peggy froze.

"Yes, I said what I said," he breathed in frustration. "I don't pity you. I love you."

She had no words. Did not even have thoughts. He had known about it all. All this time, even before their first kiss, he had known her darkest secrets and accepted them, accepted her. It was almost too much to fathom.

"Say something," he murmured, taking a tentative step toward her and another when she did not back away.

"I cannot believe it," was the best that she could muster. She was filled with wonderment and still disbelief. "Does Nora know?"

"No, none but me," he said taking another small step. "Nora, for once, has no say in this," he said with a laugh.

"Oh." Peggy felt what little hope she had melt. It was one thing for Lord Belton to accept her and quite another for others to go unbothered. She had seen the affect others'—especially familial—disapproval could have on a mindset.

"She will not care. She adores you," he continued. "Everyone does. The whole town loves you."

"The town?" she said. "But you are a baron. One day you will be a viscount. This small northern town may be able to see past what I have done, but not London."

"From what I've gathered from the letter and from your contacts in London, everyone who has ever met you finds you remarkable and worthy. London included."

Peggy shook her head. "It is not that simple. The Ton…"

"Oh, the Ton can go hang," he snapped. "Sorry." He reached for her as if drawn by some irresistible force.

She stared at him. In one minute, he was accepting her as less than a lady and in the next apologizing like a London gentleman who misspoke before a lady. She was so confused, but the truth was, he was a gentleman, and no matter what he said now, one day he would regret being with her. She could not allow it. She shook her head mutely.

"Let it be for now," he murmured as he slipped one hand about her waist and coaxed her to him. She did not resist. "For this moment, let us not be who the world thinks us to be. Let us just be Nash and Peggy." He tipped her head up and kissed her with such tenderness that she thought her heart would break.

"Oh, Nash," she groaned in agony and allowed her forehead to fall to his chest. She wished that she could just hide there forever. Her life here in Riversbend seemed far too easy and good to be true. She knew that this was not the way of the world. The world was filled with hateful, evil people who would tear her to shreds the moment her full story was revealed, and he would be hurt by that gossip. She did not want him hurt.

With a finger to her chin, he coaxed her to look up into the security of his blue eyes. For that was what she felt in his arms, safety. So badly she wanted to trust that feeling. So many times, she had learned that there were few places in this world that one might feel safe.

His eyes searched hers, looking for and finding answers that she could not know herself.

"You can stay here," he murmured, his mouth descending as he spoke, "with me."

She started to shake her head in negation, but then their lips met, and there was nothing but him. The Ton and all the problems of the aristocracy were obliterated by the power of that kiss. Peggy hummed with pleasure.

"Is that a yes?"

She could feel his smile against her mouth. Her mind was filled with confusion, and her heart was heavy with what must not be. She was no lady, but he was a gentleman. They could never be married. All they could have was this moment. Well, so be it.

She would have the moment, and the future would have to take care of itself. She was already a fallen woman. Gossip could not demean her more than it already had. She had endured too much to let this small chance at happiness go, even if it was only temporary. In this moment, they were not a laundress and a baron. They were only a man and a woman in love. Were they in love?

A desperate sound of want and sadness for what would never be escaped her lips, and then his lips closed over hers. She wanted this. She pulled Nash to her and twisted her position so that she was pressed with the counter at her back and Nash at her front. "I'll need some convincing," she said.

In response, his hands moved swiftly toward her bottom. He lifted before she knew what he was about, and he set her with a resolute thunk upon the countertop. She squealed, both shocked and pleased with the rugged nature of his behavior. It was simply not done! Now seated, and finally eye to eye, he placed one hand at either side of her hips and pretended to give her a stern glare. Then, his features took on an earnest expression that conflicted with the shifting movement that settled his hips between her knees.

"In all seriousness," he said quite casually, considering she was flustered, and it took all of her willpower not to link her ankles at his back and pull him closer, "I won't force the issue if it is not what you want. But if it is at all a possibility, I would like the chance to convince you."

Peggy wondered for a moment what sort of convincing he might be implying, and her cheeks flushed at the thought. Certainly not *that.*

He must have read her thoughts because he chuckled. "Then you'll consider it?"

Peggy was breathless with wanting and merely nodded before she recalled that she had a stipulation.

"I don't want Adam to know anything until I've decided," she explained. "To stay or not, that is. I cannot bear to get his hopes up. I need to know where he stands with *me* as his mother before I decide anything else." Peggy needed to know that Adam wanted her and not just the chance to stay in Riversbend. It was important that their bond as mother and son come first, before romance and before the Baron.

"That is a bother," Nash teased. "I figured between Adam, Nora, and I, you wouldn't stand a chance."

"Exactly!" She giggled as she pretended to be cross. "The three of you are quite enough on your own without my having to deal with you all banding together."

Nash nodded, solemnly accepting his fate.

"I mean it," she said. "I will not have Adam's place tainted. I want him to stay with me here, and I need time to build a relationship with him."

"And what about a relationship with me?"

She groaned at the thought. Allowing Nash to visit the shop would certainly put a damper on her relationship with Adam and vice versa.

She started to shake her head, but he put a finger under her chin. "Can I begin to convince you now?" he asked, kissing along her jawline and toward her neck. "Adam is not here."

"I suppose." Peggy could hardly breathe. She was all in knots. His mouth came over here and she clung to him. They kissed and murmured incoherent things to one another. She was fairly certain that Nash mentioned some-thing about *thanking God for the bloody curtains*, but she hardly had time to laugh and breathe at the same time.

Then, without warning, he stepped away and smoothed his waistcoat, which was in shambles and quite possibly missing a button.

"Now that that's settled," he said, kissing her lightly on the forehead. "I shall see you tomorrow for the ledgers, and we shall have to behave ourselves in front of Adam."

"Yes," she agreed somewhat shakily.

"I suppose it is time to release Nora from her confinement." Then, he exited the shop before Peggy had a chance to recover.

She remained for a long while on the countertop, thrumming with desire. Her mouth hung open in astonishment, wondering as time flew by if she had imagined it all. Surely, if he were really here, he would have slaked his desire, but he had not. She had no idea where this tryst would take her. What was his plan? A tryst? An arrangement? If this was Nash's idea of convincing her to remain in Riversbend, then she was in way over her head.

Finally, she thought her legs could hold her and she leapt down from the countertop. She did not think she could sleep. Perhaps, she would make some of that delicious new tea. As she wandered aimlessly in the room, the moonlight caught a glint on the floor.

Apparently, she had not swept as well as she thought she did. She leaned down to capture the shiny object. It was a silver button; *his* silver button. She stared at it. She had not dreamt the last encounter. It was real. Nash was real. She wrapped her arms around herself, reliving the feeling of comfort in his embrace. He had said he loved her.

# CHAPTER 27

ANOTHER FORTNIGHT PASSED IN WHAT PEGGY COULD ONLY describe as pure bliss and carnal torture. Adam made the decision to move in with her at the shop for a trial period, which meant there were no more private evenings with Lord Belton. Peggy was disappointed, but Adam was her first concern.

She had worried that the boy would be uncomfortable with the shared space, but the addition of a second bed and a small chest of toys was all the boy needed to feel at home. Their evenings were spent talking and playing. At bedtime, he would ask her to read to him or to tell her stories of her travels with the gypsies.

He shared with her stories of his life at the gamekeeper's house and the kindness that he had been shown by the entire family. She learned that he had broken his arm three summers past, and Mr. Finch and Nash had driven him to the next town over to see a physician who had set the bone with care. He spoke of fishing trips and the hunt for the infamous white stag. To his amazement, Peggy informed him that she had seen the beast and confirmed that it did in fact exist.

"What does it mean?" Adam asked.

Peggy recalled her time with the gypsies. "Mrs. Banning would say the stag loses his antlers but grows them anew each year, showing that loss is nothing but a gateway to bigger and better things—more important things. No matter how broken you feel, there is healing in nature. You have that power, the power to make your own choices. Nothing can stop you..." She broke off, wondering how many things she had learned about herself on the journey north. "And everything you experience, the good and the bad, makes you the person you are."

It seemed an apropos time to explain more fully about the horrors that she had endured for four long years. The boy listened in silence, punctuated only by a few meaningful questions such as if she had missed him or if she had wondered how he had been. When she completed her tale, sharing much more than she had intended, he threw himself into her arms and promised that he would protect her always and she need never fear anyone harming her ever again. Peggy had kissed his hair and held him close, promising to protect him in return and assuring him that she would do whatever it took to keep them together.

What surprised Peggy most was the town's acceptance of the transition. As soon as it became known that she was Adam's birth mother, she had expected whispers and long stares. Instead, it was as if she were welcomed even more as a true part of the community, for everyone knew and loved the boy and had grown to love and respect her as well. Other mothers in the village stopped her to talk and muse about their children, an aspect that she had missed out on when they had thought her merely a single woman. This journey had brought her so much more than her son. She had friends and a place in the community—and Lord Belton.

He began to visit again, but his visits were chaste and somewhat unsatisfying. They were learning to know one another as friends, and there was no repeat of their passionate kisses, but Peggy could hardly look at her own counter without blushing.

Adam boasted about the success of the store, calling it *theirs* and showing distinct pride in his mother's success. He sat with Peggy and Nash as they went over the books, and he showed a remarkable acuity for the arithmetic involved. Nash and Peggy snatched a stolen kiss here and there, but there was no repeat of their passionate evening. Lord Belton was ever the gentleman.

Mr. and Mrs. Finch came to visit regularly and invited Peggy and her son to dinner no less than twice a week. The couple were pleased to see Adam thrive in his mother's care and were even more pleased that they had not been excluded from his life while the pair remained in Riversbend. Talks of leaving had become fewer and farther between, but Peggy knew that the Finches would always be a part of their life no matter what she decided. She could see now that they were not only good for Adam, but they were good for her as well. They were far too good to allow their relationship to fall to competition for the boy's affection. They merely wanted the chance to watch him grow, and Peggy found she wanted that too. She had no family nearby, but Mrs. Finch, like a doting auntie, had an unending stream of motherly advice that Peggy soon learned. The elder woman also knew well enough to prevent Adam's antics before he had a chance to pull one of his many pranks on his unsuspecting mother. But Peggy's favorite morsel of guidance came from Mr. Finch and had to do with throwing up one's hands and merely hoping for the best.

Peggy laughed when the elderly woman had declared that her husband had the right of it with his hands off approach, especially with the boys. Later that same day, Martha revealed that she was getting married to the man of her dreams as soon as the love potion that she had baked into a muffin took effect.

Mrs. Finch groaned and shook her head. "Where on earth did you get a love potion child?" she asked.

"The gypsy woman of course!" the young girl declared. "She said it works every time and she had loads of sons to prove it. It's been weeks, but I think it just takes time for the love to grow. He's really coming 'round I think."

Peggy and Mrs. Finch had shared a long glance filled with humor at the girl's foolhardy beliefs, but as Mr. Finch said, sometimes children had to learn in their own way. Nonetheless, Mrs. Finch had to comment.

"Well, if you wasted your coin then that's your own doing," the woman declared with a shrug. "You'll not be getting your purse back when it fails. Who *are* you marrying anyway?"

"It's a secret!" Martha had giggled. "And a fine match, Mama. I promise you'll be proud of me."

"Mrs. Banning gave me a love potion too!" Peggy laughed and played along for the girl's benefit.

"Didn't it work?" Martha asked, eyes wide. "You don't have a man." She blushed most profusely at the words, realizing that Peggy had a child but no husband. Little did the girl—or anyone for that matter—know, but Peggy did in fact seem to have a man, with or without a potion. But that was not the point.

"I dumped it out in a bucket of water on my stoop and you shall never guess what happened…" Peggy teased.

"What!" Martha cried on the edge of her seat. "What happened?"

"The tomcat that hangs out behind the shop… Well, I learned he wasn't a tomcat at all! She had six kittens last week!" Peggy giggled at the ridiculous story while Mrs. Finch swatted her with a towel.

"That cat has a litter twice a year, mind you," Mrs. Finch declared. "It was no potion that did the deed."

"Well, if your man has a litter, then we'll know for sure," Peggy had said with a concerned shrug.

"Oh no…" Martha snorted and ran off, annoyed with their teasing.

Peggy felt like she had truly found her footing in the town. Not only were things with Adam going swimmingly, but her stolen moments with Nash were just as wonderful.

What passed between them was the best kept secret in Riversbend, and that was saying something because Miss Nora had yet to catch on. She complained about it constantly and bemoaned the pair not giving their love a chance.

"I really do think you'd make a fine pair," she said one day at tea after having sworn that she was done with the topic for the hundredth time. Little did she know that Nash had kissed Peggy quite thoroughly only that afternoon when the shop had been empty. "I told him he's a blind fool for not making more of an effort with you."

Oh, Peggy had wanted to say, he was making plenty of effort. The number of times and places they had stolen kisses was adding up, and the excitement of finding yet another secret spot heightened their secret passion.

Twice Peggy had awakened to find a bouquet on her back doorstep. The silvered pocket mirror that she kept at her bedside had come from him too, which was a rather expensive gift, but he had not allowed her to return it. Furthermore, every chance Lord Belton found, when no one was looking, he allowed himself to brush his fingers across her hand or tuck a wayward lock behind her ear. She never went more than a day without being kissed so thoroughly her toes curled, and her nights were filled with fevered dreams.

With Adam living at the shop, there were no more wanton repeats of the night that Lord Belton had come to profess himself. He maintained all proprieties in front of any watchful eyes, particularly those of the boy, but that didn't mean that Peggy's life was without romance.

Still, whenever he was nearby, Peggy could not help but be struck by how well the males were together. Adam admired the Baron as only a young boy could, and Nash doted upon him. At first, she had been afraid that his attentions had only begun with her and that it would catch the interest of the townsfolk or at the very least Mrs. Finch. But she soon learned that Nash had always interacted well with his tenants and all of their families. He was loved and respected, and she in turn was loved and respected.

Adam and Jemmy told stories of fishing trips in the summer with a dozen smart boys and all the men of the estate, including Lord Belton and his own father, the Viscount. They laughed and shared tales of the fabled stag hunt that ended in nothing more than disappointment and years of teasing the gamekeeper for having imagined the beast.

When Jemmy returned to the shop one afternoon holding back tears and attempting a brave show of confidence, it was Nash who had coaxed him to reveal that Marie Harper preferred David Rothels instead. The Baron had thrown an arm about the young man's shoulder and taken him for a stroll. Whatever they had talked about, Peggy could not say, but Jemmy had returned to the shop with a smile and declared that Marie Harper could have David Rothels and he wished them well.

"In a few years, when I have my own cottage, I'll have the pick of the crop," Jemmy had declared with a puffed chest as he returned to restocking the shelves.

"Nicely done," Peggy had whispered to the Baron when he had returned to her side, brushing against her as he passed and sending a shiver up her spine.

"If only I were as good with the ladies as my advice suggests," Nash had chuckled, sneaking a kiss. Thank goodness the naïve child had taken no notice of the adults' strange behavior.

Peggy took in a deep breath and held it, turning and catching Nash's eye as she did so. How fortunate they were that the boy did not equate the Baron's obsession with helping out at the shop as one and the same to spending time with his mother. The fact that the rest of the town was not seething with gossip just proved that the Baron was always one to help when the need arose. He was not one to generally pass off such tasks to a footman, so it was not unusual that he took an interest in his investment. No, he seemed to like to be in the thick of things.

## CHAPTER 28

WHEN MISS NORA APPEARED ONE MORNING WITH AN invitation to a harvest ball, Peggy took a leap of faith and accepted.

"Now don't you go thinking that this is a trap to throw you and Nash together," Miss Nora had begun.

"Of course, it is," Peggy countered, now wise to her friend's machinations.

"Well, perhaps it is, but Mama and Papa are visiting for the next delivery and wanted to celebrate the success of both haberdasheries. We have had several new shops open on both ends thanks to your supply. Everyone is thrilled."

"I am pleased to hear it," Peggy had replied, holding back a grin at her secret.

"But if you and my brother happen to dance a time or two…" Miss Nora had shrugged. "I think it would make a good showing of your collaboration on the project. Of course, that is just my humble opinion. You've both worked so hard."

"We have," Peggy agreed.

"That being said, I think you should wear the green gown with the silvered overlay," Miss Nora had said, as if she had just thought of it. Peggy bit her cheek to prevent herself from replying. The green gown showed a ridiculous amount of cleavage, in Peggy's opinion. She had never worn the gown and for good reason. It had been demure and elegant on Lady Charlotte Grave's thin frame but left nothing at all to the imagination when draped across Peggy's motherly curves. Her breasts would be on full display, as would her trim waist and childbearing hips. On second thought, she considered, it would be amusing to watch Nash try to feign disinterest while practically falling all over himself at the sight of her.

"I think I will!" Peggy replied with a nod of agreement.

"Now before you refuse…" Miss Nora began the argument that she had prepared in expectation that Peggy would take ages to convince. "Oh, you will? Well, then." She seemed taken aback. "I'm ever so glad. I was worried you were going to wear that." Miss Nora gestured at Peggy's usual day frock and frowned. "It is nice enough, but you were made to shine. It's as if you purposely downplay your feminine features, and I cannot understand why."

At that, Peggy laughed outright and shooed her friend out the door before she could begin to choose hair ribbons and jewelry.

"Three days!" the lady called over her shoulder with a grin and a wave. "Mama will have me busy with arrangements until then, but I will see you in three days for the ball!"

.  .  .

The following evening after Adam and Peggy had finished their supper, Peggy could tell that something was amiss. Adam had been quiet and withdrawn during the meal. He had picked at his food and left most of it on his plate. It was unusual to say the least, for she had known the boy to have a sturdy appetite.

Peggy had wanted to ask him what the matter was outright, but Mrs. Finch had once told her that it was best to let a child work through their thoughts and come to you in their own time, and so she had determined that to be the best course of action. That was so long as they did not take too long to come about it. Then, one must find a way to leave hints.

It was not until he had settled into his bed and she was tucking the sheet about his sides that he spoke.

"Mama?" He looked up at her with large brown eyes. "Can I call you Mama? Since Mrs. Finch has always been Mum?"

Peggy nodded, unable to speak past the lump in her throat. It had been the first time that he had called her Mama, and she had nearly lost her composure at the word. He had studiously avoided calling her anything at all, and she knew that Mrs. Finch would always hold a special place in his heart. Luckily, the heart is capable of infinite amounts of loving.

She settled down at her son's side and leaned over to brush his hair away from his face.

"Can I tell you something?" he asked, his eyes bright in the light of the oil lamp.

"Anything, dear," Peggy replied in all seriousness.

"I know that I said that I didn't want to go with you in

the beginning," he muttered, toying with the fringe at the edge of his blanket.

"I remember," she said when he appeared unable to go on.

"I just wanted you to know that I never want to leave you. Not ever again. No matter what." His voice was so small, and she could tell that there were big emotions behind the words.

"Adam, you don't have to concern yourself with that at this hour." She sighed. "Just sleep. I'm right here, and we won't be separated again. I'm here," she repeated when he squeezed her hand with his small fingers.

"That's not what I mean," he said with a deep swallow. He sat up and set his shoulders as if he were making a decision fit for a man and not that of a child. Peggy braced herself. "I mean that if you want to go… I'll go with you. Wherever you say. I'll do it. I'm not leaving you. Not ever. And I can protect you. Like the white stag. No one will ever hurt you again."

Her heart broke into a thousand pieces at that moment.

"Darling," she crooned pulling him into her arms. "I did not want you to go with me because I needed protection. I've learned to do that on my own." And she had. After their release, the Duke of Manchester, a naval man, had shown the recovered women several moves intended to disarm an opponent. She was not sure she could actually use them, but it was a comfort to know she had some preparation. "I only wanted us to be together again, Adam. Do you understand?"

She felt him nod against her shoulder as his little arms wrapped around her.

"I know, and I want to be with you always," he said

with a squeeze about her waist. "I don't ever want to lose you again. I couldn't bear it. I said that I didn't want to go with you, that I would run away, but I lied. I want to be with you more than anything, and Jemmy promised that he would write and maybe visit if it isn't too far. So," he took a deep breath and gave one sharp nod, "when you go, I want to go with you."

Peggy hugged him close and pressed a kiss to his temple.

"You know how much I love you, don't you?" she murmured against his brow. He nodded once more. "All right then, get some sleep, and we can talk about it tomorrow."

Tomorrow, she thought, after she spoke with Nash. She had thought that she wanted to hear that her son wanted to be with her above all else, but the truth was that his words had rocked her to her soul. That he would willingly give up such happiness for her was both a blessing and a curse. She ached for what the boy would do to renew their small family and yet found joy in the fact that he wanted her again to be his family.

Hearing his choice, however, had made hers. His love was beyond selfless, and now hers needed to be as well. She would not leave Riversbend. Not now, not ever, so long as Adam wished to stay. Whatever may or may not come of her situation with Nash, she would not deny the boy this place, this happiness. It was imperative that she speak with Lord Belton as soon as possible so that she could communicate her decision.

If they remained, either Adam would learn of their affiliation, or they must put an end to it now before it became an issue. She was fairly certain where Nash stood.

He had long approved of telling the boy and encouraged her to remain in Riversbend. Still, they had never spoken of the details. Remain in Riversbend, yes, but above the shop as his occasional flirtation or as something more? She had hoped in secret that his behavior had indicated that he had wanted to include Adam in their bond, as a family, but so far, she had no promises to confirm one way or the other. She could not fault Nash for having kept his intentions to himself. For all he knew, Peggy intended to leave the town in little less than a month. It would not have been prudent for either of them to have put their assurances or their hearts on the line until they knew if there was even a future to be shared.

Now that she knew where she stood on the matter, Peggy was anxious to speak with the Baron as soon as possible.

The morning was a sleet-filled haze of cold and wet that kept the shop empty for the first few hours. When the sky had finally cleared and the sun came through, the day warmed to a harsh last reminder of summer's beauty.

The cold kept people home in front of warm fires. The muddied streets made for poor shopping conditions, and so Peggy decided to close up and allow her son one last day to run about the town before the cold set in. They had only just donned their boots and cloaks when Adam pointed out a large carriage that had come to a halt in front of the windowed door.

Peggy stepped outside with her son at her side.

"Can I be of service?" she asked the pair of burly men

who stepped down. They were unfamiliar faces and seemed more ruffians than visitors. She took an instant dislike to their appearance but chided herself that she was judging so quickly by appearances alone. After all, didn't she hate it when people judged her without really knowing her? When they split up as they walked, placing Peggy and her son between them, all of her fears began to scream in her mind. She told herself to remain calm, her instincts were merely overreacting because of her past. They were customers, nothing more. Still, with one hand she pressed Adam behind her and repeated her question. "I was just going to close for the day, but if you need something…"

"What's your name?" one of the men grunted.

"I am the shopkeeper of this here haberdashery," she said by way of diversion.

"Margaret Wilhelm?" he asked, taking a step closer. Her heart seemed to stop. He knew her name. Her true name. "This your welp?" He gestured towards Adam, who stood frozen to the spot.

"My name is Peggy Williams," she protested with the best smile she could force. "I'll admit that they sound similar at first, but no. Such a common name, it seems an easy enough mistake."

"Like shit you are," the other replied.

Peggy turned to push Adam away and make off down the street, but she was grabbed from behind before she had even completed the turn. The other man scooped Adam up and tossed the kicking boy over his shoulder.

She had enough time to release one earsplitting scream before she was shoved into the carriage, and it set off down the road and out of Riversbend. She could only hope that someone, anyone, had heard. The feeling of déjà vu was unmistakable, and yet previously she had only herself about which to worry. Now there was Adam. She would die before she would allow anything to happen to him. This she swore in a silent prayer.

The carriage jostled along for what felt like an age before it came to a grinding halt. Peggy and Adam had clung to one another for the entirety of the ride with the mother whispering as much support as she could muster for the frightened boy.

The most pressing problem was that she had no idea who had taken them or why. Her mind raced over and over the probabilities, and the most likely solution was that one of the Lady Blackwell's cronies had decided to pay retribution upon those that had escaped their treacherous ring. While much of the criminal circle had been broken up by the investigation—and to the best of her knowledge sent off to Australia—she knew there were others that had slipped through the cracks. At the beginning of her months of freedom, she had feared such an act of retaliation. It had been part of the reason why she had not raced to Adam straightaway but had taken her time to be certain that the ring was disbanded. Now, she cursed herself for having brought this danger upon him. If she were thrust back into servitude, she might survive it. She would never forgive herself if Adam were forced to endure the same plight or worse.

The good sisters at Halthaven would be proud that she remembered so many prayers. She prayed them all. She prayed as she had never prayed in her life, not for herself, but only for her son, her innocent, sweet son.

## CHAPTER 29

THERE WERE VOICES OUTSIDE OF THE CARRIAGE TOO SOFT
and indistinct to make out with any clarity. At best, she
could discern from their tones was that they were frustrated. Wherever it was that they had stopped, they were
now forced to wait. The waiting was an agony in itself.

Adam had begun to shiver with fear. It had started to
rain, the patter soft against the carriage.

"Are we gonna die, Mama?" he whimpered.

She did not know the answer and hated to lie, but for
him, she would. "Not today," she promised. "We just need
to be strong and keep our wits about us. That has served
me well in the past, and it will serve us this day."

In the darkness of the carriage, she saw his little head
nod. She pulled him into a hug. At least the villains had
not bound them hand and foot.

"I'll protect you," he said with a confidence that she
admired but wished he did not have to bear.

"No," she replied with a stern voice. She held his face
in her hands and forced him to hear her. "At the first

opportunity, you run. Do you hear me? You do not look back, and you do not wait for me. You run with everything you have in you. Do you understand?"

"You'll run with me?" he cried.

"I will," she replied, but it was a lie. For the first time, and likely the last, she lied to her son. She would do whatever it took to allow him his escape, even if that meant that she had to be a distraction herself. Even if it meant giving her life for his freedom. "You just run, and you never look back. Not for anything."

"I'll run for help."

"You run," she repeated, "and don't look back, no matter what you see or hear. Promise me."

He nodded uncertainly.

When she was certain he understood, she clasped him to her breast and wished that she had had more time with him. She told him that she loved him and that if he ran hard enough everything would be all right. It had to be so. She would make sure of it with her last breath.

After what felt like an age, the sound of another carriage pulling alongside could be heard.

"Where you been?" the gruff voice of their captor complained. "We been here an hour at least."

The rain was falling harder now, obscuring the sounds. A response was made, but Peggy could not hear it clearly enough to make sense of it.

"A hundred pounds," their captor demanded. "You said a hundred if we got both."

"So I did," came the reply, closer now, and Peggy's blood ran cold. She recognized the voice in an instant, and it was one that she had wished to never hear again. The sound of a bag of coin being tossed rang through the silence, and a pleased grunt of satisfaction echoed as her captor pocketed the reward. "Move them over to my carriage and be off. We're done here."

The handle of the carriage rattled and then stopped. Peggy and Adam scooted as far away from the door as possible, but it was no use. The door opened and a pair of arms reached inside, wrenching Adam from her arms and then returning to pull Peggy without ceremony from the carriage.

His back was to them as he opened the door to his own carriage, but Peggy recognized him. Lord Sterling Pentworth, the Viscount of Banbury, and the sire of her son.

As she and Adam were held by the firm grips of their captors, some motion in the distance drew their attention.

"I told you to grab them unseen!" Lord Sterling spun on his heel to look out at the distant road, and his shout of anger rent the air.

"No one was about," came the reply from behind Peggy's ear. "Besides, you said no one would care about the bit o' muslin."

"Blast it, that's at least twenty riders, you fools!" Lord Sterling was irate and spun on his companions with barely contained rage. "They must have followed the tracks." He swore and cursed the ever-present English rain along with his criminal companions.

"You were the one who was late," snapped the leader of the thugs. "You should have been on your way by now."

Lord Sterling growled his ire, but a moment later, the thugs released their charges and shouted for their driver to make a run for it. They clung to the moving carriage and were off, leaving Peggy behind with Lord Pentworth.

True to his word, in the confusion of the moment,

Adam made a break. He was around Lord Pentworth's carriage before the driver could leap down and snatch him, but Peggy was not so fortunate. Lord Sterling had flung himself at her and grasped her by the hair. She cried out in pain but could not break free.

"Get in the carriage and no one gets hurt," he hissed in her ear.

"Let me go," she argued, trying and failing to wrench free.

"You are mine, Margaret, and you always will be," he snarled. The riders were drawing closer, racing at full speed, but they were still too far away to be of any help to her.

"You did not want me then; why would you want me now? Just leave me be!" she snapped. She threw an elbow behind her, but it missed its mark and glanced off of him. It only resulted in a laugh. He struggled to drag her toward the carriage, but she fought the progress with every step. Years of hard labor had made her strong, and she resisted for all she was worth. She could not best him, but she could delay. Perhaps, the riders would arrive in time.

"I would have had you, but my father would never allow it," he spat in her ear. "Low stock." Peggy bristled at the insult but refused to let him bait her. Instead, she tried to angle her head toward the open field to see if Adam had managed to escape. Lord Sterling yanked her head back further until she cried out in pain.

"That bastard doesn't matter. It's you I need. I only thought he might keep you compliant." He chuckled but then fought her with renewed urgency when shouts were heard from a distance. "Not worth the trouble now."

"Need?" she grunted as she kicked back at him landing

a blow to his shin. It only infuriated him further. "You have no need of me. You have a wife."

"I have a useless empty sack," he snarled, shoving her forward but only succeeding in flinging her to the ground where she landed upon all fours in the mud. She attempted to stay down to prevent him from dragging her further. "Five times she's failed to hold a babe," he said with disgust. "A useless twit."

"I can't solve that," she argued, landing sprawled out in the mud as he tried to wrangle her flailing limbs.

"You are fertile and produce sons," he snapped. "She is nothing but a wet blanket. A barren wet blanket. I've never been satisfied since I've been denied your pleasures."

"Perhaps it's because she loathes you," Peggy hissed. "As do I."

"Lies. You love me."

"I once thought that I loved you," she hissed. "I was wrong. Now I know you to be nothing more than a hateful scoundrel."

"You love me, and I love you," he continued with full belief in his own words. He was delusional. "I should have never let you go, and I will have you again, so help me…"

"I will never," she spat. By this point, he had dragged her back to her feet, and she realized that she was beginning to tire. Even with all of her strength, he was bigger and stronger than she could ever hope to best.

"Blast you, Margaret, stop fighting me. You'll bear my heir. You should be happy."

"You are married!" she repeated, as if he could be made to see reason.

"Yes, and I have suffered for it long enough. You will provide my heir and Mary will present it as her own," he declared. "I will take care of the children that you provide, and you will love me for it. Father is dead now, and I *will* have you both. I love you. I have always loved you." Something was broken inside of this man, she realized. Perhaps something always had been, and she had never noticed. He was unhinged, but help was on its way.

"This is not love. This is obsession," she cried, trying to keep him distracted. She could hear the horses now. She only needed to postpone their departure a little longer.

"There is no difference," he snarled. "You ought never to have left me."

"You told me I was nothing." She bit down on the hand that had crossed her front and come too near her mouth.

He swore and called her an obscene name.

She spat blood.

"I said, I could not marry you," he said in denial of her claim. "Father would have never allowed it. I had every intention of keeping you on as a mistress, but you disappeared."

"A fact that I shall never regret," she murmured.

He shoved her nearer to the carriage, and his driver came around the back shaking his head, and his hands gloriously empty. Adam had escaped. She exhaled with relief, exhaustion suddenly rolling over her.

"How did you find me?" she asked as she kicked out at the driver who had moved in to help his master force her into the carriage.

"I looked for you for years," he revealed with a manic quivering to his voice. "It was not until your father suspected his *Wilhelm Charm* had resurfaced that I was able to track you to that ridiculous little village. If it can even be called that. I did not find you. Your father did."

Peggy's heart sank. So, her own father had given her up to this villain.

"How did he know?" she pressed. The driver had entrapped one of her feet in his arms, and she swung the second leg up to collide with his temple. Somehow, the blow landed true, and he dropped like a stone. Still, Peggy was not free.

"You were daft to contact all the best merchants in the south. Only he or his daughter would know all of their names and locations." Lord Sterling shouted at her to quit fighting, but she would not. So, he continued speaking instead, her ploy to take advantage of his need to boast working in her favor. "Then, there was the matter of recognizing your writing, though the signature and seal were not your own. Some baron you had duped into the deal. Did you bed him too?"

Peggy screamed in frustration at both the implication and the nearness of the carriage door. She was running out of time. Once she was locked inside the carriage, driver or no, Lord Sterling would be off.

"He wants you back too," the Viscount revealed with a relish, "your father. Business never has been quite as profitable since you left. I offered to loan you out when you weren't cloistered with child."

"I hate you!" Peggy screamed as she gave a push against the wall of the carriage in the hopes of putting some distance between herself and the door, but it only resulted in throwing her off balance and giving Lord Sterling the momentum that he needed to shove her closer.

Just as he was about to thrust her inside the carriage, Lord Sterling released a terrifying cry of agony, and Peggy fell to the ground free of his grip. What had happened?

She looked up in time to see Adam draw back, a blade in his hand dripping with blood and a gruesome looking wound on her attacker's thigh. Adam made to scramble away, but Lord Sterling's hand snaked out and grabbed his ankle before the boy could be free. The knife clattered to the ground out of reach.

No, no, no! thought Peggy. Her boy was supposed to run. He was supposed to be out of reach, out of danger, but he was not. Lord Sterling could reach him.

"No!" Peggy screamed. "Leave him be!"

Lord Sterling, with more control against a child than he had been able to muster against an adult, pulled a pistol from his belt and held it to Adam's chest.

# CHAPTER 30

"IT'S YOU OR THE BRAT," HE DECLARED WITH A GRIN. "I've no use for a sideslip, even if he is mine, so choose." Adam's eyes shot to the gentleman's face with horror, but Lord Sterling did not even bother to look at the boy.

"Take me," Peggy said without hesitation. She held up her hands in submission and allowed her malicious ex-lover to pull her to him as Adam was shoved away toward the approaching horses.

"Run," she ordered, and though her son looked like he wanted to do anything but run, he finally acquiesced when she repeated the demand in a tone that would not be argued with.

Peggy watched until Adam was out of sight. When Lord Sterling took a long draw of her scent and expressed having dreamt about her these long years, she cringed.

"You disgust me," she spat, but he only laughed.

"You agreed to give yourself for your son," was all he offered. "You'll tell those men to leave, or I'll make sure you never see that boy again. I promise you, I will hunt him down and kill him. I found you once. I can find him the second time."

Peggy looked up at his words to see Nash riding at the front of the group, his face wracked with a mixture of fury and fear. At his sides were his father, Mr. Finch, Jemmy, and several other men of the town, including what appeared to be a few local lords. They had rallied the forces, but it seemed not in time.

Peggy felt the press of the cold metal against her temple.

"Leave now or the ladybird dies," Lord Sterling shouted so that all would hear. "She's mine, but you can take the boy unharmed. The brat stabbed me, but you can take him."

"That's my boy," Nash and Mr. Finch said in unison, before glancing at each other with some pride.

Peggy thought she had never loved Lord Belton more. He was here, for her and for Adam, but she was resolved that she would go with Lord Sterling before she put either of them in danger.

Lord Belton had other ideas.

"We aren't going anywhere," Nash declared as he dismounted no less than thirty paces away. Peggy prayed he would not come any closer. She did not wish for the man that she loved to be anywhere within range of the pistol, and he was already near enough to put Lord Sterling on edge. She could feel it in the way he trembled, not with fear but with excitement, and he didn't seem terribly competent with the pistol. It could go off at any moment.

"Tell your men not to move an inch or I'll put a bullet in her head," Lord Sterling shouted when the riders had begun to move as if to circle around. "I'll do it. I'll kill her before I give her up."

Peggy knew without a doubt that he meant every word. Lord Sterling seemed like a passionate man in his youth. Now she realized that he was crazed.

"Lower the weapon," Nash said in a calm tone, taking one slow step forward. "We can talk about this, gentleman to gentleman."

Lord Sterling pointed the pistol at Nash to force him to stop his approach and then swiftly returned the gun to Peggy's temple when he realized the mistake. Nash had meant to draw the weapon away from Peggy's head even if that meant having it leveled at himself.

"No closer!" the assailant cried. "We are going to climb into the carriage and be off. You can keep the boy, but don't follow or she's dead."

"With what driver?" Nash wondered, looking down at the unconscious man who still lay sprawled at the foot of the carriage.

Lord Sterling seemed to all at once take note of his precarious position. True, he held the hostage. But it was dozens of men against one, and even if he got them into the carriage, there was no one to drive it. If he drove the rig himself, then Peggy would not be so well guarded and might even attempt to fling herself upon the road. He had found himself in a pinch, to be sure. He looked uncertain.

"You don't want her anyway," Lord Sterling shouted for the benefit of the crowd. "She's ruined. I ruined her."

"That is where you are wrong. I want her very much," Nash replied.

"We want her," Mr. Finch said. "We find her quite respectable. A widow, whose husband died in the war."

Peggy stared, realizing that the whole town was perfectly willing to hide her secret, but Lord Sterling knew the truth. "I ruined her!" he shouted.

Nonetheless, there were nods of agreement from the men of Riversbend that brought tears to Peggy's eyes. Not that her fear, the fingers clawing at her hair, or the gun at her head helped much.

"Who are you?" her captor demanded while waving the gun wildly. "Some other sap caught in her spell?"

"I am Baron Whitehall," Nash revealed. "And yes, I suppose I am quite caught by her. So you see, I won't be letting you take her. Not today. Not ever."

Lord Sterling bristled. "The damned baron from the letters," he snarled, and his tone turned sly and mocking as he turned his attention to Peggy and began to berate her. "You think *he* is going to claim you? Ha. You weren't worth a viscount. You won't ever be more than a whore, no matter whose bed you warm."

He turned back to Nash and addressed his rival with distain. "She's good enough to bed, but not good enough to wed, right? Shameful thing these upstart merchant's daughters. They think money makes them equal, but the breeding just isn't there. Now, as a mistress I will tell you… that is a fine choice." He shrugged against her as if he expected that as men of status, they must have an understanding.

"Now. Here's the thing. I've found mine. You'll just have to look elsewhere. I'm sure there are plenty of willing convenients for your by-blows," Lord Sterling said with a grin. Peggy could tell that he was enjoying the attention, the power he felt in this moment with everyone waiting on his action. "Now, as I said…" He fumbled to pull back the hammer on the pistol with the thumb of the same hand that held it and then changed his mind. Peggy wondered how proficient he was with the pistol. "Allow us passage or we all lose." He released her hair and wrapped his elbow around her neck. With the newly freed hand, he pulled back on the hammer once more to ensure it was in place.

Peggy's eyes met Nash's, and her heart ached at the sight. She could see in his eyes that he would fight to the death for her, to his own death, and she could not allow it. Tears began to flow freely as she shook her head, begging him not to act. They would both be killed. She could not see Adam from the skyward position which Lord Sterling held her head, but she hoped that he had run free of the sight, for she could see that Nash would not surrender her to this fiend. If she died, he would go down fighting unless she could convince him otherwise. She had not a moment to waste. "Take care of Adam," she said. "Be there—"

She caught Nash's eye, and for a moment they were of one accord.

*I will be there. Always.*

"Always," he said.

She slammed her head back into Lord Sterling's face, hoping to catch him in the nose or strike some other painful blow. In surprise, he released her, and she fell forward to the ground. At the same moment, she saw Nash spring forward from the corner of her eye, but he was too far away. As she turned back to face Lord Sterling, she watched as he leveled the gun at her and... pulled the trigger.

Nothing happened.

Peggy sat on the ground shaking, too filled with fear to even bother crawling away. She knew Nash and the now others were running toward her. She could her him cry out her name, but the world seemed to have shrunk in size to nothing more than herself, Lord Sterling, and the weapon. He shook the offending item and slammed it against his palm, pulling the hammer back yet a third time as he reset the pistol for a second attempt. This time, he aimed straight at her face, his grin unearthly and terrifying. She closed her eyes and hoped only that it would be painless.

He pulled the trigger, and a resounding crack shook the air. Peggy smelled gunpowder and heard a thud but there was no pain. It was over, she thought.

She was dead.

Then, a pair of arms were flung around her, and knees landed at her side. She felt herself being pulled into the lap of a large form that she had come to know so well. *Nash.* Perhaps she was not quite dead, but at least she felt no pain, she thought. Perhaps this was what it felt like when one's soul left their body. If so, she was in heaven. She sighed and burrowed into him, listening to the heaving breaths that were torn from his chest.

"It's all right," he murmured in her ear. "Open your eyes. You're all right. I can't believe it, but," his voice cracked with emotion, "you are unharmed."

Peggy did not understand, but after he repeated the words, she did as he had instructed. She opened her eyes and looked up into the most stunning blue she had ever seen. The same blue eyes that she had grown to love these past months.

"What… What happened?" She turned to look at Lord

Sterling, but Nash's hand cupped her cheek and prevented her from glancing over her shoulder.

"You do not want to see it," he explained. "The gun must not have been properly loaded. It misfired. It exploded when he pulled the trigger. He's dead."

"Adam?" she asked, craning her neck to look over his shoulder for her son. He was her only concern in the moment.

"He's fine. Jemmy saw him in the field and went to get him. They are headed back to the village. He didn't see it."

All at once, the tears flowed freely. Adam was safe and he would not be traumatized by the horrific death of Lord Sterling Pentworth. She clung to Nash for all she was worth, not even opening her eyes.

"I tried, Nash. I really did," came a frustrated male voice. "I left her with her mother." Peggy looked up to see one of the gentlemen in the group glaring at Miss Nora as she dismounted at their side. She looked as if she had ridden through a maelstrom, so flushed and disheveled the lady appeared in her effort to catch up with the menfolk.

"Lord Abernathy," she snipped in acknowledgement of her nemesis. Then she turned to Peggy and cried. "I tried to join from the off, but they left me behind, and it took ages to give Mama the slip. I'm so glad you are safe, Peggy. I've been worried sick." She shook off Lord Abernathy's hand as he attempted to steer her away so that Peggy and Nash might have their privacy, but Miss Nora paid him no mind. "I passed Jemmy and Adam on the way, and they said that some beast was..." She turned and must have caught sight of Lord Sterling's mangled form because her face suddenly went ghost white. The boys had warned

273

her of the villain but had known nothing of his terrible outcome.

"Oh," Nora said turning now a vivid shade of green.

"Come." Lord Abernathy caught Miss Nora's elbow to pull her away from the gruesome sight. The fact that she did not resist was the best indication of her state.

"Oh my," she groaned, and then in a flood of unaccustomed feminine weakness, she became sick all over Lord Abernathy's boots.

## CHAPTER 31

THE RAIN BEGAN TO ABATE AS PEGGY RODE BACK TO
Riversbend with Lord Belton on his massive stallion. He
said he was not letting her out of his sight, and he held her
firmly in front of him as they walked sedately towards
home. Home, Peggy thought. At last, she had a home and a
family. Nora rode at her side while Lord Abernathy argued
that Miss Nora should not be allowed to ride alone after
her own shock. Nora loudly opposed this notion. Mr. Finch
and others of the town fell back, allowing the argument to
play out. Lord Belton promised a celebration at the inn for
all involved, but Peggy just wanted peace and quiet. She
leaned her head back against Lord Belton's warm
shoulder.

Nash's father, the Viscount, and several others had
remained behind to make the reports and handle the return
of Lord Pentworth's mangled body to his wife in Hampshire. Peggy momentarily pitied the woman for the shame
that her husband's behavior would bring upon her house.
Then, it occurred to her that the lady might be more than

pleased to be free of the wretched man who was her husband. There was status as a widow, and she would finally be free to marry for love if she so chose. Peggy knew that she need not to fear her father. Such a showing and defeat of the Viscount would keep the merchant far away from Riversbend. He had never been one who liked to get his hands dirty anyway, she recalled.

When they came into town, all of the residents had come out to gawk or greet their men upon the return. Even with all of the people lingering about, the street was filled with an eerie silence. Peggy looked about for Adam. She saw him standing at the front of the haberdashery and clinging to Mrs. Finch with Jemmy and Martha laying hands of comfort upon his sobbing shoulders.

Mrs. Finch drew his attention up to the road and pointed out his mother's approach.

Without hesitation, Adam raced toward her, his arms flung out and tears flowing down his cheeks.

Peggy scrambled down from the horse before Lord Belton could help her dismount and caught Adam just as he leapt into her arms. She held him close, burying her face in his hair and relishing the knowledge that they had both come through the ordeal unharmed. Adam cried against her, expressing his fear that he might never have seen her again.

"I'm safe," she murmured against him. "I'm here, and I'm not going anywhere. We're both safe."

She sensed more than saw Lord Belton come up beside her. He had handed off the reins of his horse to someone in the crowd and pressed a hand to Adam's shoulder, offering the boy his support.

Adam turned and hugged the Baron about the waist.

Nash wrapped his arms around the boy. His eyes met Peggy's over her son's head, and she offered him a sad but grateful smile.

"You came for us," Adam spoke into the chest of his hero. "The whole town came for us."

"That they did," Nash replied. "You're one of us now, and we protect our own."

"What if our new town doesn't like us?" Adam complained, turning to his mother with pleading in his voice. "What if they aren't like the people here and they wouldn't protect you? What if that man comes again?" He was near hysterics, and so Peggy pulled her son back into her arms and whispered soothing words.

"That man will never harm us again," she promised. "He... He's dead."

"Is it true that he is... was my father?" Adam's voice was small. It broke her heart.

"Yes," Peggy replied. She wanted to tell him that though Lord Sterling was the father of his birth, he had never been and never would be a true father to the boy. But that was not what the boy was asking, so Peggy had kept her answer brief.

"Then I am glad he is dead," Adam scoffed. No longer was he tearful. He straightened his shoulders and stood strong, looking up at his mother with determination. "He wanted to hurt you, and so he is no father of mine."

Peggy swallowed past the lump in her throat and nodded. She was sure this day would stay with the child, but she would not contradict him in this moment. In this moment, it felt as if Providence had smiled upon them. Was it an evil thought to be glad of it? She wondered. To be glad a man was dead? Were not the lives of all so preordained? She could not think of it now. She would not. She could only be glad her son was safe.

"Come now, child," Mrs. Finch's voice broke in from a few yards away. "Let us fill your belly and get you some rest. I think your mother needs some time to collect herself." The woman's eyes made a pointed gesture at Peggy's blood-spattered gown, a detail that she had yet to notice, and Peggy was pleased to know that her son would be well cared for while she cleaned herself up. The gown she would burn, she thought with a flare, for she never wished to look upon it and think of its horrors again.

Adam allowed Mrs. Finch to take him under her arm as she led him away. He looked so small to have endured so much trouble in his life. He had been right, though, when he noted that the town had ridden out in their defense. Without question and with haste, a small army had given chase, even including several faces that she had never before seen. That was something, she thought with satisfaction. That was what made a place a home.

Peggy left the murmuring crowd in the street and let herself into the shop. It took her less than half of an hour to toss her gown into a freshly lit fire, scrub her skin until it was near raw and held no indication of the day's trials, and don a new frock. When she checked her appearance in the mirror, she did not look so very different, and yet she felt as if she had transformed into a new person entirely.

Gone was any question of leaving Riversbend. No more would she attempt to imagine a new life far away with just herself and her son. They had a community now, and Peggy had never felt that so deeply in her soul before this day. So many had come to their defense. Even those that she had not yet met had pledged their support and their lives in the protection of herself and her son. She had long been left to feel quite on her own, a captive worker with no agency of her own, a moving pawn in a game of chess for her father's progress, or an aberration in society as a woman ruined by a man without consequence. Now, she felt a oneness with those around her, and she was grateful to have been accepted even after the town had learned that she had begot a child out of wedlock. Still, they had come for her in numbers greater than she could have ever imagined. For the first time, she had not been abandoned to her fate.

When she finally felt that she had put herself back together, she descended the stair with the intention of opening the shop to the crowd. There would be few purchases today, but they would all have questions or wish to offer their support, and she owed them her gratitude. It was the least that she could do to put on a brave face and bear through it.

It took several moments for her to realize that she would not be opening the shop at all. Lord Belton waited below with the curtains drawn against anyone who found themselves too overcome with curiosity. She was pleased that she would not be expected to perform and felt simultaneously guilty that she had the need for privacy at all. That her troubles had come to Riversbend was no one's fault but her own.

"They are all worried about you," he explained, "but I told them that what you needed right now was some quiet."

"Thank you," Peggy said with hesitation. He stood in

the center of the shop awaiting her approach, but she was frozen on the last step, unsure.

There was a part of her that wished to run into Nash's arms and allow his embrace to chase away all of the concerns of her day. There was a part of her that cried out for him and screamed within her head that he had more than proved his devotion to her this very day. There was a part of her that had believed what he had said when he had declared to all that he had been taken with her. There was a part of her that wanted to hope that the affection that had grown between them was enough, could be enough.

And yet… there was also a voice in her head that could not help but believe what Lord Sterling had professed. That she was worthy enough for a distraction, for pleasure, but nothing more. She was not a woman of noble birth. She was not even a poor but innocent woman. She was ruined. How could a man as wonderful as he, ever care for her in the way that she had come to care for him? Try as she might, she could not stop the doubts from taking over.

She was forced to admit that Nash had never formally declared himself. In all of their weeks of happiness, she had made the foolhardy assumption that his intention was for them to remain together in a much more public manner than they had begun. In her most secret of hopes and dreams, she had imagined them wed and happy, but she now saw that he had never actually suggested such a thing outright. He had claimed that he loved her, that he wanted her, and that he wished that she would stay. Lord Sterling had wanted the same, and that had never once meant more than a superficial arrangement. Like the Viscount, the Baron had never offered her his home or his name.

Her ex-lover had been quick to point out that his

expectation of Peggy's role might not be so different from that of her new beau. Lord Sterling had expected to keep Peggy tethered to the wings, and while the cover of secrecy had been her own demand for Adam's sake, Peggy could not help but note that it would benefit Lord Belton in the long run if he ever chose to forsake her for another. He could keep her as his lover and the manager of the haberdashery without ever needing to give her more. Gentlemen were known to expect such things on the side of their formal agreements. They married noble ladies. They bedded whomever they pleased.

Though she had tried to argue with herself that she and Lord Belton had never dared move past a passionate embrace, it was only a matter of time before they succumbed to the need. She could not even place the blame solely on Lord Belton. She realized that despite her determination that she would never place herself in such a position again, she had fallen too deeply for the Baron to deny him much. If he had pressed further, she would have complied. The knowledge made her lose what little respect for herself she had gained over recent months. As Lord Sterling had suggested, she was weak when it came to matters of the heart.

"What is the matter?" Nash broke her from her reverie with a voice filled with trepidation.

"I don't know," she lied. But she knew very well. She had done the thing that she had sworn she would never do again. She had fallen in love with a gentleman who was well above her station and who would never, if he had an ounce of sense about propriety, claim her in public.

He shook his head, stepping forward to meet her where she stood at the stair. Peggy remained aloof but allowed

281

him to brush his fingers down the length of her arm until his hands clasped hers at her sides. A shiver ran over her skin, leaving raised bumps across its surface.

"You are doubting my intentions," he said with the strange and acute knowledge that had so often caught her off her guard. "What that lout said was meant to make you doubt me. Doubt us. It wasn't true. I thought you would see that."

She allowed herself to meet his eye. No matter what Nash thought he felt when he was with her, it would not solve the issue that it would never make sense for them to be together. No one would ever expect him to lower himself to her standard.

"I could see his point," she said in a voice that was barely a whisper. "I know that you are his superior in every way, but I know who I am. What I am. And that makes his words ring all the more true. Why would you stoop to choose—"

"Why would I choose a woman who is kind and strong and has already proven herself to be the most devoted mother?" he cut in before she could finish. "A woman who has survived the worst and still gives her best? A woman who has every reason to hate the world and still sacrificed herself and her own choices for the happiness of a little boy and the benefit of a town in need?"

He spoke with passion, and Peggy tried to listen, although the hopeless part of her mind refused to believe. "Why would I choose the most beautiful woman I have ever met who turns my insides out and who I dream about each night? The woman I want to bear my children and call my wife? Yes, my wife. Not a mistress. Not a lover. I want it all.

Peggy felt the need to protest, but he went on. She had heard what he had said and wanted to celebrate in the knowledge, but she knew that his wants, or her wants, mattered little when other people had a say, and they would speak out against her. Society would reject her and him in kind. "Why would I not willingly choose only a woman who my family has grown to love and respect? One that they would support and champion even against the harshest critics of society. Let them say it is wrong. We will prove *them* wrong." He was so filled with certainty that her heart ached. Only one of truly noble birth could see the world through such gilded eyes. She had seen the dark side of life, the dark side of the aristocracy, and she knew that it would eat up all those who were foolish enough to think that good could prevail. It was a wonder that this man, this gentle, wonderful man still believed in fairy stories, for what they had could only end in heartache.

"We cannot—" she began.

"Bollocks," he interrupted, sounding nothing at all like a gentleman and every bit the earthy man she loved. "We can. Did you not say that you didn't give a bloody farthing what people thought?"

She blushed. He was not supposed to hear that.

"It was not very ladylike," she whispered. "That is why…"

"Why I stand before you now, as a man before the woman he loves. Not a lady and a gentleman, but a man and a woman who love one another. Say you love me, Peggy," he whispered, the pain suddenly in his words.

"I do, but I cannot be a baroness. I certainly can't be a viscountess."

"Why not?'

"The people would never accept me."

"I do not care what the people think, but I think you are wrong."

"Those that fall under my care would respect you as more than just their lady. They have already proven that. They have accepted you as a woman who has proven that she could earn a place among them. That they would risk their lives for. That they would come running to protect when the call rang out. For that is exactly what we saw today. Each and every man who rode with me championed you and your goodness. Not me alone, but dozens. They believed in you and were willing to fight to protect you." Peggy suppressed a sob that threatened to break loose at his words. But he went on. "One whose decisions I could trust and who had the knowledge to work alongside me to make this village thrive?" He threw his hands up in the air. "Why would I choose *that* woman?"

Peggy was stunned. In one speech riddled with sarcasm, he had cast aside all of her arguments and left her feeling as if she had insulted his very nature for the mere implication that she was beneath him. Yet that is how she had felt after Lord Sterling's words. She had felt unworthy. No. She knew she was unworthy.

Peggy reflected on all of their interactions and tried to recall each moment as she had seen them before, when they had been filled with wonderment and happiness, not with the taint of hateful words and insulting insinuations.

Nash had always been kind to her, more than kind. He had gone out of his way to ensure her comfort and offered his ear even when she had refused to speak. He had trusted her with the responsibility of a man when many would have laughed in her face and told her to focus her efforts on more feminine pursuits. He had known her darkest secrets and still allowed her the chance to prove what type of person she was within. He had been gentle and respectful in his courting yet never withheld the proof of his passions. Nor had he taken advantage even though he had known that she was not an innocent.

Most importantly, he had only kept their attachment a secret at her behest, not from any drive to hide her away from embarrassment or to convince her to be a kept woman. Peggy had wanted time and the ability to pull away freely if she chose. She had wanted an out and Nash had given it to her. He had never once asked for a single thing she was not willing to give.

With a sinking feeling, Peggy realized that her doubts were the result of no one's behavior but her own. The struggles of her life had formed insecurities that had gone unnoticed. She had thought herself healed and whole, a strong woman who knew her own mind. She had been wrong. Nash had known about her child and about her time in London, but he had known nothing of her life before those tumultuous events. He had not known of her father's expectations and how they had weighed on her. He had been unaware of the ease with which she had been cast aside in her shame by both the father of her child as well as her own family or the damage to her confidence that being cast out by those that she had thought would always love her had left upon her psyche. He could not have known that she had been declared unworthy time and again after having been told that she must appeal to a certain standard, or that the false declarations of love that had been used to manipulate her youthful mind had left her unwilling to trust or leave herself vulnerable to others. Then had come her captivity, in which she had soon learned that the only person that she could rely on was herself. It had not been until the very end that she had even remotely begun to allow herself to collaborate with others for her freedom. And yet this town had come to her air. *He* had come to her aid.

Had he known these things, he might have been able to preempt her plummeting confidence by making his intentions clear. Instead, he had held back only the most formal of declarations until she had made her decision to stay and be with him or leave. As it was, Lord Belton had been sure that he had left little room for doubt, only enough opportunity for Peggy to make her choice without the pressures of his own hopes to cause her confusion. He had wanted her to choose him, as she had wanted Adam to choose her.

She felt like the most ridiculous fool, needy and demanding of constant proof.

"I am truly sorry," she said when it had all begun to make sense in her mind. "Nash, I believe that I have some explaining to do. You know of my past, but not all of it. There are things that shaped me, things that I thought that I had long ago moved past. It seems that some part of me still believed them. Still believed that I was unworthy of anyone, let alone someone like you."

"If you could only see yourself though the eyes of others, through my eyes," he amended, "then you would never have reason to doubt."

Peggy descended the final step and made her way to stand in front of him. He seemed to be waiting for her cue as he looked down upon her.

"What can I do?" she asked of him.

"Well…" He shrugged, looking a bit uncomfortable. "You could tell me what *your* intentions are." He looked terrified at the prospect of her answer. "I would not fault you for deciding that you wished to find a more secluded place where you and Adam would have no fear of being accosted. Being a Baroness, and then a Viscountess, I cannot promise you anonymity, but I can promise I will protect you"

"While I am certain that such a thing will never happen again," she began with a smile, "I cannot guarantee that any village will protect us quite so well as Riversbend and you."

He waited with bated breath, which Peggy could not help but find endearing.

"I think this is just the place for us to remain, if we are still welcome," she concluded.

"You're staying?" he said in a breath. "For always?"

She smiled, thinking he sounded for all the world like a boy who had just been told Christmas had come. She nodded and gasped when, in his excitement, he swept her up into his arms and spun her about.

"I had been certain that you would until today," he revealed. "To think that such a horrible thing could happen here." He shuddered and kissed her, as if the need to confirm that she was real and before him was too strong. "I could not bear it if it made you feel unsafe."

"Quite the contrary," she replied. "Had I not been in Riversbend and surrounded by such good people, I would have been lost for sure. It was only by being here that I was saved. I have never felt safer in my life than knowing that I have so many lovely neighbors who would never allow harm to befall me or my son."

287

"Your son," he mused. "I was thinking that you might wish to rethink that a bit."

"Oh?" Peggy wondered aloud, her heart racing with hope and uncertainty. A gentleman of his position might wish that her son be cast aside. Though she did not think that Nash was the sort to suggest such a thing, it was not unheard of.

"Well," Lord Belton brushed her hair away from her face and clasped her to his side. "I cannot claim him as my own, but I *can* provide for him as if he were. I could give him a good life, if you'd let me... raise him alongside others even. He'd have an education and an allowance. A real future of his own desire. It's just a thought."

Peggy turned into the frame of his arms and looked up at him, her features overtaken by the love and gratitude that he would even consider caring so fully for a child that was not his own.

"Is that what you want?" she asked.

"I want you and everything that comes with you," he confirmed. "I've always cared for Adam, and to raise him like a son would be more than I could have ever dreamed."

"But could you?" she wondered. "Raise him as your own, that is? Love him even though he came from another?" She was fearful that if there was a future between herself and the Baron, any further children might cause a rift since she knew according to the laws of succession, Adam could never be the Baron's heir. Providing for a child was one thing. Making them feel like a welcome part of a family was quite another.

Nash drew back and looked down upon her with confusion. "Do you not think that the Viscountess loves me?"

"Well, of course your mother loves you," Peggy sighed. He must have misunderstood her meaning, she thought. She had not meant if a male could love a child in the way a female could love a child. She had meant if he could love a child that was not bonded by blood.

"Lady Umberly is not the woman who gave birth to me," he revealed, to her utter shock.

"What?" Peggy reeled. "Of course, she is. She called you her child on several occasions. I am sure of it."

"I am her son, for all it is worth." He shrugged. "But my own mother died a few years after I was born attempting to give birth to another. They were both lost."

"I do not understand," Peggy frowned. The Viscount was clearly in love with his wife. She had never heard of him speak of another. Was Nash implying that he himself had been begotten outside of the marriage bed? She blushed with the thought, although if he were from the wrong side of the blanket, well, she could hope. The son of a Viscount was clearly beyond her reach.

"My father loved my mother very much," Nash explained. "It just so happened that they were only married for a few short years before she passed. She was quiet but had a humor about her that she only revealed to those closest to her. It was how my father learned that both laughter and passion must exist for a marriage to bring pleasure to both parties. He knew that if he were ever to love again, it would require that much and more."

Peggy clung to him, her arms about his waist and her face turned up in anticipation of the tale. "It was several years later that Father met Augusta. She was open with her laughter, and it brought joy back to the manor. Further- more, she was the mother that I had never had the chance to recall. She gave birth to Nora and raised the both of us as her own. She can dote and scold in turn as easily as any mother, and I never once felt separated from her treatment of my sister. If anything, she is harsher with Nora, but that is only because my sister has brought that upon herself. Blood has never stopped our family from being whole."

Peggy was shocked at the revelation. Of course, it made sense. Had she not herself noted that Nash and Nora looked nothing alike? They did not even act alike. Quite the opposites, in fact. He was tall and dark, while his sister —his half-sister—was petite and fair in feature. He tended toward a quieter nature, like his mother, and Nora was as lively as the Viscountess or more. And then there was the gap in their ages that made sense when one considered that the Viscount had gone through the long transition of widower to husband.

"Then…" She tried to consider what he was offering but did not wish to jump to conclusions.

"Adam would always be welcome and loved," he clarified. "I would never subjugate him to the shadows. He will never want for anything. He would be mine in every way except to the entail, which of course, I could not change. That responsibility would fall to *our* son."

"I—I see." Peggy reeled.

"Unless you are opposed," he added with hesitation. Peggy looked up to see that Nash's features were unsure, as if he feared that he had assumed too much.

"Why would I be opposed?" she laughed.

"Well…" He released a long breath and pulled her to him as if he could draw comfort just from having her in his arms. "Quite some time has passed in this conversation since I mentioned that I would like nothing more than to have you for my wife, and you haven't exactly responded."

Peggy's mouth fell open in horror. He was right. He had mentioned it when he had ranted about all of the reasons why she had been worthy of his love. Then he had gone on to quell her fears about being accepted, about Adam being accepted, and still she had remained silent on the subject, but she had never dreamed he meant marriage. Marriage to her, a ruined woman with a child.

"Well…" she decided with a devious grin. She grasped him by the cravat and tugged until his mouth met her own.

She kissed him. Thoroughly and with every ounce of passion that had ever cried out for this man, she kissed him. Her body pressed against his, she melded into him, and his arms held her close. Mouths and hands and bodies moved in a dance as old as time. Peggy was breathless and on edge, but she held nothing back, allowing herself for the first time perhaps ever to give herself over fully to a man. Heart and soul, she sang for him, and he met her beat for beat.

"That had better be a yes," he groaned when a long while later they had been forced to draw apart, gasping for breath, before neither of them could prevent the embrace from going further.

"I'll say," Miss Nora said from where she stood in the doorway at the back of the shop. Her cheeks were red, and her eyes were wide with shock, but the way that she blew out her cheeks and turned straight around to make her exit revealed that although she had witnessed enough, it had been no more than the last few seconds of their embrace.

Peggy dropped her head to Lord Belton's chest and

laughed at the absurdity of having been caught in the embrace, but this time, she felt no shame.

"Now you'll have to marry me," he said with a laugh, "or I'll be ruined." The irony of the situation was not lost on her.

"Nora will not tell a soul." Peggy chuckled as he rested his chin upon her head.

"I suppose not," he said. "She wouldn't dare risk ruining her own claim to success."

"No," Peggy differed. "She would not tell because she is my friend.

"I suppose that is true, but if you change your mind and slink back into the shadows, I might just have to make certain that she does tell! She is my sister, after all. I have ways of making her talk." He winked cheekily.

Peggy slapped at his arm and then pulled him down to kiss her once more. No, Miss Nora would not tell a soul. But soon enough it would not matter, for Mrs. Margaret Williams intended to marry the Baron Whitefall just as soon as possible, and she wanted all the world to know.

# EPILOGUE

THE GUEST LIST FOR THE BALL THE FOLLOWING EVENING doubled when it became known that it was not only to be a celebration of the growth and success of the villages but also an engagement party for the Baron Whitefall and his bride to be.

Peggy wore the green and silver dress as promised but had found herself draped with jewels and spritzed with expensive perfumes by her future sister and mother-in-law.

"For someone so resolutely against marriage, you certainly have a way of showing it," Peggy had teased when Miss Nora had squealed with delight at the announcement and promised to help in any way necessary for the planning of the nuptials. Her first task had been to send out word for a new shopkeeper. Peggy, Nash, and Adam would still monitor the business dealings, but the new lady of the house would not have time to man the counter for endless hours each day.

"I am not against the institution," Miss Nora retorted. "I am against the concept for my own person."

For someone so determined to avoid love and trappings, Peggy thought, her future sister certainly seemed to be a romantic at heart. It had been largely a result of Nora's forceful manner of throwing the pair together that Peggy and the man that she loved had overcome every obstacle to find one another. A true cynic would not have put quite so much effort into interfering, but Peggy kept that tidbit to herself, for Miss Nora would not find it amusing.

Although Adam would not be attending the ball, since he was too young, Peggy could not help but smile at the thought of her son as she descended the sprawling stair that led down into the ballroom.

The boy had been elated when she had told him that it was her intention to remain at Riversbend. His reaction to that news had been nothing when compared to the pure joy and shock he had exhibited when he learned that his mother and the gentleman that he admired most would soon be wed. When he learned that they would be moving into the manor after the wedding, he had been left speechless.

"Into the servant's quarters?" he had wondered, unable to consider that in one fell swoop his life would change so fully.

Peggy had shaken her head.

"No," Lord Belton had leaned down to whisper to the boy. "You'll take the room across from Miss Nora. But only if you promise to tell her that there are spiders in her bed now and then."

Adam had grinned and taken the task to heart. "Jemmy has a wooden snake that I can borrow that is sure to give her a fright!" With that he had raced off to find the older boy and make plans for their mischief.

Martha, on the other hand, had been despondent. Having hoped that the confection that she had given to Lord Belton would have resulted in him falling madly in love with her, she had been shocked to learn that he had chosen to take another—much older, she lamented— woman as his bride.

Peggy and Nash had tried not to laugh at the girl's plight, but her belief had been so true that Nash had been forced to admit that he had given the cake to the stable-master's son and had never eaten it for himself. Martha seemed to accept that as an explanation for the failed potion, and in no time at all she had gone off toward the stables to see if her prospects were better there.

"Little George admitted to me last week that he finds her fair," Nash revealed when Peggy had been shocked that he had sent the determined girl after the boy. "I honestly have no recollection of what happened to the cake." He laughed. "But he eats enough of the sweets about the manor that I am sure even he would not know if he had or not."

They chucked with the thought, and Peggy said it seemed that Nora was not the only matchmaker in this family.

"Apparently not," Nash agreed.

When Peggy reached the bottom of the staircase, her betrothed broke free from the crowd and offered his arm. Her expectation that Lord Belton's reaction to her gown would be worthwhile did not disappoint. He could not take his eyes off of her. Peggy had accepted the escort with a shy smile, unused to so many people staring at her. She had better get used to it, Miss Nora scolded her before they had made their way down to the throng, for she was soon to be a baroness, and one day, many years in the future they all hoped, a viscountess.

Peggy allowed herself to be led from the hall into the ballroom, which had been bedecked from floor to ceiling with ribbons and candles that made the room sparkle and dance.

The musicians had been waiting for the entrance of the celebrated couple to strike up their first chords. As they did so, Nash swung Peggy into his arms.

This time, she did not go rigid. This time, she had no reason to pull back or hide the love that threatened to overflow. She gazed up at the man that she loved and melted into his arms as he twirled them about the floor. Others joined them, and soon the room was a crush of dancing couples.

Peggy saw out of the corner of her eye Miss Nora decline a proffered hand that had been extended by Lord Abernathy. Miss Nora had turned her back and walked away without a backward glance. Rather than look irritated by the clear snub, the gentleman had grinned.

"You know," Peggy mused after Lord Abernathy had simply settled upon another partner, "I don't know why Nora makes such a fuss. Lord Abernathy seems fine enough. Besides, he came to my aide, and for that he will always have my favor."

Lord Belton held his betrothed in his arms and pulled her closer than was perhaps appropriate. It was their engagement celebration, however, and so he knew that no one would dare tell them that they must not dance so close.

"She only dislikes him because he knows her so well," Nash chuckled. "She does not like a man that she cannot trick with her ploys or who calls her on her mischief. They both play the game of hating one another, but I suspect that deep down they both enjoy the game."

"Seems to me that would be just the sort of man that she needs." Peggy laughed and wondered what Miss Nora would do if someone else were to plot against her as she had them. Then, she changed her mind. She could not fault Nora her meddling when Peggy herself was so pleased with the result.

"One day my sister will find herself entrapped in one of her own games," he offered. "When that time comes, we can only hope that she does not balk and ruin her own chance at happiness."

"Speaking of happiness..." He leaned forward and whispered something truly devilish in her ear. She flushed bright red, and her eyes snapped to his.

"If that is your plan, then Adam will have an army of siblings with him to torment his Auntie Nora." She could not help the flush that had taken her over at his suggestion.

"Outnumbered by nieces and nephews, I'd say their aunt won't stand a chance." He grinned down upon her. Peggy felt his look and its implication all the way to her toes.

"We'll either have endless entertainments or my dear sister will find her revenge. Either way, I shall enjoy the show."

"Oh, I think we will have endless entertainments, no matter what Nora decides," Peggy said with a glint in her eye.

"Tell me again this plan of yours," Nash said.

"How about I show you," she whispered. Instead of answering, she pulled Nash's lips down to hers for a passionate kiss. Nash might be the one who believed in fairy tales, but Peggy was sure she had found her happily ever after in this wonderful man.

# ALSO BY ISABELLA THORNE

### THE SEDGEWICK LADIES

LADY ARABELLA AND THE BARON

HEALING MISS MILLWORTH

LADY MARIANNE AND THE CAPTAIN

### SPINSTERS OF THE NORTH

THE HIDDEN DUCHESS

THE MAYFAIR MAID

SEARCHING FOR MY LOVE

### THE LADIES OF BATH

The Duke's Daughter ~ Lady Amelia Atherton

The Baron in Bath ~ Miss Julia Bellevue

The Deceptive Earl ~ Lady Charity Abernathy

Winning Lady Jane ~ A Christmas Regency Romance

The Ladies of Bath Collection

### THE LADIES OF LONDON

Wager on Love ~ Lady Charlotte

### THE LADIES OF THE NORTH

The Duke's Winter Promise ~ A Christmas Regency Romance

The Viscount's Wayward Son

***Collections by Isabella Thorne***

Winter Holiday Collection

# DON'T MISS THE COUNTESS AND THE BARON

The Countess and the Baron ~ Prudence
The Baggington Sisters Book 1
By Isabella Thorne

**A single kiss on a dark night at a lonely inn changed Prudence's life forever...and not for the better.**

Deemed *"the Baggage"* by the ladies of Nettlefold, Prudence Baggington held secrets they could never know.

She thought to marry an earl. Instead, she married a monster.

Fearful for her life, she runs, seeking safe haven at a convent.

As a married woman she cannot join the convent, nor can she marry again. How could love ever be in her future?

Her only hope is for peace and simple friendship with the Abbess' nephew, the Baron Halthaven.

But the evil that made her fear for her life is coming for her.

**Will Prudence be forced to run again? Or will the Baron Halthaven show her that love really can conquer all?**

An uplifting tale of survival and perseverance.
Trigger warning for those who are sensitive. Prudence runs from a past abusive relationship.
No graphic descriptions.

Part of
THE BAGGINGTON SISTERS COLLECTION
by Isabella Thorne

Collection Includes:
The Countess and the Baron ~ Prudence
Almost Promised ~ Temperance
The Healing Heart ~ Mercy
The Lady to Match a Rogue ~ Faith
*And Coming Soon*
Love over Lords ~ Hope

~

Keep Reading for an inside look…

## Prologue

Miss Prudence Baggington's fine light brown hair had been arranged atop her head with a garland of minuscule white flowers that her maid called baby's breath. She still wore her dressing robe, but the voluminous folds of her wedding gown were draped over the edge of the bed and ready to be worn. She still could not quite believe that this day had arrived. She expected someone to come and snatch the victory away from her.

Outside her window, dawn colored the sky with the most beautiful array of red and orange sunbeams that Prudence had seen in weeks. She had thought to have once heard a saying about a crimson sky in the morning being a cause for alarm, but shook her head and laughed at the silly, childish notion.

Of course there was nothing more beautiful than a rose-hued sunrise. The weather was beautiful and she was about to be wed. At last. She let herself breathe in the cool scent of the morning and sighed with relief.

Marriage. Escape was perhaps a better word, but marriage would do. Once married she would be safe. She had dreamed of little else for most of her life, and she had prayed most dearly for these past few years. At last her prayers were answered, though not in the way she expected.

Of course Prudence did not want to stay on as a spinster in her father's home. Perish the thought. Still she had thought her groom would have been the wealthy and oh so handsome Duke of Kilmerstan, but Garrett Rutherford had evaded her every move, and eventually married that little mouse of a woman, Juliana Willoughby.

Prudence huffed. Juliana was on the shelf for years. How could she have succeeded where Prudence failed? The thought still irritated but Prudence pushed it from her mind. She could not be bothered by that now. It was her wedding day.

She may not be marrying a duke, but an earl would certainly do. She would be a countess. That status had to count for something. A bit of cheer bubbled in to halt her consternation. She would make all the hypocritical biddies who called her "the baggage" eat their words. She smiled at the thought, took up her wedding dress, and twirled around the room. She could not ever remember being so happy. She smiled at herself in the glass.

"Yes, Countess," she said. "Right away, Countess."

She carefully hung the gown again. It was true that her situation was not what she had once hoped, but there was good in it, she thought. One unexpected kiss of passion with a near stranger, an earl no less, had led to the marriage arrangement and the reading of the banns.

She had expected each Sunday to have someone object to her impending marriage, but looking around the church she saw no one speak to oppose it, not even the Earl of Fondleton himself.

At first, Prudence had been nervous about the marriage and about the earl's absence at each reading of the banns, but the happy day had arrived. Marriage to an earl had not been her plan, but he was titled, and wealthy. He was not old, nor was he terrible to look at. What more could a lady ask? They would grow to know and love each other in time. She was sure of it. Certainly, this was a better option than her current situation.

She shuddered.

The truth was that Prudence would have married just about anyone to get out of her father's house. She, and her mother, had been plotting for months to catch eligible gentlemen in the Nettlefold countryside, but all to no avail. No expense had been spared. They had ordered the most extravagant gowns and perfumes to catch the attentions of the gentlemen. Prudence had been hesitant at first to follow the advice of a London socialite, but her mother paid heavily for the designs, so Prudence capitulated.

She had shrugged her shoulders and gone along with the ploy, even attempting to enact an overly feminine accent that she had been instructed would appeal to the gentlemen's ears. She thought she sounded akin to a banshee, but the gentlemen did take notice. Still, it was a relief to know that she could return to her normal tone, even if some said she had a voice like a man. Perhaps speaking normally would bring an end to the hoarseness and sore throat which plagued her in the mornings.

Prudence had thought all the glitter and glam a farce, but perhaps her mother was right. Perhaps such maneuverings worked. After all, the machinations did end with her engagement. She would be Lady Fondleton.

"Lord and Lady Fondleton," she had whispered to herself in the mirror as the hope for her future lay ahead in an endless road of promise. While their meeting had been abrupt and, of course, improper, there was some romance to it as well. One could not be kissed in a stable without the thought of romance, she supposed.

She brought her fingers to her lips, remembering. The kiss was rather abrupt and rough, but she supposed the earl had not thought so well of her at the time. He did not know she was a lady. In the dark he seemed to think her someone else, perhaps a kitchen wench or some drab. She would not censure him, she decided, if he wanted to take a mistress, as long as he was discreet and she was with child first. He would want an heir, of course. She tapped her fingers nervously with the thought. She remembered the first and only time she had met her soon-to-be husband.

Upon literally bumping into one another in the stables of the Inn, Prudence had nearly fallen off balance. She was sure she wind milled her arms in a most unbecoming way, and her hat had fallen askew, but instead of being put off by her unladylike stance, the man caught her. Overcome with passion in that moment, he had swept down upon her, gathered her close to his very masculine form and planted a hard kiss upon her lips.

She had not been prepared. Never before had she felt quite so overwhelmed. She had perhaps just this once earned the nickname of baggage, because she was so thrilled in the moment, that she had not decried his boldness. Instead, she had allowed the kiss. Well, she supposed she did not really have a choice in the matter. She did not even have time to be afraid.

He had her in his arms, one hand laced through her hair and the other clasped her to him in a very ungentlemanly way. She should have been afraid. He was so audacious and overwhelmingly male, she found herself as meek as a kitten. She could not even utter a squeak. Such was not a disposition that others expected of Prudence – lioness perhaps, or jackal, but not kitten. She was certain that the earl's passionate kiss had been a sign of their destined future, and then they were well and truly caught.

Once caught in such an embrace there had been no explaining it. Prudence had swooned in his arms and he had held her. He had kissed her quite thoroughly and she imagined that she looked quite flushed and disheveled with the whole affair when Mrs. Hardcastle came upon them and exclaimed her outrage. She couldn't even blame Mrs. Hardcastle for outing them. After all, the woman knew Prudence was contending for a husband. Mrs. Hardcastle knew her situation, and she saw a solution. Prudence took it. Perhaps she should thank the woman.

Prudence twirled a recalcitrant curl around her finger, tucking it into place.

Perhaps the earl loved her, Prudence thought suddenly. She wondered, could it be love at first sight on his behalf? She could only hope that love might grow between them, but no matter. It would be better than home. She had to believe that.

Still, as the passion of their wedding night approached, Prudence could not help but worry. She remembered the earl's embrace. It had not been full of love, but full of lust. She shuddered with the thought, but she reminded herself, she would be his wife. She would have stature.

He was simply overcome with passion in the stable. He would not treat his wife so callously. On their wedding night she was sure he would apologize for his previous behavior, and she would forgive him. He would be her husband and offer her his protection. She would suffer his embrace. This she could do.

He would be more caring this time, she thought. He would be gentler and gentlemanly. She had thought of little else but the wedding night for weeks prior to today, though she had never had the opportunity to be alone with her betrothed. In fact, she had not seen the earl at all. If she were not currently looking at her wedding finery, she would have wondered if this was really the morning of her nuptials.

Father would walk her down the aisle. With any luck this would be the last time the man would touch her. She remembered Father's reaction when the news of her indiscretion reached him. He was, as was to be expected, furious. But after today, his wrath would not be able to touch her. She would be under her husband's protection. She smiled.

Prudence was just pleased to have escaped her father's grasp once and for all. Now, with a wealthy husband, she could lead the sort of life that she, and her many sisters, had always dreamed of. Her sisters. She would allow them all to visit as often as they could. She would shelter them. She would not abandon them like her older sister Temperance had done, running off to a convent rather than marrying. No. She, Prudence, would help them, just as soon as she was married to the earl.

"Mama," Prudence had called. "I am ready."

Her mother had entered the room with a smile as bright as the rising sun.

"You shall be beautiful," she whispered into her daughter's curls.

Prudence bit her lip. With several sisters well known for their timeless beauty and remarkable features, Prudence was more than aware of her plain face. Plump cheeks and a voluptuous frame softened any definable structure that was applauded in the willow thin bodies of her siblings. Even her eyes were nothing that would cause prose to be written in the throes of passion and love. Brown. Brown. Brown. Nothing more, nothing less. There was nothing special about her, Prudence thought. It was for that reason that she had allowed her mother to doll her up in extravagant costumes that might help her to stand out amongst the crowd of beautiful debutantes.

As Prudence stepped into her wedding gown, which was soon pulled tight by her mother's practiced fingers, she began to worry.

"Mama," she whispered. "Lord Fondleton... he is a good man, is he not?"

"He is an earl," her mother replied as if that were all the answer needed.

Prudence thought on her mother's words for a long while. Titled gentlemen were expected to be above all others in regard to their morality and character. Still... she wondered. He seemed nice enough. He offered plenty of smiles and compliments, but so did her father. In public, he seemed the perfect gentleman. In private, he was a monster.

"Papa is a viscount," she muttered but, if her mother heard her, the Viscountess Mortel did not respond.

## THE COUNTESS AND THE BARON

PRUDENCE WAS MARRIED FOR THREE MONTHS. THREE months of torturous marriage was more than she could bear. As the mail coach bounced along the rutted roads she only hoped that she could get far enough away before the earl realized that she had left. If he found her, he would bring her back. If she stayed away, perhaps he could say she was dead. She might as well be dead.

Jasper Numbton, the Earl of Fondleton, was a monster and a rake. Prudence did her best to keep her features illegible of their torment. Not a tear or muffled sob would slip free. Years upon years of practice had taught the Baggington sisters to hide their woes. Prudence had thought marriage her salvation. Now, she carried nothing but a small carpet bag that rode in her lap as if it contained items too precious to be lashed to the top of the carriage.

"Halthaven ahead!" the driver called. The carriage began to slow and Prudence felt her heart begin to thump in her chest anew.

She had taken a risk coming to Halthaven, a monumental risk. It would either be her deliverance or her undoing for if the earl discovered her escape she might never get the chance again. She was sure he would lock her away. His would be the only face she saw for the remainder of her days.

The other occupants climbed from the coach to stretch their legs but they would not be staying in the remote village. As soon as the horses were watered they would be on their way again, with no recollection of the quiet lady with her face shielded by a bonnet.

Alone in the coach Prudence struggled to pull the wedding band from her plump finger. It had been a source of protection during her journey but she had no need for it any longer. In fact, she wished nothing more than to forget that she had ever been married in the first place. With the ring's removal she felt somewhat lighter, more like herself, Prudence again rather than Lady Fondleton.

She slipped the plain metal ring into a velvet pouch and considered pushing it into the carpet bag, but decided it was best to leave it closed just now. It was best the contents of said bag remain secret. Instead, Prudence put the velvet pouch into her pocket and pushed the golden ring to the very bottom.

She wished she could forget about it entirely. She wished she could have left it behind, but of course, she could not. The ring was the only jewelry she carried. She had left the more costly ornaments at the manor. She did not wish to be accused of theft, even though as the countess the jewels were rightfully hers. She knew the earl did not love her, but if she took anything of value, Prudence knew he would hunt her down. She hoped that leaving empty handed would keep the earl from seeking her too vigorously.

Then, with as much pride as she could muster, she tucked her small bag close and descended the mail coach. She thanked the footman for handing her down. She had no coin for a tip except the one that was promised to the nuns, but she was grateful for his kindness. He smiled absently and looked away. For once, she was happy to know that her plain features would help her to be easily forgotten.

She had never been to Halthaven before, nor had she ever intended to visit. It was a shock to see the rush of activity in the isolated town. The arrival of the mail coach had spurred the excitement of the locals. Doors opened and slammed shut as patrons rushed to collect their letters or packages. An old woman with a cane and one milky blue eye watched Prudence with interest. Prudence turned her face away and held her bag close to her chest with two hands as she slipped down the street away from the crowd.

A sign swung and creaked in the wind, announcing a tavern named the Broken Bridle. Prudence was not sure of the level of clientele that would be housed within, nor did she care. The patrons could not be more repugnant than her own husband. She pushed her way into the dark and dank hall and made her way to the barkeep.

The burly man in a once white apron, polished the glasses that sat in a row on the counter. His face was mostly covered with a surplus of facial hair. Both his hair and his beard looked like they could have used a trim weeks ago. He grinned at her, and she felt somewhat at ease by his ready smile.

"What can I help ya fer?" he grunted while replacing a

glass and choosing another to shine. His eyes were on the glass.

Again, Prudence noted that she was not worth the lingering stares that would follow her sisters every time they showed their faces outside of the manor. Once again, she thanked God for her plain features.

She cleared her throat.

"If you would be so kind," she muttered hoarsely, cleared her throat again, and began anew. "If you would be so kind as to direct me toward Halthurst Abbey, I would be most grateful."

The man raised his gaze to look her over. Prudence stood under his appraisal from her bonnet to her toes with a nervous patience. Then, he gave one curt nod and turned his attention back to the glasses.

"Gon' be a nun, are ya?" he asked.

As a married woman Prudence would never be allowed to take such vows against those she had already stated, not while her husband lived, but there was no way for this man to know that. Rather, she would give whatever excuse might kept her identity concealed until she arrived at her destination.

"Yes, sir," she whispered. "I wish with all my heart that I would be worthy to dwell with the holy sisters." She lowered her head and did her best to give a modest and pious nod. Perhaps he often directed ladies toward the abbey. Prudence wondered if her own sister had stood here all those years ago and made the same request.

"You'll not get there any time soon," he revealed. "All this rain we've seen has got the throughway flooded. Bridge is washed out and no way across 'cept on foot."

"Oh," Prudence felt deflated. She turned to glance out of the window and saw that the sun was already well in the sky. "If I were to walk could I arrive by nightfall?" she asked.

The barkeep held one finger to the tip of his nose while he thought.

"Perhaps ya should wait 'til mornin'," he offered.

"I'd rather not wait another moment, if it can be helped," she revealed. "If you think it can be done, please point me in the proper direction, and I shall go."

"I ought ter say no," he shrugged, "but ya look like a sturdy enough gal for it. Ya got a strong pair of boots on them feet of yours?"

Prudence shifted her feet beneath her gown. She was wearing her best walking boots in preparation for the journey but they were still made more for fashion than crossing the countryside. Another product of her London advice, she mused sadly.

"Of course," she lied. Prudence did not care if she had to climb barefoot up a mountainside if it meant getting to the abbey before darkness fell upon her. She was road weary and ready to be free of her burdens, if that were at all possible.

The man narrowed his eyes. For a moment she worried that he might call her bluff, but it seemed that he decided to allow her to make her own bed, if she so wished it.

"Well," he nodded, "my daughters are brawny girls so I learned not ta expect less from a woman. It's not a trek for the weak but I see you'll not be swayed." He explained that she should follow the main road to the end of the village. Then, she should take the fork in the road to the left. Once she came to the bridge she'd have to find a more shallow place to ford, but the road led straight to the abbey if she just stayed upon it.

"Don' go to the right or you'll end up in the Baron's Wood," he warned. "It's mighty easy to get turned around in the woods. We might not find ya 'till Michaelmas since we've no way 'o knowin' if you didna get to the abbey, what with the road out and all."

She thanked the barkeep and offered him her last coin. The rugged man, who could scare the leather off a cow, let his shoulders droop as he looked upon her extended hand.

"Keep it, miss," he gave a soft grin. "If nothin' else, give it to the sisters up where you're goin'. They've done a world a good for this village. That's to be sure." Prudence realized that there was more heart in him than met the eye. She folded her hand back around the last coin to her name, tears welling in her eyes at such a simple kindness.

With a croaked word of thanks she left the tavern and made her way toward the edge of the village.

For a moment, she almost felt a hope that her faith might be renewed in humanity. Then, she recalled why she had found herself in the tavern in the first place, and she cursed the world of men, mostly her father and her husband. Then she bit her tongue and asked forgiveness. She should not go to the holy sisters with a curse in her mouth.

"If only you would take them both, Lord," she prayed. "I do not wish harm upon them, for that would be ungodly. I only wish they were in Your Presence rather than mine. I am too weak to suffer them."

~

Would you like to be notified when my next
novel is published?

**Click Here to Join my VIP Readers**

Printed in Great Britain
by Amazon

38390074R00182